1799

D0231169

# THE CRUISE OF
# THE COMMISSIONER

Captain James St John Stanier has now
been elected a Commissioner of Celtic
Lighthouses and from this elevated position
he is determined to get even with Septimus
Macready, captain of the *Caryatid*. When
Macready's ship literally steamrollers Bishop
Island's bakery, Stanier sees a heaven-sent
opportunity to achieve the ruin of his old
rival. As tension builds and old loyalties
are put to the test, both sides anticipate
stormy seas ahead ...

# THE CRUISE OF
# THE COMMISSIONER

# The Cruise Of The Commissioner

*by*
Richard Woodman

**Magna Large Print Books**
Long Preston, North Yorkshire,
England.

British Library Cataloguing in Publication Data.

Woodman, Richard
The cruise of the Commissioner.

A catalogue record for this book is
available from the British Library

ISBN 0-7505-1398-5

First published in Great Britain by Severn House Publishers
Ltd., 1998

Published in Large Print 1999 by arrangement with Severn
House Publishers Ltd.

Magna Large Print is an imprint of
Library Magna Books Ltd.
Printed and bound in Great Britain by
T.J. International Ltd., Cornwall, PL28 8RW.

All situations in this publication are fictitious and any resemblance to living persons is purely coincidental.

# CONTENTS

To Brian Davies,
who first showed me the Celtic coast.

## A Cloud On The Horizon

'Bullshit!' exclaimed the Chief Engineer with such violence that small crumbs of toast shot across the white napery of the saloon table and struck Mr Farthing sitting opposite; the First Mate was drawn reluctantly into the argument.

'Take it easy, Chief,' the Mate said, placing a protective hand over his cup of tea.

'You keep out of this! This is an engineering matter and nothing to do with you damned deck ornaments,' expostulated the Chief Engineer, turning once more on the Second Engineer who was fighting a gallant rearguard action in the face of superior rank. Mr Farthing rose from the saloon table leaving the two engineers to savage each other in the technical language of their race. As he passed the partially open door of the saloon pantry he saw the face of the Steward and gave him a wink.

Caught eavesdropping, the Steward flushed then quickly covered his embarrassment by saying, 'At least it ain't oil and water having a go, sir.'

'No indeed,' replied Charlie Farthing,

11

lifting his uniform cap from the row of hooks in the alleyway.

'Well, it makes a change, like,' breathed the Steward to the Mate's retreating back, retiring to his interminable task of washing up.

After initialling the muster book left upon his desk by the quartermaster, Charlie Farthing put on his cap and went on deck to view the cause of this disruption to the normally peaceful saloon of the SS *Caryatid*. The Steward's remark about the incompatibility of oil and water, that is to say the engineering and deck departments, was a gross and unwarranted slander. For most of the time, that is. Mr Farthing liked to think the ship was run harmoniously. That, after all, was the chief part of his own job and much of its success rested upon the maintenance of a smooth routine. Intrusions like the steamroller were inimical to smooth routines.

And there it was, sitting upon the deck just forward of the *Caryatid*'s single hatch where, under normal circumstances, she would have half a dozen brightly painted buoys ready to be deployed at sea, replacing the rusty and weedy seamarks which had done their stint of warning mariners off the dangers of the Celtic coast. Mr Farthing regarded the thing with some distaste. It gleamed with the gloss of paint, its boiler and housing fir green, its heavy iron wheels bright scarlet; the pipework polished and proclaiming pristine newness. Mr Farthing walked round it, testing the securing chains with his feet. Its immobility reminded him of Gulliver lashed down upon the Lilliputian beach.

'All right, sir?' The Bosun appeared from the port side, similarly fascinated by the unusual deck cargo.

'Yes, seems fine, Bosun. I don't think she'll go anywhere.'

'Not till we discharge her, anyways.'

'Quite,' responded Mr Farthing, unable to resist slapping the boiler of the monstrous machine.

'Any heavier and it'd have put the old lady down by the 'ead, sir.'

'Yes. Have the lads had breakfast?'

'Just finishin'. I'll start singing up about ten and she'll be all ready for the tide.'

'Grand,' said Mr Farthing. 'High water's at a quarter-past and we'll have to follow *her* out.' He nodded across the small dock which formed the inner harbour of Porth Ardur, drawing the Bosun's eyes to the *Kurnow*. The Bosun spat skilfully over the side. Mr Farthing smiled to himself. The fact that the Bosun's brother was carpenter aboard the *Kurnow* did nothing to ameliorate the hostility between the two ships.

The *Caryatid* was a lighthouse tender owned by the Commissioners for Celtic Lighthouses, a practical, no-nonsense ship whose crew basked in the self-confidence of the supremely able. The *Caryatid*'s appearance bore witness to the fact: a working foredeck from which rose a heavy mast and derrick together with enough wire and manila hemp to do credit to a windjammer and a boat deck chock-full of boats. A tall buff funnel stood among its harem of boiler-room ventilators abaft the varnished teak bridge with its wheelhouse and chartroom. True, there was a touch of elegance aft, a long raking counter that boasted some gold leaf around the ship's name, but by and large the overall impression was one of rugged utility, a proud maid-of-all-work.

By contrast the *Kurnow* was a debutante; a flighty, flush-decked, turbine-powered steamer with the grandiloquent title of 'Royal Mail Ship'. Her task, daily in the summer and weekly (weather permitting) during the winter months, was the conveyance of the mails, supplies and holiday-makers to Ynys Meini. The Island of Stones was the largest of the Bishop's Islands, an extensive archipelago off the Celtic coast. The new service inaugurated by the *Kurnow* two summers previously had so boosted the number of the

14

islands' tourists that the steamroller was now considered indispensable in the construction of a proper road across Ynys Meini. It was therefore a matter of the profoundest satisfaction to the crew of the *Caryatid* that they, and only they, were capable of delivering it to the island. The *Kurnow* had no such heavy lifting gear as *Caryatid* possessed, and the deficiency marked her for a flibberty-gibbet.

'Aye, pity she's leaving on the same tide,' the Bosun mused.

'There's one glimmer of light on the horizon,' Mr Farthing said, catching the Bosun's drift. The Bosun looked up at the Mate, a glint of suspicion forming in his eyes. 'What's that?'

'She's under orders to vacate the berth before the next high water at Ynys Meini and make way for us.'

'About bloody time,' remarked the Bosun, expectorating a second time over the side. 'And we'll get a night alongside.'

'And you and the lads will get your run ashore,' confirmed the Mate, suppressing a smile.

'About bloody time too,' said the Bosun, repeating himself as evidence of satisfaction. 'So we'll discharge this thing next morning, on the low water, is that it?' It was the Bosun's turn to slap the steamroller.

'That's it. The quay and deck will be about level then and the ship will be sitting on the bottom.'

The Bosun tore his mind away from the prospect of a night at the Mermaid's Tale and scratched his head.

'Aye, sir. It's botherin' me how we're goin' to get this bloody thing up the quay. My brother tells me there'll be no driver until yon hooker takes the road-makin' gang out, and that ain't tile next month. If it's left on the quay it'll block the bloody place.'

'Ah,' said Mr Farthing, thinking of the row which, for all he knew, still raged in the saloon. 'That's what the Chief is concerned about. He and the Second were at it hammer and tongs over breakfast, deciding which of them was the better qualified to drive it. We just have to land it safely on the quay and then the spanner-tappers can sort it out.'

A slow smile spread across the Bosun's face. 'Well now ... I think,' the Bosun said after a brief, thoughtful pause, 'I'd rather see the Second do it, sir. I've never seen the Chief so much as go down the engine room in the seven years he's been here—'

'Now, now, Bose,' said the Mate grinning, checking the Bosun's assault on the wardroom officers, 'that's an

16

exaggeration and you know it. He's got a Chief Engineer's certificate, he should be able to manage this thing.' Once again the steamroller received a pat upon its rotund boiler.

'I sailed with a skipper once, Mr Farthing, on the old *Loch Killossan* it were, an' the old bugger had never been on a royal yard, not even to overhaul buntlines when he was a 'prentice boy.'

'So?' said the slightly nettled Mate, losing the thread of the Bosun's argument.

'He put the old barque on the Pratas Reef off Hong Kong. I tell you no good'll come of it if the Chief drives this bloody monster.' The Bosun sent a third gobbet of spittle over the side in an impressive arc.

Both men looked up at the tall funnel that rose from the forward end of the heavy machine. A few clouds drifted across the blue sky high above it, like prophetic smoke. When Charlie Farthing went to say something about the weather he found the Bosun had gone.

Mr Farthing met Captain Macready as that worthy came aboard at precisely ten o'clock, resplendent in his uniform and brass-bound cap. 'Good morning sir,' the Mate, said saluting. 'Steam's raised and we're just singling up. The *Kurnow*'s on the move.'

17

'Morning, Mr Farthing,' Macready responded, acknowledging the salute then looking across the dock at the *Kurnow*. Her screws suddenly churned a welter of white water under her cruiser stern. Macready dismissed her with a glance then looked up at the sky. 'Fine morning. All right, Mr Farthing, all hands to stations for leaving harbour. We'll get going. Deck cargo secure?'

'Yes, sir.'

The passage to Ynys Meini passed without event. The stern of the *Kurnow* disappeared out of sight ahead of them, leaving them alone on the ocean as the coast dropped astern and even the dominating height of Mynydd Uchaf faded into a blue cone before dropping over the rim of the world behind them. Although a few clouds drifted across the blue sky, the sea sparkled under sunshine pocked with the clouds' shadows so that the occasional transformation of the day made men look up, only to resume their work as they passed into sunlight again. Such a contrast gave them an appreciation of the privilege they enjoyed. An ebb tide gave the old steamer and her incongruous deck cargo a favourable shove, while the presence of the steamroller prevented any distraction, such as the proper business of the lighthouse

18

tender, from spoiling the even routine of the day's passage.

'Like a regular cruise, it is, Chippy,' the Bosun remarked to the Carpenter, 'Jus' as if we was off on holiday ourselves, like.'

The Carpenter, a man of taciturn disposition emitted a grunt which the Bosun, from long association with his fellow petty-officer, knew to be whole-hearted and enthusiastic agreement. Then he said something, so unusual an occurrence that the Bosun, not expecting any articulated comment, had to ask him to repeat it.

'I said, bit of a swell comin' in off the Atlantic,' the Carpenter said, adding for fulsome measure, 'must be a blow to the westward.'

'Aye,' agreed the Bosun who had not really remarked the low undulations that ribbed the vastness of the sea and were barely noticeable on the *Caryatid*'s deck, 'you're right.'

Up on the bridge the low swell was distinctly visible. Its period was so long that the *Caryatid* merely rose and fell as each undulation passed beneath her, hardly dipping her bow or raising her stern as she did so. But the parallel lines of each successive and advancing swell could be seen like faintly drawn shadows lying

19

across the ship's line of advance.

Captain Macready sniffed the air and screwed up his eyes. Far, far ahead of them, beyond the as yet invisible archipelago of the Bishop's Islands, beyond the fluffy white of the passing cumulus clouds, a faint muzzing above the horizon was the first indication of high cirrus.

'Bit of a swell building up, sir,' said Mr Farthing, coming up on the bridge alongside Macready.

'Aye, Mr Farthing. The dog before its master.'

By the late afternoon the blue hummocks of the islands rose over the horizon and an hour and a half later, as the sun westered, *Caryatid* steamed up the Sound, with Ynys Meini to starboard and the smaller island named after St Illtyd to port. Slowly, around a low hill on the Island of Stones, the little town of Porth Neigwl opened to view. Macready rang the engine room telegraphs with a clanging of bells and *Caryatid* slowed. Both Master and Mate trained their glasses on the huddle of houses and the granite breakwater.

'*Kurnow*'s still alongside,' observed Captain Macready, and Mr Farthing grunted agreement. 'I suppose they're going to drive the road over the spine of the island from the town,' Macready ruminated as both men continued their conversation with their binoculars to their eyes.

'That's what I heard, sir,' Mr Farthing agreed. 'Apparently someone's bought the old castle with a view to turning it into an hotel and the road is to link it with Porth Neigwl and the fishermen's cottages on the north side.'

Captain Macready rang the engines to dead slow. Up on the bridge they could hear the faint jangling of the telegraph bells down below in the engine room. As the engineers reacted, they swung their own telegraph and the bridge bells rang, the telegraph indictors swinging to conform with the bridge levers. *Caryatid*'s speed dropped to a gentle forward motion which barely disturbed the surface of the sea as Macready ordered, 'Hard a-starboard!'

'Hard a-starboard, sir,' the quartermaster in the wheelhouse replied, following this a few seconds later with: 'Wheel's hard a-starboard.' *Caryatid*'s head began to swing against the jumble of rocks, skerries, islets and the larger islands which made up the archipelago. Forward the solitary figure of the Carpenter emerged onto the foredeck and, with two heavy clunks, dropped the slips from both anchor cables.

'Both anchors cleared away,' he called and Mr Farthing waved acknowledgement.

'Midships ... Steady ... Steady as she

21

goes ... ' Helm order and response followed in disciplined measure. 'Starboard anchor and three shackles in the hawse pipe, Mr Farthing.'

'Starboard and three in the pipe.' Charlie Farthing slid with practised ease down the ladder to the boat deck, his feet never touching a step, his hands running down the brass handrails with a faint but audible squeak. From the boat deck he dropped to the foredeck and next appeared to Captain Macready, watching from the bridge, as he clambered over the wires and bottle-screws securing the steamroller.

Macready rang the engines to stop. The rumble of the ship's propulsion ceased as she ghosted to the marks which Macready had for years used to find a patch of sedimentary ooze of which he appeared particularly fond. Here he knew his anchors would hold and the crew, if they were inclined, might find the odd sole. As the square church tower came into line with the gable end of the Mermaid's Tale, Macready jangled the telegraphs and *Caryatid* began to shake. Water boiled green and white under her stern as the screws went into reverse. Slowly the marbled water surged forward, indicating all forward motion was off the vessel and she had begun to move astern. Macready stopped the engines, the rumbling and shaking ceased and all that could be heard was the seething of the whorls of disturbed water as it ran along the ship's side below the bridge.

Raising his right arm, Macready dropped it sharply. Mr Farthing, now watching his commander from forward, nodded to the Carpenter and that worthy swung the brake off the starboard capstan. In a cloud of rusty dust and with a roar that broke the tranquillity and sent a dozen quietly soaring gulls sheering away, *Caryatid*'s starboard anchor dropped from the hawse-pipe and plunged into the water with a splash, dragging forty-five fathoms of heavy stud-link cable behind it. Mr Farthing hung over the side, closely observing the lead of the cable as the ship continued to drop astern and the cable drew ahead. He watched as it came taut, dragging the anchor so that the flukes turned, dug deeply into the mud on the bottom, and checked the sternway of the ship. A moment later the cable slackened as the catenary pulled *Caryatid* forward again, and she brought up securely to her anchor.

'Secure, Chippy,' he said, turning to the waiting Carpenter then, turning to face the bridge, he held both forearms in a crossed stance. 'All brought up,' he called and Macready waved his acknowledgement. The Captain took off his uniform cap and ducked into the wheelhouse. 'Finished with the wheel, Quartermaster, until that hooker has sailed.' Macready jerked his head in the direction of the distant *Kurnow* alongside the only berth Porth Neigwl boasted on the granite pier-cum-breakwater.

'Aye, aye, sir.'

Macready scribbled the time of anchoring in the rough log, then stood in the wheelhouse looking down at the steamroller. He was still staring at it when Mr Farthing joined him. 'That thing,' said Macready as though all his contemplation had produced the remark, 'is going to clog up the pier,' he observed, 'unless there's someone here who can drive it.'

'The matter's in hand, sir,' Mr Farthing explained. 'I understand that although there's no driver available until next month, the Chief has plans to drive it away, clear of the berth.'

'Oh good,' Macready said, bestirring himself and turning to go below. 'I'd hate to mess up the *Kurnow*'s delivery of beer and cigarettes.' Mr Farthing smiled dutifully at the Captain's little joke. 'The Chief's organizing it, you say?' he asked, pausing at the head of the companionway.

'Well, yes, sir,' responded Mr Farthing, thinking of the row in the saloon that morning.

'Ahhh, well then ...' said Macready enigmatically, drawing the syllables out so that they seemed to contain immense and prescient foreknowledge.

When, to derisory cheers from *Caryatid*'s crew lining her rail, the *Kurnow* sailed and *Caryatid* was able to inch into the now vacant berth before the tide had ebbed too far, the lighthouse tender weighed her anchor and slid quietly alongside. As Mr Farthing had indicated to the Bosun earlier that day, the monstrous machine dominating the ship's foredeck would be discharged the following morning at local low water. By a curious anomaly, when it was high water at Porth Ardur, it was almost low water at Porth Neigwl. The curious run of the tidal streams made possible the schedule of the *Kurnow* and meant that the matter of the steamroller's delivery, which could not of course be undertaken in the hours of darkness, would take place at about eleven o'clock next morning when the granite pier and steel deck were as level as would be possible.

As the sun set amid a tangle of cirrus that confirmed Captain Macready's prediction of a coming gale, a festive mood settled upon the steamer. Showers were much in demand, steam and pink flesh filled the lower alleyways while above the hiss of spraying water a gently obscene banter marked a keying up of spirits, such was the spirit of anticipation abroad in the *Caryatid*. Of course the men whose duty confined them to the ship were disconsolate. They sat about the messroom still in their working clothes, brewing tea and rolling cigarettes with the resigned air of men contemplating several years isolated on desert islands.

It had been some months since *Caryatid* had last anchored in the islands (and some years since she had last laid alongside), allowing her people a run ashore in Porth Neigwl. Her crew were supremely good seamen. They did not have to stay at sea for months to prove it and many had already trod the path of distant, deep-water voyages in their impetuous youths. Service aboard the vessels run by the Commissioners for Celtic Lighthouses was appropriate for men of mature years with wives, families and commitments. But they still managed to view their forthcoming hours of freedom with an air of hungry enthusiasm that belied the fact that only that morning they had left their own domestic hearths. In its post-tourist, autumnal evening, Porth Neigwl waited like an unsuspecting maid.

At seven o'clock, Mr Farthing summoned the Bosun.

'Red and white watches ashore, Bose. All hands back on board by midnight.'

The Bosun's 'aye, aye, sir' was flung

26

over his retreating shoulder as he hopped blithely over the sea-step at the end of the officers' alleyway. A second later his stentorian bellow hollered the order down the companionway to the messdeck below, then the Bosun headed for the gangway. The Bosun's voice had not ceased to echo off the steel bulkheads before there was the clattering of boots on ladders, the liberated whoops and hoots that only shore-bound sailors can make and only ship-bound watch-keepers recall, filled the air. Three minutes later, the silent resentment of the confined blue watch settled back upon the ship.

Mr Farthing decided to go ashore and went along to the wardroom to see if any company could be found. The Chief and Second Engineers were standing before the fireplace that the Commissioners for Celtic Lighthouses seemed, somewhat incongruously, to consider an indispensable furnishing to an officers' wardroom.

'Now look here, Roberts,' the Chief was saying, wagging a finger ominously at a man with whom he had sailed for years, with whom he was frequently drunk in the Conservative Club in Porth Ardur and who was commonly called Gwyn, 'for the last time, I'm making this an order. If I so much as *see* you on the bloody pier

27

tomorrow, I'll have the Old Man suspend you from duty!'

The Second Engineer, his face an empurpled mask of truculence, opened his mouth to speak, thought better of it and looked vainly round for support. The Second Mate, a sallow young man by the name of Wentworth, who miserably filled the evening duty as the watchkeeping officer, avoided Robert's eyes and buried himself deeper in a paperback novel, the cover of which featured a remarkably voluptuous corpse draped half dressed across an iron bedstead. The Third Engineer, who shared the watch with Wentworth, pretended no interest in the word 'suspension' which might earn him at least a temporary promotion and a weekly increase in pay of one shilling and sixpence for its duration, noisily turned the pages of the *Western Courier*. The Second's imploring glance then fell upon Mr Farthing as the Mate entered the wardroom from the adjacent saloon. Mr Farthing was about to say something to mollify the two men who must, judging from their colour, have given the matter of the steamroller little respite since breakfast. But the Chief was terrible in victory, sensing he had at last gained the upper hand and that Mr Farthing was best swept into his own camp.

28

'And furthermore, Mr Farthing,' the Chief said, detaching himself from the fireplace and heading for the door, 'I look to you to see the order carried out.' Mr Farthing stepped aside as with awesome dignity the Chief Engineer strode from the wardroom.

The silence he left in his wake was punctured by Wentworth. 'Do I assume,' he said with airy facetiousness, 'that the Chief Engineer will be driving the steamroller clear of the pier tomorrow morning?'

'You can sod off!' snapped Gwyn Roberts, his face furious with rage and humiliation. 'I'm going ashore to get legless.'

'Good idea,' responded Mr Farthing. 'Mind if I join you?'

Disappointment was the first emotion experienced by the Bosun and the lads as they tumbled ashore. At its landward end the granite pier swung through an angle of about sixty degrees and ran along the wall of a long stone building which had been built some time in the last century as a boathouse. The boathouse and its adjacent dwelling had been bought by a speculator and turned into a public house and hotel shortly after the turn of the century when the fashionable and artistic set were discovering Ynys Meini as the ideal place for bohemian holidays. The resulting 'hotel' had, however, only enjoyed two summers' popularity by this set of shocking young people before half its clientele, the male half, had found more permanent accommodation in the mud of Flanders. The only relic of these intellectual days was the name of the place, which reflected a literary hand in its punning name. The pun was the bane of the local school teacher, for almost every child on the island spelt 'tail' as though it were a story. After its failure as a hotel and before the renewed popularity of the island as a destination for more numerous holidaymakers of less flamboyant style, the building had become a common tavern. The converted boathouse, however, made an excellent public venue, particularly for the island's regular and sometimes hasty wedding breakfasts.

The Mermaid's Tale enjoyed great popularity among *Caryatid*'s crew largely on account of the fact that the bar sported two well-endowed blonde barmaids and rarely closed while a customer was left standing. It was also a place where reputations were made and lost, for both the young women were commonly held 'to do a turn'. Who had done what to whom was largely a matter of mystery, much talked of on hungover and work-ruined mornings after, and the matter is only mentioned because it explains the alacrity with which the Bosun led the men ashore that evening. Though many claimed to have benefited from the favours of one or other of these beauties, *Caryatid*'s Bosun was believed to have once bedded them both simultaneously, a fact which conferred upon him almost legendary status and greatly augmented his authority on the ship's foredeck. By association with him, men basked in the reflected glory of this stunning deed and while it was only mentioned in whispers among male-only gatherings in Porth Ardur, in Porth Neigwl there existed a greater liberty.

All of which explains the corporate disappointment when the human tide, fetching up against the door of The Mermaid's Tale, found it firmly closed against them.

'The bloody sign's gone too,' the Bosun said to no-one and everyone as he sought to find some explanation in the indifferent heavens above. It was true.

The sign depicting the beautiful siren, winking one eye and beckoning enticingly with one promisory finger, was no longer there. Instead its iron bracket stuck out from the masonry with all the pointless uselessness of an unoccupied gibbet.

'And look at that!' All eyes, seeking in vain the fishy temptress, swivelled as one. There, on a freshly painted board bolted to the gable above, was a new legend: *The Mermaid Bakery*.

'Mermaid Bakery my arse,' said the Bosun, speaking for them all, adding, with that limitless resource that is the foundation of all good seamanship, 'right lads, follow me.' And turning away he led them shoulder-hunched in their silent regret up the road toward the Anchor and Hope.

The Mate and Second Engineer made the same discovery half an hour later, though with less frenzy and more curiosity than the hands, for it was not their intended destination. They were both slightly abstracted. Charlie Farthing because he hated a run ashore anywhere other than on the island of Ynyscraven where his wife Sonia lived, regarding liberty spent elsewhere as a waste of time, and Gwyn Roberts because he was mortified by the threat of suspension that hung, like the sword of Damocles, above his head.

As they reached the bend in the quay, the Second had looked back. 'It's so bloody narrow, Charlie, I don't suppose there'll be more than six inches either side of those damn great wheels.'

'Eh?' Charlie said, not understanding the allusion, thinking as he was of Sonia and feeling his belly hollowing out for a pint, or something.

It was with something like relief that they discovered the transformation of the public house. It gave them a topic of conversation that united them, a neutral subject upon which they could venture opinions, though about which they knew absolutely nothing. They were still discussing the economics of running a public house and how it would be a fine way for a seafarer to end his days, when they pushed open the door of the Buccabu Light. It was not because the pub was named after the famous lighthouse whose maintenance was one of *Caryatid*'s principal tasks, that they drank there. It was simply because with the nicety of pragmatic diplomacy and by the usage of the Lighthouse Service, the officers of *Caryatid* traditionally drank in the Buccabu Light when in Porth Neigwl.

It was with mixed feelings that *Caryatid*'s people greeted the new day. For the majority of those who had enjoyed a run ashore the previous evening, the predominant sensation was one of cranial agony, an unpleasant feeling made worse by the sanctimonious self-righteousness of those who had had the duty watch. During breakfast on the messdeck, a story went round that the Bosun had attempted to assist the new deck boy to lose his virginity with the landlady of the Anchor and Hope. She was a widow with certain characteristics in sympathy with the granite landscape in which she had grown up, though these became less obvious as a jolly evening wore on, and she was certainly not without a degree of comeliness elsewhere about her person. The story varied in the telling. Some inclined to the version that the boy had proved his manhood, despite first having been compelled to swallow more beer than he could comfortably hold. This version was said to be verified by the sheepish look on the youth's pallid face. Others pointed to this as concrete evidence that the lad had failed and that the Bosun had had to complete the job himself. This was apparently proved by the Bosun's early turning-to on the foredeck where the seamen stumbled about easing the wires and bottlescrews which restrained the steamroller, and his zealous frenzy in drowning a conscience in work. Whatever the truth, neither party seemed inclined to reveal it.

In the saloon, the Chief presided over the breakfast table, scarcely able to contain his excitement. Since Captain Macready rarely took breakfast, being conscious of his figure which it was necessary to maintain in as trim a state as possible in order to keep his place in Porth Ardur's ballroom dancing team, the Chief was able to bask in his seniority, throwing out good-natured remarks which arose from a good night's sleep, a clear conscience and a clear head. The Chief ignored the unpleasantness of yesterday and, as a consequence of this and the combination of a hangover, was ignored in turn by Mr Farthing and Mr Roberts. The Chief had risen at the uncustomary hour of six and turned out the hungover Donkey Man, instructing him to break up two bucketsful of bunker coal, ready to fuel the steamroller. Needless to say, the feckless Donkey Man had muttered something about there being all day to play bloody train drivers, and had turned in again.

Neither Mr Farthing nor Mr Roberts said anything to mute the Chief's self-esteem. They were too preoccupied with their own suffering, though their jaded countenances were taken as tokens of submission as they munched their respective ways desultorily through their breakfasts. At the head of the table the Chief Engineer completed his with a flourish of his napkin and rose with the energy of a second Napoleon flinging the Grand Army across the River Niemen.

'Right!' he exclaimed, rubbing his hands as he left the saloon.

35

The fact that the Donkey Man had gone back to sleep was the first thing that went wrong. Had the Chief Engineer possessed a shred of prescience, he might have seen in the sleeping man a providential warning of the chain of events which was to follow. Alas, the skills that form a man into a marine engineer are not normally those found in seers and mystics. The Chief did not recoil from the recumbent form when, in the absence of the broken coals, he went in search of their bearer only to find the Donkey Man much as he had been over three hours earlier.

A roaring bellow that resounded throughout the lower-deck accommodation brought the Donkey Man into the middle of the morning and full consciousness at a rush. The poor man had once been torpedoed and was in the alleyway with his life-preserver before he recollected himself. He was, however, soon in the stokehold with the Coal Trimmer, breaking nuggets of coal into small pieces while the Chief, in the boiler room next door, loudly organized two firemen into drawing out of the starboard boiler a quantity of red and glowing coals. These were soon on their way up the steel ladders and heading for the open air.

By the time the Chief and his acolytes

emerged on deck, Mr Farthing, the Bosun and the hands had unlashed the steamroller, slung it and lifted it. By heaving on one derrick guy and slackening the other, they had slewed the heavy spar through an angle of some seventy degrees with the ease of long practice, treating the gleaming machine as if it had been a particularly heavy buoy. As the steamroller traversed the *Caryatid*'s deck, the ship, though hard aground on the soft mud of Porth Neigwl, nevertheless heeled a little. Moreover, as the steamroller's wheels touched the granite pier and its weight came off the heavy purchase, the old ship eased back to the vertical. The Chief was confronted by his charge sitting upon the pier, in the very act of being released from the chain slings by which it had been suspended from the purchase hook.

As the Chief Engineer emerged with his followers—the Donkey Man with two buckets of black lumps and the Trimmer with a third bucket of hot and burning coals—quite a crowd had assembled. From Captain Macready on the *Caryatid*'s bridge above, to the cook leaning out of the galley port slightly below the level of the pier, *Caryatid*'s crew waited like a jubilee throng anticipating the arrival of monarchy. The only exception was the Second Engineer who, in a mood of sullen obedience, was staring out over the opposite rail to the advancing bank of cloud coming from the west.

From this position he could just hear the Chief's voice raised in the giving of his commands. 'Let's be having them live coals now ... That's it ... Now the rest, Donkey ...'

Mr Roberts could also hear the squeals and laughs of schoolchildren, particularly when they heard a grown man called 'Donkey'. 'Oh, bugger the bugger,' Mr Roberts said and, struck by an idea, returned to his cabin.

By the time steam had been raised in the steamroller's boiler, the Chief was bathed in a lather of sweat and his white boiler suit was sullied by unaccustomed grime that the steamroller, immaculate in its newness, had maliciously produced from its inner recesses.

Many of the now not inconsiderable crowd, which had mustered to see the arrival of the steamroller, had not seen a steam engine before. In this category were a number of small boys who had been led down to the harbour with their classmates for educational purposes. They had broken away from the strictures of their crocodile and were clambering all over the steamroller even to the extent of pinching lumps of coal and hurling them at each other. That they would undoubtedly be caned for their behaviour only added to the fun and when their teacher, a plain but dutiful young woman, sought to bring them back into line, *Caryatid*'s watching seamen thought the day improving by the minute.

The Chief, intent on his fire and the quick raising of steam, merely swatted these boys when they became excessively importunate; otherwise he fiddled with the draught controller and tapped the pressure gauge, drawing from the observant Macready the murmured comment that, 'It's not a bloody barometer that you've got to be tapping it like that, man.'

At this point one of the boys became over-exuberant and both Chief and teacher grabbed him at the same instant. A moment later they were arguing with each other over the rights and wrongs of having a steamroller on the pier at the same time as a crowd of schoolchildren. This altercation was terminated by the late, but inevitable arrival of the law. The island's only constable had naturally felt it necessary to return home to collect his helmet, before proceeding to investigate the imminent affray then brewing on the pier. He led the heated teacher back to her charges who were now in impeccable formation, having long since spotted the approaching policeman.

Muttered approval of the lady's heaving bosom was generated along *Caryatid*'s rail and more than one suggestion was made to the Bosun and the Deck Boy in which the honour of the ship played a small part.

The intervention of the constable was signalled by a watery, but irrefutable hoot from the steamroller's whistle which terminated these speculations. Steam was almost raised and the spluttering whoop was greeted by a small cheer from the expectant throng. Several children jumped up and down in the excitement and one or two thought the entertainment over, and that they would soon be back in the classroom, victims of disillusion and disappointment.

The brief hoot also drew the Second Engineer back into the mainstream of human affairs. He watched from the concealment of a boiler room ventilator trunk, then moved nearer, as though drawn by the mounting pressure in the green boiler, to crouch furtively behind the boat-deck bulwark, peering through a panama lead.

When at long last the Chief gave a triumphant thumbs-up to the ship's company and was met by an ironic cheer, Mr Roberts could, had anyone taken any notice of him, have been seen with his camera, poised to take a shot of the departing steamroller.

The Chief was now in the throes of carrying out the preliminaries necessary to starting a steamroller moving. Draincocks dribbled, spluttered and then hissed satisfactorily, whereupon the sweating Donkey Man was ordered to shut them off. The Chief settled himself in the driver's seat and motioned the Donkey Man up behind him. Regarding his sins forgiven, egged on by the acclamations of his mates on board and the presence of the audience, the Donkey Man obliged. For the Chief, the presence of the Donkey Man was not so much an act of indulgence as a snubbing of the Second Engineer.

With a frown of concentration, the Chief let off the brake and opened the steam valve. Slowly the juggernaut eased forward to a tentative noise of enthusiastic approval. At this point two things happened. Mr Roberts defied the Chief's order and, unable to contain himself further, leapt onto the pier with his camera. The sudden movement caught the Chief's eye just as, with the steamroller trundling slowly forward, he turned to wave to the ship's company. His gratification was swiftly turned to anger at the Second Engineer's defiance. His bellow at Mr Roberts was drowned in the cheer raised

41

by Mr Farthing, taken up loyally by the Bosun and all hands and augmented by squeals from the schoolchildren. Then the Donkey Man drew the Chief Engineer's attention to the fact that the steamroller occupied almost the entire width of the pier. Simultaneously, with eighteen turns of his steering wheel lock-to-lock, the Chief discovered that guiding the steamroller was a difficult task.

Sweating profusely despite the sudden chilly, rain-bearing wind that was freshening every moment, the Chief corrected the steamroller's slew. The green and gleaming machine lumbered along in a straight line and the Chief relaxed, feeling himself in control. Ahead of him ran the straight granite pier. He opened the throttle and the crowd moved back. With a delightfully sibilant hiss-hiss and the trembling rumble of its progress over the granite cobbles, the steamroller made its juggernaut progress towards the bend in the pier.

Having, as it were, seen the steamroller off on its regal progress, Mr Farthing went up to the bridge and joined Captain Macready on the starboard wing. From this vantage point both men had a grandstand view of what followed. Indeed the elevation alerted them to the possibility of disaster at least a minute before any indication of danger impinged itself upon the Chief's consciousness.

*Caryatid*'s crew spilled down the gangway onto the pier, filling in the vacuum left by the departing steamroller like leaves that are sucked into the wake of a passing vehicle. Close behind the roller itself ran Mr Roberts, the Second Engineer, whose presence on the pier had been specifically proscribed by his superior.

'Oh dear,' said Mr Farthing, aware that he too was in dereliction of his duty.

'I think,' added Captain Macready, unaware of the situation of the Second Engineer and more concerned with the approaching bend, 'that the Chief is about to experience a navigational hazard.'

'Oh dear,' repeated Charlie Farthing, grasping the significance of the Captain's remark and, with an intuitive leap, guessing why Gwyn Roberts was so attentively following the Chief.

As the juggernaut reached the bend the Chief shut in the steam slowly, grinning confidently at the Donkey Man whose face bore an expression of sudden apprehension.

'I should put a bit of brake on, Chief, if I were you.'

'Nonsense, man,' said the Chief, elated by their progress as he started to whirl the little steering wheel. The long boiler began

43

to nose round the corner.

'A bit of brake, Chief!' The Donkey Man called, his voice raised in alarm.

It was now clear that the rate of the steamroller's turn did not conform to the geometry of the bend. The Chief whirled the wheel faster and, at the moment the Donkey Man decided to use his own initiative and leaned forward to apply the brake, the Chief leaned outboard to observe the progress of the heavy forward roller. In so doing he all but unseated the Donkey Man who, clutching for his life, narrowly avoided being dropped neatly under the huge, nearside rear wheel. He recovered just in time to watch the forward end of the steamroller penetrate the long stone wall of what had once been the dance hall of The Mermaid's Tale.

But it was no longer a dance hall. What the Chief had driven into and was now in the process of demolishing, was the flour store of the Mermaid Bakery. To the slightly distant observers on *Caryatid*'s bridge a silent explosion seemed to occur, a soundless release of elemental forces that was as delicate as the flap of a butterfly's wing. Great soft white clouds rose up in huge billows to be torn to leeward in the wind.

'Oh dear, oh dear,' Mr Farthing said yet again, scarcely able to conceal his

44

amusement. Aware of its impropriety he did his best, skewing a sideways look at Captain Macready whose face bore a look of resignation, like a man brought before a circumstance he had long foreseen. Mr Farthing looked again at the white cloud which was now beginning to subside. Figures moved within and around it. A gleeful covey of schoolboys leapt up and down and turned and smiled and shouted at each other. The *Caryatid*'s crew stood in a half moon of spectators, many rocking backwards and forwards with obvious laughter. The police constable advanced rapidly, withdrawing his notebook while Mr Roberts could be seen bent over his Kodak.

Then, like a supremely skilled actor making an entrance, upon the timing of which rested the credibility of the scene, the Chief emerged bellowing from the centre of the cloud. Brushing the policeman aside, he advanced on the Second, shouting incoherent abuse as the latter, still snapping and rewinding his Kodak, fell back before his enraged superior. As though at a signal, although it may have been at the policeman's protest at being manhandled, the Chief broke into a run, whereupon the Second went into full retreat. In a single body, those members of the *Caryatid*'s crew who had followed

45

the steamroller's progress along the pier, turned and fled with the Second before the wrathful Chief, a flock of sheepdogs being chased by a single, mad white ram. Behind the Chief in feeble imitation, ran the constable.

'Oh Lord!' said Mr Farthing, who could now hear the words, 'Sabotage ...! Your fault ...! Suspension ... Bastard!' coming from the approaching Chief Engineer.

The proximity of the ship to the pier and the level nature of her deck enabled the athletic to dispense with the gangway and merely vault the bulwark rail. Bodies leapt inboard again, as though quickly taking up their original places as spectators before being seen as accessories to what promised to be further entertainment. Gwyn Roberts, encumbered by his camera and its precious evidence, was making for the gangway when he was caught by the Chief. The two engineers began an unseemly grapple for possession of the Kodak box camera and the hand of the constable was already reaching out for the Chief's collar when all was suddenly transformed.

At that moment Mr Farthing's admiration for Captain Macready increased. He had observed the Captain in a number of situations fraught with incipient disaster. In all of them he had remained calm, unruffled and supremely confident of his own abilities. This, however, was scarcely one in which Charlie Farthing would have expected *Caryatid*'s master to manifest any talent. But Mr Farthing was wrong.

In a monstrous bellow that put past muster anything the breathless Chief could now produce, Captain Macready froze the little group on the pier. Even the police constable responded to the authority inherent in the stentorian monosyllable.

The Second recovered his camera with the thought of the price the negatives would fetch when offered to the *Western Courier*. Behind him the Chief stared mawkishly up at the bridge.

'Chief,' called Captain Macready, dropping his tone without losing the attention of all within range, 'how many times have I told you that many are called to drive, but only a few chosen to navigate?'

# The New Commissioner

Far to the east there was no hint of a gale. The sun still shone, in tune with the mood of James St John Stanier as he sped along the streets of the capital in his chauffeur-driven limousine. He leaned back exuding satisfaction. It had been a good morning and, on his way to his inaugural meeting as a Commissioner of Celtic Lights, he anticipated a good afternoon. During the forenoon he had chaired a meeting at his offices at which a Member of Parliament and a peer of the realm had promised their support for a project to mine coal from an open cast site near Porth Ardur. The produce of the mine would be exported in the ships of the Cambrian Steam Navigation Company, of which Stanier was the chairman. After this, he had lunched well at his club and the excellent burgundy put him in an even more expansive mood, so much so that he had engaged the chauffeur in some casual small talk about the weather.

Being a stickler for punctuality, a characteristic developed during his early years at sea as a young officer in the legendary liners of the Isthmus and Occidental Steam Navigation Company, Stanier arrived at the porticoed entrance of the Commissioners' headquarters at exactly half past two. The imposing Georgian building, its red brick warm in the afternoon sunshine, added to the inner warmth induced by the burgundy. He had made it, by Jupiter! To have been elected a commissioner was the icing on the cake of his career. Ship-owning gave him kudos in the city even if they were not quite the sort of steamships owned and managed by the great I & O Line, and in its own way, the Cambrian Steam Navigation Company now reflected much of what was practised in the I & O liners, not least among which was a strong reliance upon punctuality. But his appointment as a commissioner set him truly apart, a man of approved rectitude, a pillar of the establishment, a paradigm among his peers.

Only one small shadow marred Stanier's prospect of the afternoon and that was the question of his title. He had been appointed to the Board of the Commission for Celtic Lighthouses largely as a representative of shipowners' interests, but what chiefly recommended his candidacy was the fact that he was himself a master mariner. His fellow shipowners had therefore felt that he was uniquely qualified among them to do battle on their behalf, mostly it has to be said, in the matter of keeping their costs in the form of light levies to a minimum. The majority of the other commissioners were former shipmasters, but the Commission's constitution required that three of its Board came from the commercial world in order to maintain sensible control of its finances. In this way the running expenses of the Celtic Lighthouse Service were properly managed by a Board which constituted representatives of both paymasters and customers. It was an ancient body, with some odd rites, but it had worked well for 350 years, since its inception in the late seventeenth century.

It was Stanier's good fortune, therefore, that the resignation of one of the number of the commercial trio had left a timely vacancy and the outgoing Commissioner had nominated Stanier for election as his successor. Duly elected, Stanier had assumed his new dignity eagerly. However, while he was proud of his status as a master mariner, he felt privately most uncomfortable about using the formal title of 'captain'. He would have admitted this to no-one, not even his wife Caroline, but it had been Stanier's personal tragedy to have wrecked his first command, the steam yacht *Sea Dragon*, owned by the millionaire shipowner, Sir Hector Blackadder. A few years earlier, *Sea Dragon* had been driven ashore from her anchorage off the island of Ynyscraven, to have her bottom torn out on a reef known as the Hound's Teeth. Stanier still had the occasional nightmare about that terrible night, though, to any other person, his fortunes might have been said to have taken a decidedly upward turn as a result of it. Despite the fact that several people had been lost along with the yacht, including Sir Hector himself, James St John Stanier's career had risen from that dreadful and awesome moment, for he had married Sir Hector Blackadder's beautiful daughter Caroline and taken over much of the late Sir Hector's business interests, among which the most significant was the chairmanship of the Cambrian Steam Navigation Company. Caroline, sweet darling that she was, had suggested that he took command of one of the company's ships for two voyages, and the experience had largely buried the spectre of the loss of the *Sea Dragon*. This period of command had the salving effect of rehabilitating himself in his own mind. It was only at such awkward moments, as the present might prove to be, that he worried about the disaster and his use of the title of 'captain'.

He got out of the car and was immediately met by a commissionaire.

The man was not only clearly expecting him, but solved his problem with almost providential tact.

'Good afternoon, Captain Stanier,' the flunkey greeted him. 'If you would be so kind as to follow me.'

Stanier strode up the wide stairs behind the coat tails and lacquered shoes of the commissionaire, passing some fine ship models and beneath the glowering gaze of half a dozen full length portraits which, he might have observed, were he the observant type, reflected the change in male hair styles from the full-bottomed wig of the seventeenth century to the establishment short-back-and-sides of the present day. He might also have observed that one thing remained the same—the portly demeanour of his predecessors. They all seemed to be men stuffed full of good food and self-esteem and Stanier felt immediately at home with their painted images.

Three hours later, as the meeting drew towards its conclusion, Stanier was well content. He felt he had given the Board, the members of which had greeted him with affable cordiality, the benefit of good counsel. It was clear that the Board were not hostile to the general principle of economics and, Stanier thought, his advice in this area was both welcomed and would form the basis of an initiative. Stanier felt his heart-beat quicken. He was not an impulsive man, but it had occurred to him when he had accepted the appointment as Commissioner, that the post might give him the opportunity to get even—he eschewed the concept of revenge—with a man who had once got the better of him, Captain Septimus Macready. Stanier did not wish to get even with Macready because the master of the *Caryatid* had been involved with the tragedy of the *Sea Dragon*. Not a bit of it. The animosity felt by Stanier for Macready arose from some real humiliations Macready had subjected Stanier to when he, Stanier, had had his first shore appointment as harbour master of Porth Ardur. The two men had clashed then and Stanier was not one to let matters die away when fate gave him an opportunity. Indeed, Stanier regarded such a thing as signifying providential approval, but he could hardly have hoped such an opportunity would present itself at his very first attendance at the Commission's Board.

From the nature of the discussions that afternoon, Stanier had gleaned a desire on the part of the Commissioners that the scrapping of their oldest lighthouse tender, which happened to be the *Caryatid,* and the closure of the small establishment at Porth Ardur, could form the substance of his suggested initiative. He kept his voice subdued when the Chairman, Captain Sir Charles Mudge said, 'You know Porth Ardur, Captain Stanier, do you not? Weren't you harbour master there for a while?'

'Yes, Sir Charles, I do know the place. I should guess the *Caryatid* to be reaching the end of her serviceable life, certainly ...'

He proceeded cautiously, seemingly un-eager, and when a fellow commissioner, Captain Blake, said in a tone that challenged contradiction: 'Old Macready's a fine seaman, though. I'd hate to see him go,' Stanier was quick to agree.

'A fine seaman, yes, undoubtedly, but he's not in the first flush of youth.'

'Wasn't there some damned tittle-tattle about his having a floosie on that bloody island, what's it called? Ynys ...Ynys—'

'Ynyscraven, Captain Jesmond,' Sir Charles Mudge said, helping the oldest member of the Board to recollect an island graced with one of its lighthouses.

'Yes, yes, that's the place. Well, if he's got a bit of fluff tucked away, he can't be too damned old, can he?' The old sea dog laughed at his own humour to the general embarrassment of his fellows.

'Well, gentlemen, that's hardly germane,' Mudge said, 'and certainly we shall not

54

record that in the minutes.' He motioned to the assiduous clerk who, under the sombre shadow of the Secretary to the Board, nodded compliance.

'No, don't put it in the bloody minutes, of course not,' persisted Jesmond, 'but it's a consideration when thinking about a man, don't you think? It shows vigour, by God!'

'Well, that is true, of course,' Stanier put in quickly, seizing the advantage the old fool had given him. 'But I imagine moral turpitude is not to be condoned in the public service—'

'Quite so,' agreed Blake and Sir Charles quickly.

Having achieved this moral ascendancy, Stanier drew in his breath and frowned, as though giving great consideration to what he was about to say, gaining the attention of all his fellow Board Members. 'Of course, I suppose with the *Caryatid* ageing, her running costs are mounting to a prohibitive extent and therefore her demise would effect considerable savings. In addition, though I agree that Captain Macready is a fine seaman of the old school, indeed I had the pleasure of knowing him quite well during my brief stay at Porth Ardur, he does lack a master's certificate and this would provide a technical reason for premature retirement.'

'Yes, that is a good point,' agreed Sir Charles. 'He was promoted under the old system of internal examination by the Board and while it has its merits, it exposes our people to charges of not being fully competent. One might run risks if the press got hold of such a thing nowadays.'

'Damn the bloody press!' barked Jesmond. 'If you want officers with master's certificates, you may have to pay 'em more, and then they'll have the same qualifications as ourselves! We'll have 'em up here arguing with us then! Unthinkable!'

'Most of the up and coming generation of officers in our ships hold master's or mate's certificates, Captain Jesmond,' Sir Charles Mudge said soothingly, 'but Captain Stanier has a moot point. The matter provides an excellent pretext, especially as the only item under any other business also concerns the worthy Captain Macready.'

Stanier listened with suppressed triumph as Mudge instructed the Secretary to the Board to read out the letter of complaint received from a certain Ifor Davies. In a sonorous voice that lent a tragic air to Mr Davies's complaint, the Board were informed that Mr Davies was the only baker on Ynys Meini and that his bakery had been wrecked by the incompetence of the crew of the Celtic Lighthouse Service Steamship *Caryatid*. These men, having enjoyed a drinking spree the night before, had wilfully driven a steamroller into his flour store. This action had ruined his entire stock of flour which had only just been shipped to Ynys Meini at great expense, expense which had been secured against a bank loan raised at the exorbitant rate of two per cent per annum. Mr Davies had lost business and now faced bankruptcy and the imminent starvation of his wife and six children. The islanders were faced with a crisis and to cap it all, this unprovoked incident had culminated in Captain Macready making a public joke at which his entire crew had laughed uproariously. In short, a sum of compensation was sought.

'Doesn't sound like Macready to me,' said Jesmond testily.

'Nor me,' offered a heavily bearded Captain Gostling, who stared at Stanier over half-moon glasses.

'Nor me,' said Mudge, 'but perhaps, with the benefit of local knowledge, Captain Stanier can give us his opinion?'

Stanier leaned forward and pursed his lips as though reluctant to gossip. 'Well, Sir Charles, it is not entirely outside the man's character. I recall him once driving the bow of the *Caryatid* against the dock

57

caisson and insisting the port was open, even though the closed caisson indicated it clearly wasn't—'

'High-handed, d'you mean?' asked Captain Blake.

'Not Macready,' Gostling insisted, his face clearly expressing disbelief. 'There must have been a reason for such a thing.'

Stanier shrugged. 'I leave it for you to decide the man's motives, gentlemen,' he concluded obscurely.

'Well, your loyalty to an old colleague does you credit, Stanier,' Mudge pronounced approvingly, bringing a deep inner satisfaction to the dissembling Stanier who merely nodded graciously. It was not necessary to state that it was his own inefficiency that had caused the port signals to show Porth Ardur remained open to traffic.

Mudge laid the file down and went on. 'Nonetheless, this chap Davies has a good claim against the Service, with unimpeachable witnesses which include both the local police constable and the schoolteacher. We shall have to pay him something by way of compensation. Captain Macready's ship's company have caused us to incur substantial unforeseen expenses. It is not something to recommend them to us in a more general sense.'

Mudge paused. 'I propose one of us chairs an enquiry aboard *Caryatid* at Porth Ardur to establish our side of the case. It will at least give Macready a chance to tell us his version. Mr Davies, I fear, may be a little self-raising in his claim.' They dutifully laughed at Mudge's joke as he looked round the table.

'Captain Jesmond?'

The old man shook his head. 'I'm damned if I'm going down there as the hangman, Charlie. Get the new boy to do it.'

'Captain Blake?'

'I'm afraid my diary is full, Sir Charles. I agree with Jesmond. Captain Stanier seems the ideal candidate ... It'll be good experience for him too.' And so it went on until Mudge confirmed the matter.

'I agree then. You'll be the best man for the task, Stanier. You know the place better than most of us who have only visited on inspection cruises, you know the man, you know the local background. In fact Macready's probably lucky to have an old friend to attend to the business.'

And thus, it being a tradition in the Celtic Lighthouse Service, Captain Sir Charles Mudge brought his polished wood gavel down three times on the table top, where an area of the glossy wood had been thus defaced by centuries of the

59

practice, and the matter was concluded. The blows rang loud and triumphant in Captain Stanier's ears. It hardly seemed possible that the day had ended so well. His moment of uncertainty had been smoothed away; and he had been rewarded to an extent far beyond his most fanciful anticipation. The downfall of Captain Septimus Macready was in his hand.

He was filled with a boyish glee as his limousine sped towards his town flat.

Caroline Stanier received her husband with the customary Martini cocktail. He did not really enjoy Martini cocktails, but the ritual was but a prelude to a greater event, and this helped make the drink more palatable. Caroline had long ago recognised her handsome husband for a vain and biddable man and had engineered their marriage with a precision that in anyone else might have been called cold. Stanier himself, being a man of natural conceit with an early realisation that he was attractive to women, had largely taken their marriage as a matter of course. The business of satisfying women had been ingrained upon his not unwilling perception as a young officer in the I & O's liners. It was expected of them, a matter of duty. It never occurred to Stanier that Caroline had picked him up from the wreckage of his career and his first command from motives of her own. She had lost a father to whom she was close, and understandably he thought that she sought some consolation in the arms of a sympathetic lover. Their losses were, Stanier thought, the coincidental points of their lives. That Caroline also took a great interest in her late father's business enterprises pleased Stanier. She was intelligent, a modern and progressive woman, with whom he could discuss matters. Not that he ever actually sought her advice, of course, but Caroline would almost always have a gratifying grasp of a situation. Naturally she had never sought a seat on the Board of the Cambrian Steam Navigation Company, remaining content to let her adored husband guide its affairs.

Senior staff at the steamship company's office might be heard to venture a contrary opinion. They might, over a drink, even be persuaded to reveal that they considered Mrs Stanier more than an *éminence grise*, but this fact was not obvious, least of all to Stanier himself, and it was generally considered politic to say nothing. Mrs Stanier had quietly engineered the dismissal of at least two senior employees, both of whom she was rumoured to have been unusually fond of.

Within five minutes of his arrival home,

Stanier had outlined the events of the day and was already basking in his wife's approval. He stood holding his glass, his arm resting on the marble overmantel. One leg was crossed elegantly over the other while she regarded him from a sofa, the long length of her lower leg tantalisingly exposed. She drove the sweet feelings of incipient revenge from his mind, forcing him to reiterate the deliberations he had had over his lunch with Lord Dungarth and Mr Duncan Smith, the member for Porth Ardur.

'They are much more important than silly old Macready and his little ship, my sweet,' Caroline prompted, setting down her cocktail glass, getting up and leaning against him. She kissed him on the cheek. He felt the warmth of her lean body against his own and marvelled, for the umpteenth time, that so boyish a form could so arouse him. She felt this and smiled, placing her hands on his hips and drawing him away from the fireplace.

'Caro—'

Her skirt fluttered about her ankles and she stepped out of it, lying back on the sofa already naked where he sought her as he dropped his trousers and helplessly thrust at her.

'Caro—'

'We're dining out tonight, my sweet,'

she said a few minutes later, sliding out from under him. Bending down she recovered her skirt and strode towards the bathroom.

'Oh? Who with?' he mumbled, still face down, kneeling where his rutting had left him.

'The Pomeroys,' she said, pausing for a moment by the bathroom door.

'Oh no.' He looked round at her frowning. 'Why them?'

'Because Pom's got a lot of money and he's looking for a good investment.'

'How d'you know he's looking for a good investment? I thought he put all his money into those ridiculous African heads.'

'They aren't African, they're Tasmanian and while they may be ridiculous, they are also valued and sought after. As for what is ridiculous, my sweet, you are at the moment, with your shirt-tails hanging out and your dear little bottom showing. We've to be there by eight.'

Stanier always felt ill at ease in the company of Mrs Pomeroy. Five years ago, when he had first gone west to Porth Ardur as an ambitious young harbour master, he had started a passionate affair with a certain Tegwyn Morgan. It had culminated when Sir Hector Blackadder, on appointing

63

Stanier master of his yacht, invited him to bring along a 'companion'. He took Tegwyn but in the emotional aftermath of the shipwreck, Stanier had found their love played out, gone like the yacht herself. Instead he was infatuated with Caroline Blackadder while Tegwyn had formed an attachment to Sir Hector's guest, an odd character called Pomeroy. It was as though their affair had simply vanished, like the *Sea Dragon* herself.

Stanier always considered Tegwyn's relationship with Pomeroy as 'an attachment', partly because he could not really understand why she had ceased to fawn upon Stanier himself, but mainly because Pomeroy seemed such an unlikely husband for the stunningly beautiful country girl. An ex-Etonian Guards officer, Pomeroy was at best an epicure, a collector of art, a quiet and exquisite dandy, and at worst a suspect character, a rather dodgy queen. Stanier, of course, thought he recognised the type, but what he found even more disquieting and incomprehensible was the effect this attachment had had on Tegwyn. Pomeroy had accomplished a transformation not, like Professor Higgins, in the matter of her accent, for her Celtic lilt was charming, nor in her demeanour which was naturally proud and upright, but in her manners and her personal magnetism. A fiercely passionate woman, Pomeroy had made of her a society hostess of distinction and, in their apparently blissful happiness, he disarmed all but a hardened and prejudiced clique who clung to notions of his own perversity. The only remaining evidence of this was a lack of children, which was circumstantial enough.

Pomeroy had other interests. He collected rather more than carved Tasmanian heads. The Pomeroys' huge flat contained several reception rooms each given over to distinct areas of Pomeroy's acquisitive interests. One, dominated by a Poussin but also containing a small work attributed to Vermeer, contained his older paintings; another held later works including a Renoir, a Georges Roualt and a Puvis de Chavannes. In yet a third, lit by subdued lighting and with walls of dark green, several large sculptures of the male nude stood like petrified guests left behind by some wicked fairy who had deprived them of their clothes at the same moment she had taken their lives. Finally, a fourth held Pomeroy's spectacular collection of ethnography, a subject in which he was becoming increasingly interested. At half past eight he was conducting his guests round his latest acquisitions, some strange wood carvings, he explained, fashioned by the extinct natives of Tasmania.

'It is strange, is it not, that these are almost all that is left of a people quite literally hunted down and shot like wild animals? Stranger too that they should end up here, in an apartment on the other side of the world.'

'Very odd,' agreed Stanier, though his wonder was a conclusion arrived at by a less philosophical route.

'What exactly are they, Pom?' Caroline asked, taking her host's arm in cosy intimacy.

'We don't know, Caroline; not exactly anyway. One can conjecture, of course, but without even so much as a single descendant to give us a clue, the nearest guess we can take has to be helped by matching them against what we know of mainland Australian Aboriginal culture—'

'And?'

'We are still none the wiser.'

'I think they are just tree roots,' said Tegwyn smiling archly, 'but beautiful tree roots—'

'Tegwyn discovered, due to her innate irreverence and philistinism, that if you blew through these holes which might represent eye sockets, you produce a most beautiful low note. Listen—'

And Pomeroy put the largest of these dark and grotesque objects to his mouth. The low sound vibrated in the room in a curiously soothing note of such low register that Caroline shuddered. 'Oh, that sounds horrible—'

'Like the dying note of a race of people, I think,' Pomeroy said with such seriousness that the fanciful image seemed stamped upon the strange artefacts. He laid the odd, twisted shape down again, adding, 'full of a terrible and prophetic melancholy.'

For a moment they stood, their drinks unsipped in the wake of the note, as though momentarily held in thrall by a strange, elusive magic. Then Stanier suddenly resented this lugubrious shadow thrown across his day.

'Well, Pomeroy, it's very interesting, but I've a proposition to discuss with you. I don't expect Caro mentioned it.'

Pomeroy threw a quick, complicit glance towards Caroline who disguised the wry twist to her mouth with the rim of her glass.

'Come, Caro, let's leave the men to talk business for a moment, I'm sure you and I could use another drink.' Tegwyn led Caroline out of the room and into the lounge. As Tegwyn poured them each another drink, Caroline said, 'Jimmy's going down to Porth Ardur next week.'

Tegwyn's eyes widened. 'Oh? What on earth for?'

'Oh, some sort of enquiry to do with the

67

Lighthouse Service. He went to his first board meeting as a Commissioner today. He's rather full of it all.'

'I expect Pom's Tasmanian carvings left him rather cold then.'

'I shouldn't wonder. They chilled me a bit too.'

Tegwyn laughed. 'I'll ask Jimmy about it over dinner,' she said. 'It'll make him feel better.'

'That's very sweet of you,' Caroline smiled, accepting the refilled glass.

'Will he mind?'

'Mind?' Caroline frowned. 'What, you asking him?'

'No,' Tegwyn laughed again, 'mind going to Porth Ardur.'

'Why should he mind?' Caroline asked sharply.

'Well, he must have some difficult memories ... You know, the *Sea Dragon*—'

'And you, my dear,' Caroline put in pointedly, adding wryly, 'but Jimmy's made of stern stuff—'

'Oh, I didn't imply otherwise, I assure you, it's just that we all have a peculiar attachment to the place.'

'I don't, I didn't grow up there!' Caroline said, suddenly almost hostile.

'No, my dear, but the place played its part in your life,' Tegwyn riposted with a gently compelling firmness, quite unabashed. 'Without Porth Ardur there would be no Jimmy—'

'What's that about Porth Ardur?' asked Stanier, blundering into the conversation as the two men rejoined their wives. But the question hung unanswered in the air as dinner was announced and after they had sat down Stanier gave voice to a more important preoccupation, grinning across at Caroline.

'Well, my dear,' he declaimed, 'old Pom's on board, aren't you, Pom?'

Pomeroy inclined his head. 'So it seems, James, so it seems.'

'You *have* had a good day then, James,' said Tegwyn smiling at him.

'Absolutely,' said Stanier, tucking in his napkin and picking up his soup spoon. 'Absolutely.'

# The Enquiry

The letter announcing the holding of 'an enquiry into the late events occurring at Porth Neigwl' signed by the Secretary to the Commissioners for Celtic Lighthouses, was awaiting *Caryatid*'s return to her home port of Porth Ardur. The chilly formality of the tone taken by a man Macready regarded as a cold fish at the best of times, nevertheless sent a shiver of apprehension down his spine. For some time now, Captain Macready had been subject to slight feelings of disquiet whenever he was in Porth Ardur. He was no longer quite the master of his own destiny he had once been. Since his wife Gwendolyn discovered the existence of her husband's love affair with Justine Morgan, their marriage had become a neat, very civilised and mutual accommodation. With his former dancing partner Justine quietly installed upon the island of Ynsycraven, Macready could have been said to enjoy the best of both worlds, and he kept the agreement reached with his wife to the letter. He conferred upon her, undiminished, all the respectability and attentiveness that was her due as the

70

wife of the commander of the lighthouse tender *Caryatid,* a position of considerable social prestige in Porth Ardur, establishing Gwendolyn as one of the principal wives of the town. But Macready had a conscience and he had once loved Gwendolyn, for all her subsequent frigidity. That he had later fallen for the voluptuous widow Morgan was both Macready's salvation and his tragedy, rescuing him from the bleak fidelity forced by sexual indifference upon decent middle-aged men, but saddling him with a deep and ineluctable guilt made worse by the reflection that circumstance and passion meant that he could never repudiate Gwendolyn, nor fully acknowledge Justine. Somehow his presence in Port Ardur exposed Macready's conscience to moments of vulnerability. The news of the enquiry now dripped like acid into these cracks in his self-esteem.

He set the letter down on his desk. The so-called late events had turned out rather well, he thought. It was true that the Mermaid Bakery had suffered somewhat, but a hole in mortared granite was easy enough to repair and the broken slates which had skidded off the disturbed roof could be readily replaced from the quarry not half a mile from the little port. Most of the destruction had been wrought by

71

the front roller, the collapsing masonry inflicting reciprocal but lesser marring of the runaway machine. As for the steamroller, the only damage was some scuffing of the paintwork on the boiler front and a rather heavier battering of the funnel. It was a pity that the Chief Engineer's ego was crushed, for it was in the nature of ships and ships' companies that while a man's successes might be recalled upon occasion, his humiliations and errors pass quickly into local legend. One was, it was frequently averred, only as good as one's last mistake, a circumstance compounded by the fact, Macready ruminated, that chief engineers tended to be odd individuals who believed that they were in fact the real commanders of ships. The argument that without them the ship would not work, failed to hold water. Macready naturally knew better. As a real commander he appreciated the value of the key individuals within his crew and knew that as much depended upon a cook as upon a chief engineer. A crew were hungry three times a day whether or not the engines worked. A good commander always knew his own reputation rested upon the quality of his ship's cook.

Conditioned by such considerations, Macready regarded professional matters with more detachment than the Chief who had, after detaching himself from the steamroller and the clutches of the local constabulary, retired to his cabin and locked the door. Macready disregarded this unfortunate petulance. He was confronted with the problem of removing the steamroller from its position perched half in and half out of the bakery and in this, in his opinion, his crew had excelled.

It is true he would have expected nothing else, for his officers and men regarded themselves as possessing infinite resource as seamen and what the gathering population of Porth Neigwl and the surrounding hinterland were coming to regard as a major disaster, had been swiftly rescued. In the wake of the disappearing Chief Engineer, the Second strode briskly, manning the beleaguered steamroller with commendable promptitude while Charlie Farthing, the Bosun and deck crew had rapidly laid out upon the quay a complicated array of blocks and tackles made up of two 120-fathom coils of four-inch manila hemp. The purpose of this had been to withdraw the roller from the flank of the bakery, since the precarious position of the machine no longer allowed the driving wheels to gain traction with the surface of the pier. The operation had attracted a larger crowd than its initial discharge from the ship and, in due

73

course, even the schoolchildren returned, to be given a lecture by their teacher on the mechanical advantage the sailors would derive from their impressive arrangement of 'rope and pulleys'. The labouring seamen, making the final tucks in the long splices that joined the two coils of hemp, had been heard to correct this inaccuracy with the expression 'block and tackle', the latter word pronounced to rhyme with 'take-all', but this did not deter the schoolmistress. Afterwards several of the younger and more muscular sailors had attributed her interest not to the practical application of physics, but to their own physical attributes about the upper arms and shoulders which were, by any standards, impressive.

In due course, when these preparations were completed and *Caryatid* had provided a massive inertia against which even a steamroller might be pulled, the running part of the system had been taken to her powerful forward capstan. Then, with four turns of rope about its upright drum, the steamroller had been smoothly drawn from its lodgement in the Mermaid Bakery with less fuss than a tooth is pulled. Despite the ease with which this had been accomplished, it had roused a hearty cheer from the onlookers, which deeply gratified Captain Macready, Mr Farthing, the Second Engineer, the seamen and those members of *Caryatid*'s crew who took no active part in the operation, but whose membership of the crew entitled them to some reflected glory. The spontaneous sound of acknowledgement had brought no comfort to the mortified Chief Engineer. The Captain's insulting words still rang in his ears and the flour dust still lay heavily upon his person and all about his cabin. He was a grown man and could not weep. He had had only a dram or two in a bottle of whisky which he soon despatched, and could only counter the wretchedness of his humiliation by blaming all upon the treachery of his supposed friend and colleague, Gwyn Roberts, the Second Engineer.

Macready became aware of the Chief Engineer's self-imposed solitary confinement after the gale had come and gone, and *Caryatid* lay off Mitre Rock lighthouse, while a working party cleaned out the station's freshwater tanks. He realised he had not seen the Chief for several days and, upon enquiring his whereabouts from Mr Farthing, had been informed that the Chief had taken to his bed. Being a conscientious commander, Macready had visited the cabin and ordered the Chief to unlock the door, slipping inside while the curious Steward stood unhelpfully outside.

'Pull yourself together, man,' Macready

75

had advised, sniffing the stale air of the cabin, drawing back the chintz curtains at the cabin portlights and rounding upon the supine Chief as he lay under a blanket. 'Get up at once!'

'There was no need for you to say what you did, Captain. It was an insult!'

'An insult, was it?' responded Macready, genuinely bemused. 'And how long have we known each other, Chief? D'you think I'd deliberately *insult* a man who had kept up steam for me all these years? What d'you take me for, an ingrate? Why should I want to insult you in a moment of such difficulty? Damn it, Chief, I only invited you to laugh at yourself, to ease the tension. It was an old joke between us, man. The old oil and water joke.' The Captain had paused, awaiting the impact of his words and the reaction they might provoke.

Nothing came from the shattered Chief beyond the muttered admission that, 'I haven't been able to sleep since.'

Macready had slapped his colleague on the leg and laughed. 'Come on, Chief, you know very well that if you can't take a joke you shouldn't have joined! I'll see you in the saloon at dinner.' And with that Macready had left the man to shave off the growth of untidy stubble that had accentuated his pathetic state.

Now, recalling the whole incident under the reviving influence of the Secretary's letter, Macready's sense of disquiet grew. If the Chief chose, he might make matters awkward. The Captain sighed, slipping a raincoat over his uniform, for it was almost dark and drizzling outside. The rest of his mail he would leave until tomorrow. He needed the walk home to think matters over. One of the consequences of his arrangement with Gwendolyn was that she was no longer prepared to discuss with him the business of the Lighthouse Service. It was one small slice of freedom she had recovered from the partial deconstruction of their marriage.

As he walked into the wet evening, through the puddles of Porth Ardur's ill-lit streets, Macready considered the forthcoming enquiry. He guessed it owed its origin to a complaint from the owner of the Mermaid Bakery. Macready himself had advised the excitable man to make a claim, in the knowledge that the Lighthouse Service would have covered the carriage of the steamroller in one of its ships, even though the matter itself was a favour to the local authority on Ynys Meini. Macready was used to the grasping ways of islanders; the matter was of consuming local interest and the maximum would be made of it by Ifor Davies. He supposed the Commissioners had decided to carry out a full investigation at the request of their underwriters and satisfy themselves that the matter really was an accident.

Of that Macready had no doubt and this conclusion, reached as he opened his front garden gate, cleared his mind for his encounter with Gwendolyn.

For years the twin existences of Captain Septimus Macready and his wife had run, like railway lines, along equidistant parallel lines. The years when Macready had partnered Justine in the ballroom dancing championships had been oddly innocent, enabling him for a long time to rest content with the symmetry of his marriage and the voluptuous beauty of the woman with whom he most conspicuously appeared in public. Yet, when the inevitable happened and husband and wife had afterwards settled their differences, the railway lines remained, running straight and true towards the horizon, if at a wider gauge.

Septimus's infidelity had empowered his wife and diminished him when he was with her. It was a fair payment for the joy of loving Justine, but convention compensated this by making him spend more time with Gwendolyn than he ever could with Justine. It was this uneasy feeling, compounded of guilt and a mild discontent that he knew he had no right to feel, that assailed him in Porth Ardur. It reached its greatest intensity as he turned the key in the lock and prepared himself for the customary bland anodyne greeting to his wife.

Once this private and awkward formality was over it was customary for them to discuss any domestic matters that might require them to function together. There were few enough of these nowadays, Gwendolyn filling her life with worthy activities and needing only the periodic appearance of her husband to formally endorse her status. A church service, perhaps, a wedding, or the occasional meeting of the parochial church council might be advantageously attended in his company. Since she ran the house herself and a gardener-cum-handyman was sent up from the buoy-yard once a week, he really had little to attend to when ashore, a circumstance that nowadays irked him and left him fretting over the hours he was wasting away from Justine. But it was part of the bargain he had struck with Gwendolyn, part of the price he paid for continuing infidelity and acknowledgement of the debt he owed his wife for this freedom. Above all, *her* life was to be unmoved by his great love affair and for this reason he was astonished when she put on her glasses, picked up a letter and asked him to sit down.

'There is something I wish to discuss with you.'

He did as he was told, swiftly dismissing the unbidden thought that this might at last be a request for a divorce. 'What is it, m'dear?' he asked, helping himself to a small peg of whisky and sitting opposite to her.

'I have had a letter from a firm of solicitors representing the Ardurian Slate Company.'

'What on earth do they want?' Macready asked, frowning over his glass and thinking of the rundown slate quarry that ripped into the far flank of Mynydd Uchaf, the mountain that rose behind Porth Ardur, the summit of which could be seen far out at sea.

'They have apparently been bought up by another company which intends to invest heavily in a new mine,' Gwendolyn went on crisply.

'A mine?' Macready was confused, supposing his wife had mistakenly used the wrong noun.

'Yes, Septimus, a mine. Not a quarry. A mine. A coal mine.'

'Oh no, not that old story about coal again—'

'Yes, and apparently it is no longer

a story, it is a fact. For some time I have known of geologists working over by Kynedoch and according to this letter the Ardurian Slate Company in its revived form wishes to exploit the deposit.'

A small chink of light was dawning upon Macready, sparked by Gwendolyn's mention of Kynedoch. Some eighteen months earlier an elderly but redoubtable widow who ran a farm just outside the village of Kynedoch, had died. Mrs Evans left an idiot son and the title deeds of the farm to the worthy Mrs Macready, who, seeing this as a further burden to her already saddened existence, accepted it as the Lord's will. A place was found for the son in a mental hospital and the two labourers who had helped Mrs Evans, both distant cousins of the widow, were kept on to run the farm. Maintenance of the rundown farmhouse, however, was quite beyond the resources generated by the place and, on the sole occasion he was consulted, Macready had recommended sale, albeit with modest financial provision being made for the two brothers. Gwendolyn had demurred, placing one further barrier between them. However, thanks to her restless energy, the energy taken up in other women by domestic preoccupations and the upbringing of children, Gwendolyn had had some impact on the output of the farm. By abandoning the upkeep of the farmhouse, marketing its produce more effectively and slightly increasing its output, she had provided for herself a small but gratifyingly independent income. Not an ungenerous man, this had pleased Macready. He did not wish to see Gwendolyn unhappy and rejoiced in her success. And what he now sensed Gwendolyn was about to reveal, filled him with a faint but brittle hope.

'Go on, m'dear.'

'You are not a stupid man, Septimus,' she said, lowering the letter and looking at him over her reading glasses. 'You will already have guessed the farm lies over the coal deposit.'

'So, what will you do? They are, I assume, making an offer.'

'A very handsome offer, as it happens.'

'Handsome enough to provide for the Evans brothers?'

'I shall ensure the Evans brothers are employed by the mining company.' Gwendolyn's tone was brisk, efficient; her mind was made up.

'So you have decided to sell.'

'In principle, yes. I shall try and get a little more, of course. They are obviously eager.'

'Good.' Macready forbore from pressing his wife further. If she had other plans,

plans made possible by the sudden and unexpected results of the hitherto burdensome bequest, it would not do for him to upset them. He must wait; perhaps even play a conciliatory role, for he felt no animosity towards her, fully conceding that she was a wronged woman. 'You were right not to sell earlier then, m'dear.'

'Of course,' she said, half smiling, sensing his weak position and in the full knowledge of her own empowerment. 'Do put the kettle on, Septimus.'

He rose obediently and, as he passed her, he tapped her affectionately upon the shoulder.

The enquiry was held ten days later. The *Caryatid* had spent a week at sea laying clean buoys off the Hellweather Bank and was berthed for the occasion. On his arrival back in port, Captain Macready received notice that it would be chaired by a Captain Stanier, newly appointed as Commissioner to the Board. Macready dismissed the idea that this was the same pompous fool who had once been harbour master of Porth Ardur and had lost Sir Hector Blackadder's steam yacht *Sea Dragon* on the Hound's Teeth. *That* Stanier he had last heard of as master of one of Cambrian Steam's contemptible old tramp steamers, renowned in the shipping world as being ageing rust buckets of the worst kind. He seemed to recall something that Justine had said, some gossip tittle-tattled from her daughter Tegwyn, that her former boyfriend had married well and left the sea, but then Macready had long ago written *that* Stanier off as a man who kept his brains in his scrotum. This Stanier, he thought, laying the letter down on his desk, would be a man of some distinction. After all, one did not become a Commissioner of Celtic Lighthouses without some standing in the world of shipping.

The following morning the after smoke room was prepared for the occasion. This occupied a fine varnished teak deckhouse situated on the after boat deck of the *Caryatid*. Inside, a table and chairs were secured by short chains to the carpeted deck. This bore some stains of salt and neglect, for it was often used as a store for deck brooms, buckets and holystones. As the deckhands barbarised the teak planking of the surrounding boat deck itself, the officers' Saloon Steward frantically dusted and polished the interior of the smoke room itself.

The place was usually kept locked, for officially it was provided for the private use of the Commissioners when they were afloat in *Caryatid,* giving them a discreet accommodation in which they could attend to those weighty matters upon which they brought their experience and wisdom to bear. In reality, however, the Commissioners rarely went afloat in anything other than their own yacht, the *Naiad,* a specially appointed lighthouse tender in which they inhabited a grand suite and in which they annually cruised the coast, inspecting the work of the many men in their service. In the Silurian Strait and the rim of the adjacent Atlantic, their numbers included the men who manned the Hellweather, Scarrick and St Kenelm's lightvessels, and the Buccabu, Mitre Rock, Quill Point, Goose Rock and Danholm lighthouses. In Porth Ardur they comprised the supporting storemen and labourers of the buoy yard, who were supervised by the Area Clerk. The Area Clerk, Mr Dale, was, with the lightvessel skippers and senior keepers of the lighthouses, answerable in turn to Captain Macready, whose superintendence of these personnel was additional to his command of *Caryatid* and her company.

To say that Captain Macready viewed the arrival of the Commissioners either singly or *en masse* with trepidation, would be an exaggeration. He had seen Commissioners come and Commissioners go and they generally conceded most points to his own expertise and local knowledge.

85

But they possessed a formidable statutory and collective power, so that any visitation exposed him to a potential and official criticism. Some, Macready had learned over the long years of his service, made a fetish of winkling out small and petty irregularities in a lighthouse keeper's dress, or the cleanliness of his bedsheets. While Macready knew he had nothing to fear from the annual inspection, his area being run to his own exactingly high standards, the irregular matter of the steamroller and its collision with the Mermaid Bakery might, he thought, ruffle the serenity of his life.

While Mr Farthing chivvied the crew to complete their deck scrubbing and brass polishing, Captain Macready briefed his chief witnesses in his cabin. Having shed their habitual boiler suits, the Chief and Second Engineers were unusually smart in their best doeskin reefer uniforms. They sat upon the Captain's settee attentively while he attempted to coach them.

'Now, gentlemen, it is some time since this unfortunate incident occurred and I think the lapse in time has healed those breaches that you might have felt towards each other, eh?' He waited a few seconds, expecting some reaction from the two engineer officers. The Second looked sideways at the Chief who maintained a silent impassivity which, Macready knew, had unfortunately characterised the relationship between the two men since the day of the incident. 'Well, anyway, we none of us want this matter to be made more of than is necessary, do we? I have reported the matter as an accident and recommended the baker at Porth Neigwl recovers the cost of reconstructing his bakery wall. Have you anything to add?'

'No, sir,' responded the Second. The Chief remained silent.

'Well, Chief?' Macready prompted.

'Whatever you say, sir.'

'I do say, Chief,' Macready rumbled ominously. Whatever this Stanier fellow said or decided today, he would be on the train back to the capital tonight and Macready would revert to his position of primacy. He saw the Chief's bulk shift slightly in acknowledgement of the implicit threat. There was a knock at the door.

'Come in. Ah, Mr Farthing ... News?'

'Old Dale's just waved the scarlet hanky, sir.'

'Ah. Very good. Quartermaster all ready?'

'Everything's ready, sir.'

Macready smiled. 'Of course it is.'

Mr Dale, the Area Clerk, had received a telephone call from his brother the stationmaster to let them know that their cousin the taxi driver had just picked up his important passenger from the train. Macready stood, gathering the file from his desk. 'Very well, gentlemen. Let's go.'

Realisation that it was the same Stanier hit Macready like a physical blow. He was obliged to salute the man, obliged to call him 'sir', obliged to mutter pleasantries as Stanier greeted him, his voice edged with sinister intent.

'So, Captain Macready, we meet again.'

Stanier snubbed Macready's introduction of his officers and turned aft, looking disdainfully at the houses of Porth Ardur as they climbed up the lower slopes of Mynydd Uchaf. 'Nothing much changes here, I see.' The remark implied that while Porth Ardur stood still in its provincial slumber, Captain James St John Stanier had changed a great deal. Macready noticed it in his eyes where lurked a steely intent that Macready felt as keenly threatening as a knife blade. After pausing for a few moments looking past the ensign as it flapped in the breeze, Stanier turned sharply.

'Well, Macready, let's get down to business.'

They shuffled into the smoke room and settled down round the table while the Saloon Steward served them coffee. Stanier had brought with him one of

88

the clerks from headquarters. The man doled out papers, adding to the individual files each officer had prepared. Macready, discomfited by Stanier's sudden appearance, felt his confidence ebb. There could be little doubt but that the man would seek revenge. He caught Mr Farthing's eye. Charlie too was pale with apprehension and Macready looked away. He felt chastened, like a small boy caught scrumping. Then Stanier briskly swept them up in the business of the forenoon.

'Well, gentlemen, you have before you the signed deposition of a certain Mr Ifor Davies of the Mermaid Bakery, Porth Neigwl on the Island of Stones, otherwise known as Ynys Meini ...' Stanier made the most of it. He read right through this outrageously inaccurate and exaggerated document. On completion he then read through the report submitted by Macready. A man of precise thought and instant decision, Macready's was a model of brevity, setting out the facts in chronological sequence. It took Stanier only a moment to read it and then he laid it down and leaned forward on his elbows.

'I find it difficult to square these two accounts, Captain Macready,' Stanier said. 'Yours is so lacking in detail as to suggest concealment of something.'

Macready, who had by now recovered some of his composure, also leaned forward. He did not wish to appear truculent, merely to block each thrust of his enemy with a polite parry. 'My account, Captain Stanier, gives you the facts without the embroidery of any speculation. It does not deny the central fact that, despite his best endeavours, the Chief Engineer was unable to turn the machine fast enough and unfortunately crashed through the wall of the Mermaid Bakery. Some loss of flour was inevitable, but I am certain that no-one has subsequently starved and I know that the *Kurnow* shipped extra flour from Beynon's Bakery here in Porth Ardur the following day.'

'Then you admit to carelessness?'

'In what way?'

'Why, you have just said that your Chief Engineer was unable to turn the machine fast enough. Now, Captain Macready,' Stanier went on, ignoring the presence of the culpable officer sitting on Macready's right hand, 'it occurs to me that either the corner was too sharp for the geometry of the steamroller's steering, or the machine was going too fast to allow the driver to turn the steering gear fast enough.' Here the accompanying clerk nodded, for it was really his idea that the error resulted from either of these two causes and that Stanier

90

should open with this line of questioning.

'I do not dispute that, Captain Stanier.' Macready turned to the Chief. 'Do you wish to add anything, Chief?' he asked.

Reluctance showed in the Chief Engineer's expression. He coughed with embarrassment, but bravely admitted, 'I had not allowed for the time it took to turn the steering wheel, sir. So yes, the steamroller was going too fast. I suppose to that extent I was careless.'

'That is a handsome admission, Chief,' Stanier said, smiling condescendingly, disarming the unfortunate engineer. 'But I do not seek a scapegoat, merely to establish the facts.' The Chief nodded and swallowed, relaxing a trifle. 'But there is the matter of mitigation, is there not?'

Macready looked up as the Chief swung his uncomprehending face to Stanier. 'Mitigation, sir?'

'Provocation really, Chief, wouldn't you say, eh?' It was clear to Macready that Stanier was prompting the Chief and a small ganglion of fear was unravelling itself in Macready's gut. A pregnant silence filled the room. Outside a sailor walked past carrying a tin of white paint. The officers present sat waiting for Stanier's next pronouncement, for they had nothing to contribute. Stanier drew in his breath, as though the act automatically drew after

91

his inhalation, the gaze and attention of the *Caryatid*'s assembled officers.

'Oh, your loyalty does you credit, gentlemen. Yes, indeed. Loyalty is a characteristic I esteem highly, particularly when it is given to the Lighthouse Service where it belongs. Indeed your salaries place you under an obligation to render it to the Lighthouse Service. I therefore caution you against misplacing it, gentlemen. Do not misplace it.' Stanier looked round the ring of faces. He smiled inwardly; he had their attention now. The briefest mention of salaries, the small, implied but deadly threat to their jobs would, he knew, open up the crack which existed between their corporate existence in their uniforms, and the wretched little lives that lived inside their pink skins. After the Service, loyalty went to the Captain and Stanier's insinuation was intended to prise it out, like an escargot from its shell.

'You know what I mean, gentlemen, don't you ...' Stanier's tone hardened as his eyebrows came together into a forbidding frown. It was not a question.

'I think I know what you are trying to imply,' Mr Farthing said suddenly, impetuously breaking the silence.

'Oh, and what is that?' snapped Stanier, leaning forward towards the Mate.

'Perhaps you would be kind enough

to tell us, Captain Stanier,' Macready interjected quickly, frowning at Farthing.

'Oh I will, Captain Macready. You see, it is the matter of the insult you shouted at the Chief Engineer, making him lose concentration. Such a provocation—'

'How would it make the Chief lose concentration?' responded Macready, 'since he had already hit the bakery wall?'

'Then you at least admit that you insulted the Chief?' Stanier said, his eyebrows now each individually arched above triumphantly gleaming eyes.

'I merely made—'

'Did Captain Macready insult you, Chief?'

'Well—' The Chief was about to say 'not exactly' and admit he had made more of the Captain's joke than he intended, but he was unused to these formal and intimidating proceedings, and Stanier gave him no chance.

'I quite understand,' Stanier went on, 'your reluctance to implicate the Captain, Chief. It does you credit, it really does, but if that is what happened let's openly admit the matter—'

'Oh, this is preposterous.' Charlie Farthing was on his feet. 'We all know that Captain Macready made a joke, and the joke was made after the steamroller was embedded in the wall of the bakery. It upset the Chief, but it was not the cause of the accident. This whole thing's a farce—'

'Sit down, Mr Farthing, I'll ask for your contribution when I want it.'

'No, I won't sit down, Captain Stanier. You are not impartial in this matter. See to it that your clerk writes down in the minuted proceedings of this enquiry that you have an old score to settle with Captain Macready, that you are not impartial and that you have sought to lead the witnesses in order to achieve some petty revenge—'

'Sit down, sir! You are talking nonsense!' Stanier roared.

'I will not sit down—'

'Sit down, Mr Farthing.' Macready broke in and the Mate reluctantly obeyed.

'I shall not tolerate impertinence such as we have just witnessed, Captain Macready and I shall temporarily suspend these proceedings ... Please clear this smoke room as I wish to consider matters.'

*Caryatid*'s officers trooped out onto the sunlit boat deck and Macready led them forward to his cabin.

'That was a bloody silly thing to do, Charlie,' Macready began, but Charlie shook his head.

'You know the man, sir—'

'Is he the same bugger that used to be

94

the harbour master?' the Chief asked.

'Of course he is,' responded Farthing tartly. 'He's not forgotten how things were between the Captain and himself if you have.'

'Well I'm damned. I see his game now, the cheeky bugger.' The Chief turned to Macready, flushing with embarrassment. 'I'm sorry if I've caused you trouble, sir—'

'Just tell me one thing, Chief. Did you make a complaint against me behind my back?'

The Chief frowned. 'Good heavens, no sir! Why should I be wanting to do that?'

'I've no idea. I just wanted to establish where the story of this shouted insult came from. I'm sorry if it upset you, and perhaps it was bad taste to have made fun of you at such a moment, but any malice in the occasion has been added by that bloody Ifor Davies at Porth Neigwl and he's only out for what he can get.'

'Well, what's going to happen then, sir?' the Chief asked, his face anxious with honest concern.

'I don't know. A reprimand for me and Mr Farthing will get a black mark.'

'I've some photos, sir,' said the Second, speaking for the first time. 'They show the whole thing, including the state of damage after the steamroller was pulled out.'

'Why didn't you tell us before?' expostulated Macready.

'I didn't want to embarrass the Chief, sir.'

Macready looked at the Chief Engineer. 'What d'you say to showing them to his lordship, Chief?'

'I'd show him my fucking arse if I thought it would do any good, sir, so I would ...'

And they were all laughing when Stanier's clerk summoned them back into the smoke room.

'It is my intention to recommend—'

'I'd like to stop you there, Captain Stanier,' Macready said. 'We have a sequence of photographs to show you which illustrate the problem we had ...'

The black and white shots were deployed in front of Stanier who stared at them. 'These do not show when Captain Macready shouted his insult—'

'Captain Macready did not insult me, sir,' the Chief said. 'He had a joke at my expense. Oil and water, you know the sort of thing. I admit to being annoyed at the time, but nothing more.'

For the first time Macready saw the old Stanier, the blustering stuffed shirt with no wind in his sails, with no real confidence and less of a case.

'The whole thing was an accident,' the Chief went on and Macready rejoiced as the old Chief finally emerged manfully from his humiliation. 'We were doing the island a favour and unfortunately I misjudged the corner. You can see from the Second's last shot that the damage wasn't all that extensive. You can't trust those islanders. They think the rest of the world owes them a living, you know. They're notorious for trying anything to turn a buck to their advantage. Get three quotes for repairs from local builders and then another from Taylor here in Porth Ardur and I'll put money on the last being cheaper despite the need to travel offshore.'

'Thank you, Chief,' broke in Stanier, his voice cold. 'When the Board needs your advice on such matters, I am sure it will ask for it. Very well, I shall now finally wind this enquiry up. I have noted all your remarks ...' Stanier paused, allowing his clerk to nod in agreement. Stanier coughed self-importantly. 'I have also noted the personal remarks levelled by Mr, er ...'

'Farthing,' prompted the Clerk.

'In their specifics, I hope, Captain Stanier,' Farthing broke in, but Stanier ignored him and rumbled on to his conclusion.

'And these matters will be laid before

the Board at next Tuesday's meeting.'

Stanier rose and shuffled papers. Once again the officers trooped out, though Stanier called after Macready to remain a moment. While his clerk stuffed the files into a briefcase, Stanier drew Macready to the after end of the smoke room. Outside the glass-panelled doors a ladder led down onto the after deck and the mooring bitts, capstans and towing gear. Above the rail flew the defaced ensign of the Commissioners.

'It was not my intention to mention the past, Captain Macready. It's unfortunate young Farthing did so.' Macready said nothing. 'Young' Farthing was not much younger than Stanier, but he forbore from correcting the Commissioner. 'I don't think he's the sort of officer we want in the Lighthouse Service—'

'On the contrary, Captain Stanier, he is diligent, efficient and reliable.'

'He had no right to say what he did. He has no evidence for it and in any case the matter is largely irrelevant. Between ourselves, Captain Macready, this ship's days are numbered. She is too old, too expensive and with additional costs like the one we have to address in the case of Mr Ifor Davies, a burden on the Service. She will not be replaced. Frankly I shall not be sorry. The Board is considering economies which will make her and all her company redundant.' Stanier smiled at Macready. 'Including Mr Farthing, Captain Macready, not to mention yourself.'

After Stanier had gone, Macready stood for some time staring abstractedly after the departing taxi. He thought of a hundred things he should have said. He could, for instance, have reminded Stanier that the Commissioner only held his own master's certificate courtesy of Macready himself, but these considerations were moved by *l'esprit de l'escalier*. Macready was in a kind of numb shock. Although Stanier had unwittingly reunited the *Caryatid*'s officers, his news threatened to destroy their whole world.

# An Agent Of The Devil

In the fortnight following the enquiry, Captain Macready threw himself into his work in an attempt to shove out of his mind the news that Stanier's malice had insinuated into it. *Caryatid* loaded the gleaming red, black and chequered steel buoys from the buoy yard at Porth Ardur, deploying them at sea on their lonely stations and removing the rusty, weedy and barnacle-encrusted units they replaced. Charlie Farthing in his sea-boots waded among heaps of scraped mussels and oarweed, heaving and veering heavy chain moorings and the huge, cast-iron sinkers that anchored these remote aids to navigation to their lonely stations. *Caryatid* anchored off various lighthouses and worked her boats back and forth, pumping oil and water into the reservoirs and tanks attached to each of the tall stone towers. They spent a week, as they did every month, steaming round the entire Sea Area, changing the crews of the lightvessels and lighthouses and on one occasion they towed a lightvessel to a dry-dock on the north-west coast, enjoying a run ashore, roistering like deep-sea men amid the purlieus of the great port.

Macready even took the ship to an anchorage off Ynyscraven more times than were strictly necessary in order that he could enjoy the company of Justine to whom, in the end, he confided the dreadful news. Long years of widowhood and a positive disposition enabled Justine to console herself with her situation. She had found in Sonia Farthing, Charlie's wife and her next-door neighbour, a true friend and this deep attachment in some way consoled them for the separation from their men they both endured. Furthermore, Sonia's total and committed love of the island helped to reconcile Justine to her own fate. However, in the news that Macready now brought to her, Justine perceived the possibility of a brighter future.

'But if Gwendolyn was made financially independent by the sale of her farm, Septimus, and you were to retire, we could be happy here.'

'I should leave Gwendolyn, you mean?' he asked, sitting up and throwing his legs over the edge of the bed.

'Of course. Without a ship you will have to settle somewhere. Frankly, my love,' she said, putting her arms about him and leaning her head upon his naked back, 'once *Caryatid* has gone—'

101

'I know, I know,' he interrupted irritably, 'I shall amount to nothing in Porth Ardur.'

'Women will envy Gwendolyn her full independence. She will have the sympathy due wronged women and she will be able to do what she likes. Let Stanier have his petty way. A man who nurses all that venom will never be happy. Think what *we* stand to gain ourselves—an end to these dawn partings.'

Macready shook his head, gently detaching himself from her embrace. 'There is not only us to be considered, my darling.' He paused and pulled his shirt over his head. 'What about the crew and all their families? A few of the older men will want to retire, of course, but the younger ones will have nothing.'

'What about this new mine—'

'Oh, Justine, no self-respecting seaman wants to work in a mine, even an open-cast mine. Anyway, what about Charlie and Sonia?'

'Ah, now there there is a ray of hope. The Reeve really is retiring, he's not well again and this time he has decided to go. Lord Dungarth is due here any day to see the poor old boy. Sonia wants Charlie to take the job.'

'Give up the sea, you mean?' Macready scraped at his chin, the rasps of his razor punctuating his words.

'Well, yes.' He turned and stared at Justine who lay back on her pillow, one arm behind her head. Her hair spilled about her face and her breasts lay exposed. Macready swallowed and turned back to the mirror, wiping his face and reaching for his collar and tie.

'That would be a pity, but Stanier's knife will be out for Charlie, and Wentworth the Second Mate mentioned he had heard Charlie muttering about resignation.' Macready hated upheaval. Evolution was acceptable, natural, but the work of maintaining navigational aids had a time-less quality. The philosophy of depend-ability rested upon the very principle of constancy. All things had a season; in due course it was right that he should retire. Charlie Farthing had first come to *Caryatid* as Second Mate and had now risen to the position of Chief Mate. In due course, when he himself retired, Charlie would in all probability become the ship's commander. That would be in the fullness of time, but for them both to go within a short period, precipitated by the nastiness of Captain Stanier, flew in the face of logic. Stanier, Macready recalled again, would not now have his master's certificate at all if Macready had not given favourable evidence at the enquiry into the loss of the *Sea Dragon*. It disgusted Macready that Stanier could forget the matter.

'So you are going to fight?'

Macready pulled on his reefer jacket. 'I am going to fight for the ship's sake.' He paused, bending over her, his eyes softening as she reached up and touched his smooth cheek.

'And you?' Justine asked huskily. 'What will you do for yourself?'

'Think of you,' he said enigmatically, kissing her and leaving.

Macready met Charlie Farthing on the cliff path down to the beach. After each wished the other a good morning and exchanged a brief remark about the weather, which promised a fine day, they walked for a moment in silence. When they came to the bend in the path from which the ground dropped almost sheer, both men spontaneously paused. From this point the ship, lying peacefully in the anchorage, came into view. They could see the distant activity on the boat deck as Wentworth prepared to lower the starboard motor boat which was to come in and fetch them.

'I, er ... I hear you have been considering resignation, Charlie.'

'Well, sir, I don't think I have done myself any favours and with Stanier newly appointed to the Board, the situation will only get worse. Stanier's that sort of bastard. Besides, I'd like to spend more time with Sonia and, well, there's a possibility that the Reeve's job will fall vacant at last.'

'Yes, I heard about it. It's what you've been waiting for, isn't it?'

'Well yes. There was mention of it some time ago. We more or less married with the prospect of my living here and becoming Reeve.'

Below, the faint smack of the boat hitting the water came to them and Macready began to walk again. Timed properly, both boat and passengers should reach the beach at the same time. For a little while the two men walked in silence, then Macready said, 'Charlie, there's something you should be aware of, but I don't want a word of it made known to another soul. D'you understand?'

'I understand, sir, but is it about the ship being scrapped?'

'You know?' Macready was surprised and stopped abruptly.

'Whispers, scuttlebutt, gossip.' They began walking again. 'Don't ask me how these things come up, sir, maybe Stanier mentioned something, he spent the night at the Station Hotel. The Bosun's sister waits at the breakfast tables there.'

'Ahhh. Yes, and the Clerk ... He'd want

to impress the Clerk, wouldn't he now.'

'Exactly.'

'But it's not just scrap *Caryatid*, Charlie, it's get rid of the ship altogether. There'd be no replacement. The Area would be taken over and run as a sub-Area from Cavehaven. The *Waterwitch* would cover the Silurian Strait.'

Mr Farthing shook his head as they reached the beach and trudged over the shingle. 'That must remain confidential,' Macready insisted.

'Of course, sir.'

The whispers reached Mrs Macready at about the same time. Oddly it was she who was to first learn more than anyone else, for one evening she received an unexpected telephone call from a man announcing himself as David Smith. It took her a moment to realise she was speaking to the local Member of Parliament and a moment later she found she had accepted an invitation to dine with him. She was never quite certain why she so easily agreed, except that she was left a little breathless by the fact that he had called her at all.

'I am holding a constituency surgery in Porth Ardur on Thursday, Mrs Macready, and shall be staying at the Station Hotel that night. Would you be kind enough to dine with me? I have a most important matter to discuss with you in confidence and I should appreciate your not mentioning the matter to a soul until after we have spoken. I don't want to say too much over the telephone either, if you don't mind, but I'm sure you can guess what it's about. Say half past seven? Good. Thank you so much. I look forward to meeting you. Good evening.'

And he was gone, leaving Gwendolyn staring at the wallpaper in the hall with a heart beating as though she had just been requested to attend the palace for an audience with the king. For a moment she dithered uncertainly about the purpose of the call, then her natural good sense reasserted itself.

It was the mine, of course.

But then it might also be the ship ...

Yes, that was it, it *was* the ship! The rumours were true! David Smith MP, who had never so much as visited Porth Ardur in his life before, as far as Gwendolyn Macready knew, was going to do something about the ship. Smith was, Gwendolyn knew, a junior minister, but for precisely what, she could not recall. Yes, she could, he was in the Ministry of Power and that swung her thinking back in favour of the mine. But the certainty, as soon as it had taken root, was deracinated by the man's insistence upon secrecy. No, it was almost certain that he was acting as local MP and therefore it would be the ship ...

And thus vacillating, Gwendolyn Macready found herself caught up in a heady, speculative night of fitful sleep such as she had not known since she had first set eyes upon the handsome person of the twenty-year-old Septimus Macready.

On Thursday afternoon Gwendolyn took a bath. It was her habit to do this every afternoon, but on this particular occasion she took longer than usual. She had not stopped turning matters over in her mind and, as soon as she had erected a careful argument in favour of the mine being Mr Smith's motivation, it would tumble down. She would chastise herself that she was selfishly pandering to the private fantasies of enrichment that had haunted her since she received that first intimation that the Ardurian Slate Company wished to purchase her farm. It had therefore to be the ship and this was always the eventual and final conclusion which, once reached, allowed her to sleep or get on with the ironing or whatever chore, committee meeting or visit next demanded her attention.

But she bathed and dressed with care for, despite her complex private distaste of intimacy, Gwendolyn Macready remained a woman susceptible to the honour done to her of a private dinner at the invitation of the local MP. There was a seductive hint of intrigue about the matter, not dissimilar to the scenarios painted by the novels she enjoyed reading. No one could guess how the girl that still lurked behind the public face of Mrs Macready still longed for what she had thought a marriage offered. Besides, she had not yet quite lost her looks, she thought, as she reached for her lipstick with a flutter of her heart. She rarely wore lipstick and the idea of putting it on for what she had become to consider a confidential, if not a secret assignation, a meeting with a strange man, gave her an unexpected and delicious frisson of excitement.

David Smith proved to be a short, stocky man. This pleased Gwendolyn as she caught sight of them both shaking hands in a full-length mirror in the dining room of the Station Hotel. She disliked craning up at tall men. She had chosen a maroon silk dress which fell from her shoulders in a modest simplicity which disguised her lack of height. Smith smoothly announced how delighted he was to meet her and how utterly charming she looked. Despite her naturally dismissive reaction to such blandishments, she was unable to suppress a treacherous quiver as he motioned her to sit, nor for a vain moment at least, to pretend she did not need reading glasses to decipher the menu.

When they had ordered and were taking their first sips of Chablis, Gwendolyn took stock of her host. He was a little younger than herself, she thought, though his brilliantined hair was thinning rapidly. He wore a dark, double-breasted suit and his shoes, she had already noticed, were neat, black and glossily polished. He wore a signet ring with, she thought, a seal set in it and his plain white shirt was tied with a striped tie that could have been regimental.

They ate their first course talking inconsequentially, establishing an atmosphere of relaxed understanding. Gwendolyn learned that Smith was indeed in Porth Ardur on constituency business, but his actual reasons for meeting with her were rather complicated and he would come to them in a minute. He did indeed hold a junior portfolio in the Ministry of Power, but again, this was not quite relevant to what he wished to discuss with her. She also learned that he knew she was married to the commander of the local lighthouse tender, and, as the main course was served and Smith tasted the newly opened bottle of Burgundy, Gwendolyn realised that although she had been in Smith's company for forty minutes, she was still none the wiser as to his motivation.

Smith on the other hand had learned that Mrs Macready was a cool and intelligent woman, that she was guarded in her admissions and therefore possessed a degree of discretion. Although she seemed essentially a self-effacing person, he detected a desire, perhaps even a positive ambition, to be effectual. She was also, he knew, susceptible to a little attentiveness, though wise to overt flattery. This was all very pleasing. As for her lingering sexuality, this did not interest Smith.

By the time the waiter left them to their main courses, he had established that she understood the need for absolute confidentiality.

'You see, Mrs Macready, one of the problems often encountered in democratic government when one seeks to encourage the march of beneficial progress and economic growth, is the hostility of people who perceive only part of an initiative. It is a natural reaction to resent change, of course, it unsettles us, it threatens us, but so often we end up by missing great opportunities! It therefore becomes necessary for people in government like myself to act in a ...' he paused and pulled a face as if it pained him to use the expression, 'well, semi-secret way in order to lay the groundwork so that matters can, when the time comes to reveal them, proceed smoothly. The unfortunate thing is,' Smith said, leaning forward and topping up Gwendolyn's wine glass, 'it looks as though one is acting furtively, whereas in fact one is only acting sensibly, d'you see? With an absolute economy of effort and, of course, the much more important consideration, an economy of resources.'

He smiled charmingly and, with an expansive gesture, added the non sequitur, 'You know this is awfully pleasant. I really am delighted to meet you, you know,' and he looked into her eyes for a fraction of a second longer than she could bear and she felt a stupidly girlish flush creep across her cheeks.

'Now,' he went on briskly as though not noticing her reaction, 'to specifics. I am aware that you have already been approached with a view to selling your farm. Oh,' he added hurriedly as she paused, her fork halfway to her mouth, 'please do not worry, I am not here to influence the asking price.' He laughed. 'That's the last thing a Tory would do! No, no, Mrs Macready, I am certain you will sell and that's the important thing, because the coalfield is huge and the economic

112

benefits to the locality are in proportion. Those accruing to the nation, in terms of exported coal, cannot be overlooked and will also be considerable. Of course,' Smith went seamlessly on, his mellifluous tone actually soothing in its urbanity, 'one fully understands the concern of many who regard an open-cast mine as an eyesore but, you know, there is a certain abstract beauty in the concept of a mine which yields up great wealth to those whose labour extracts it.'

Gwendolyn, who could see no circumstances mitigating the sheer ugliness of an open-cast mine even in the abstract, found herself unable to formulate any dissent as Smith went on.

'Having thus established the beneficial mine, we next have to consider the matter of exporting its produce. Now Porth Ardur is, in a sense, ideally placed. It is close to the mine, requiring only a short run of railway track to connect the two facilities, but it does possess one disadvantage.'

Smith laid down his knife and fork and dabbed his lips with his napkin. 'To be truthful, it is a small disadvantage and one easily overcome with some local encouragement and this is the nub of why I have sought you out tonight, Mrs Macready. You see, I believe you are a considerable influence for good in the town, indeed people speak highly of you in that context, and to occupy so high a place in the public's opinion is, I assure you, no mean achievement. There's many a politician who would envy you, I do assure you.' Smith laughed, laid down his napkin and refilled Gwendolyn's glass again.

'The long and the short of it is that your assistance is required to further the scheme.'

'In what way, Mr Smith?' Gwendolyn was becoming impatient, sensing a slight prevarication on Smith's part.

'In the matter of the port, Mrs Macready. You see, strictly between ourselves, a decision has been made by the Commissioners for Celtic Lighthouses that their entire operational facility in Porth Ardur is unnecessary. It is their intention to scrap your husband's old ship and to run everything from Cavehaven. I believe there is another ship, a newer ship there—'

'The *Waterwitch*,' Gwendolyn muttered almost automatically, appalled at this revelation. The smooth and handsome MP suddenly assumed the awful proportions of an agent of the devil. She began to see all the threads of her speculations converging, and running into an awful knot. The first tentative whispers of the old ship's redundancy were now more

114

than confirmed; she was horrified, aware of the impact such a decision would have upon the population of Porth Ardur, not to mention herself. The little town was bound to the sea, derived its very name from it. Some held that it was from its strand that King Arthur's body had been taken on its last voyage to the mystical land of Lyonesse. But such considerations were swept from her mind by the necessity to pay attention to Smith's words.

'... Now this gives us the opportunity to redevelop the port and to use it for the export of the coal produced by the mine and we would like you to make it your business to emphasise the manifold opportunities this will give the town. I shall, of course, keep you personally fully informed of all contiguous developments. In return I would appreciate your reciprocal confidences. I do not expect this to be easy, but it will help if you will let us know any specific concerns in order that these can be addressed and disarmed.' Smith paused to drain and refill his own glass. 'I am sure that your own private transactions will proceed smoothly. I don't have to emphasise the fact that without your land none of this can go ahead.'

She recalled little else of the evening. She had been a little tiddly, she recalled the following morning. The most surprising thing about the evening was the way both her guesses at the MP's intentions had proved correct. That they were interrelated she had never even considered.

It was not until the following morning that she sat quietly and reviewed the events of the previous evening. As she ordered her own thoughts, dragging them out, as it were, from the weighty, persuasive weight of her host's, she realised that not only had Smith tried to bribe her but he had already, unknowingly succeeded. Earlier that week she had written to propose a settlement value upon the farm. It would, she knew now, be accepted. Far from thinking she might have asked double, she realised she had no weapon to bring against the monster, that the one thing she might have done, refused to sell the farm, would now prove well nigh impossible, for in addition she had taken the Evans brothers into her confidence and explained the provision she intended making for them. And to cap it all, in her confusion she had failed to ask Smith, who would have given her anything she wanted last night, for the two men to be employed in the mine. Perhaps there was still time for that, but then, what was she thinking? She did not want the mine at all now!

She rose, wringing her hands in an agony

of confused frustration. The whole matter could have pivoted on her decision! For a moment she had unknowingly held all the key cards to the situation and she had flung all that advantage away! It did not console her to reflect she could not have possibly known all the facts any earlier and had acted in good faith. None of these considerations would carry much weight in Porth Ardur once the word was out that Mrs Macready had dined with David Smith and had consequently sold the farm, allowing the mining to begin. When news broke that the Lighthouse Service were pulling out and her husband was going to retire, the fat would be truly in the fire! My God, she could never hold her head up in Porth Ardur again!

Thus preoccupied, Gwendolyn Macready spent a day in dishevelled consternation, impatiently awaiting the return of her errant husband who, for once, she longed to see.

It was a black night of lashing rain and gusting wind as Macready brought *Caryatid* in through the open dock caisson and laid her gently alongside the berth. For the first time for many years he felt a reluctance to go home. It was nearly midnight, he was depressed, dog-tired and wanted to turn into his bunk. He was no longer young and the wearying thought of having to trudge home up the long hill depressed him still further. He longed to be sleeping with Justine, to end the seemingly endless calls of duty and obligation, to give up, concede the game to Stanier and his ilk, to retire to Ynyscraven and the idyll he knew existed there.

It was so bloody unfair. Charlie was going to do just that, and Charlie was half his age! Charlie had yet to endure the tedium, isolation and responsibility of command. Charlie, damn him, was taking the easy way, running up the providential ladder while he, Septimus Macready, once the happiest of men, slid down the snake of despair.

'Orders, sir?' Charlie knocked at the cabin door.

'Steam for fourteen hundred. Discharge all the dirty buoys and get the clean ones aboard. I'm sleeping at home tonight.'

'Aye, aye, sir,' acknowledged Mr Farthing, surprised that the Captain had thought the routine matter worth mentioning.

'And you've not changed your mind?'

'No, sir. I've the letter ready for the post.'

'Well, I'll miss you, Charlie, when the time comes.' Macready turned and smiled at his young second-in-command.

'I'll miss you too, sir.'

'I don't know who they'll send as a replacement ...' the Captain lowered his voice, 'if they even bother.'

On that lugubrious note Macready quit the ship. He looked back at her once. The cluster of lights, palely illuminating the long column of her buff funnel seemed so much a part of Porth Ardur that he wondered what the place would be like without her. It did not occur to him that most of the inhabitants of the port saw the same view without the ship and that only he, and those of his crew that drifted up the hill towards Acacia Avenue, only ever saw it with their ship looking like a permanent fixture.

He knew the moment he saw Gwendolyn that something was wrong. He had only ever once before seen her in so untidy and neglected a state, when she had been sick with a serious bout of fever which turned out to be appendicitis.

'What on earth is the matter, m'dear?'

'Oh, Septimus, it's just too awful to tell you—' She threw herself at him and he found himself embracing her and muttering silly words of comfort such as he had not done for many years as she mumbled against his chest an incomprehensible catalogue of apparently dire and terrible events. In the end he succeeded in quietening her, got her to sit, made a pot of tea and joined her.

'Now, Gwendolyn, just explain to me what this is all about.'

It was about half past two in the morning when she had finished telling him and he had completed all the questions her occasionally disjointed account provoked. For a long time he sat staring at the floor, with his wife watching him. 'What on earth are we going to do, Septimus?' she whispered at last, unable to endure the silence a moment longer.

He drew in his breath and looked up. 'Well, my dear, we must do something, that much is clear. But I don't know what.' His remark to Justine that he would fight for his ship's company had been outflanked by Gwendolyn's precipitate sale of the farm and now sounded mere boyish hubris.

'There must be some way—'

'I think we shall have to accept the inevitable,' he said. 'We cannot fight it, although I should like to minimise the effect it will have upon the ship's company. But if the festering Commissioners have decided *Caryatid*'s to go, we are quite powerless to stand in their way. What we have to do is to see if there is some way we can soften the blow to Porth Ardur.'

'What about *us*, Septimus? I am totally compromised.'

'Yes. I suppose you are. Even though

you acted quite innocently, people won't give you the benefit of any doubt. On the other hand you will have received a good price for the farm, and can perhaps move away as soon as possible.'

'And you, you'll go to that woman the moment I'm out of here.'

'Once you are out of here, Gwendolyn, I shall have no reason for being here myself.'

'Oh, this is awful!'

'It is not so very awful. Most of Porth Ardur are aware of our situation. It would be more open, more honest, to acknowledge it. You will be quite comfortably provided for. You will have the money from the farm, your father's old investment income, half my pension—'

'I don't want half your confounded pension!'

'Don't be foolish, Gwendolyn. You may need half my pension.'

'I suppose you and your tart are going to live on love! At your age, it's preposterous!'

'She isn't a tart,' responded Macready, too tired to rise to Gwendolyn's taunting. 'She's had her own fair share of bad luck, having to bring up Tegwyn on her own and all that.'

'I've been thoroughly humiliated,' Gwendolyn said bitterly, but her husband was no longer listening. Something had

121

just occurred to him. Something Stanier had said.

'I suppose it is a coincidence that the scrapping of *Caryatid,* the closure of the buoy yard and the opening of the port to the export of coal from a brand new mine is all happening at once.'

'What d'you mean?'

'Only that nothing happens here for a century and then all hell breaks loose.' He paused. 'Tell me, d'you think Smith was acting in his capacity as MP, trying to do whatever he said for his constituents and the local economy, or was he acting on his own behalf?'

Gwendolyn shrugged. 'How should I know? He's too shrewd to let much slip by accident.'

'I wonder,' mused Captain Macready. 'I just wonder ... It's all too damned pat for my liking.'

Captain Stanier apologised for his late arrival at the club. 'Bloody meeting was interminable, David, but,' he took the whisky and soda off the salver the club waiter proffered, 'we've got what we wanted: closure of the whole bloody caboodle.'

'Well done,' replied the MP, laying his broadsheet newspaper down with a rustle. 'I knew the old buggers would, the economies are too persuasive and with threats to their jolly cruises in the offing, no sacrifice is too great, eh?'

'No,' Stanier agreed enthusiastically, unsure whether or not Smith was guying him. Personally he was looking forward to the annual inspection cruise of the Commissioners enormously, but it was clear Smith, pragmatic politician that he was, was not in favour. Stanier recalled a remark made by his wife only the previous evening when he was discussing the forthcoming Board meeting with her.

'Let's not lose sight of the fact, David, that whatever you think of the inspection cruise as a waste of public money, it does have a value.'

'Oh, all that nonsense about direct contact between the Board and the shop floor, or is it the deck? Well, that's gilding a rather tarnished lily when you consider the enormous cost of the *Naiad*, isn't it?'

'No, no,' said Stanier, glad to have caught out the nimble-minded politician for once, 'I mean it gives *us* a priceless chance to prove beyond doubt the rightness of our proposed course of action in respect of *Caryatid* and the whole old-fashioned set-up of Porth Ardur—'

'It does?' Smith frowned, uncomprehending.

'Of course!' Stanier hissed, looking

123

round as adjacent newspapers rustled their disapproval at the animation of their conversation. 'We can simply damn the whole thing by turning in a negative inspection report!'

'Could you actually carry that off? Mrs Macready impressed me as one of those delightfully anachronistic characters that believe in probity and rectitude. It's as amusing as finding a dinosaur these cynical days, but I suppose it's what one expects in so appalling a backwater as Porth Ardur. If she's formidable I have no reason to suspect her husband isn't equally as straightforward. I daresay he runs—what do you call it?—a taut ship.'

'Oh, we'll catch him, don't you worry. There were half-a-dozen things wrong with his ship when I visited her the other day; besides, the Board approved a letter of reprimand to him only this afternoon. That'll catch him flat aback for a start, and we've had a letter of resignation from his Chief Officer which I have managed to influence the Board to accept. Life will be pretty unsettling for the old stick-in-the-mud, what with one thing and another, so things are definitely going our way!' Stanier swallowed his drink and clicked his fingers for the waiter. 'Another one before we dine, David?'

'Why not,' Smith agreed, smiling.

'Perhaps we shall find a dinosaur in the mine,' laughed Stanier, and it took Smith some seconds to see the lame joke.

'Oh yes. Perhaps we shall.'

Macready was stung almost as much by the news of Charlie Farthing's resignation as by the letter of reprimand. He was unable to shake off the feeling that a conspiracy lurked behind the threatened changes to his home port, but he was completely at a loss as to how to discover the truth, still less what he could possibly do once he had done so. There was no *deus ex machina* to come to his aid and the letter of reprimand seemed, as indeed it was intended, to signal the end of the epoch over which Captain Septimus Macready had presided.

# Changed Circumstances

Tegwyn Pomeroy set the glass beside Lord Craven and settled herself on the chair next to him.

'Pom won't be long—'

'I didn't come to see Pom. I haven't seen a Tasmanian wind devil in months and I certainly don't want to see his, the bloody things give me the creeps. No, I came to see you.'

'Me?'

'Yes, Teggy, don't be all bloody coy, you know that if you weren't spoken for, I'd propose instant marriage—'

'Don't be silly, Roger.'

'I'm not, but I'll spare us both and come to the point. I want your advice.' The son and heir to Lord Dungarth, owner of the distant island of Ynyscraven, deliberately closed his eyes to slits and stared at Mrs Pomeroy. 'Damn it, though, you're the most beautiful creature.'

'Shut up and say what you came to say before I throw you out.'

'Well, I have really, Teggy,' his lordship said, rolling his eyes, 'but I do want your advice.'

126

'What about?'

'In a word, Ynyscraven.'

'What about Ynyscraven?'

'Well, I hate the place. Far too quiet for me. Pa loves it, though he used to pretend it was hell when he took us down there for holidays. Anyway, to the point ... Oh, Teggy, *do* come and live with me. I adore you to distraction—'

'Anyway, what, Roger?' Tegwyn said severely.

'Anyway, my darling and cruel heart, the bloody old Reeve has finally decided to chuck his hand in. Now, I know your ma lives there in sin with some bloody old sailor ...' Craven held his hand up to silence Tegwyn's protest with a laugh. 'Pa's getting too old to take much of an interest and he wants me to look after it. Frankly the place could drift away on the tide, but I suppose I've got to show an interest so, what I want to know is, how suitable is this fellow Farthing? I gather your ma knows his wife or something like that.'

'Yes, she does. Sonia's lived on the island—'

'Oh, I remember her. Pretty thing with red hair. Had a mad artist for a mother, didn't she. I remember when I was a kid being down there one summer. She wanted to see my winkle—'

'And I expect you obliged,' remarked

127

Tegwyn laughing.

'I expect I did. A gentleman always does what a lady asks. No chance of you asking I suppose?'

'I'm not a lady. Go on anyway.'

'Must I?'

'Yes.'

'Well, I've nothing more to add really. If this cove Farthing's competent and wants the job he can bloody well have it. I wouldn't want to be cooped up on the damned place. It's always raining and when it isn't, the island's covered in fog,' his lordship exaggerated petulantly.

'He and Sonia would be ideal for the job, Roger. There was some talk of them taking over, oh, about three years ago, but it all fell through when the Reeve and his wife changed their minds about leaving. Sonia's a dear, she really is.'

'I'm not certain I can trust part of the Craven fortune to a woman who's keen on looking at strange men's winkles.'

'Try. You might be surprised.'

'I shall remind her of the occasion when I go down there.'

'Are you visiting Ynyscraven?'

'Got to really, under the circumstances,' his lordship said gloomily, adding in a brighter tone, 'I'm sailing down there, so I needn't stay long and don't have to wait for that horrible little *Plover* to take me

128

over from Aberogg.'

'You're sailing there in your own yacht, then?'

Craven nodded. 'Yup. The lovely *Lyonesse*. Want to come?'

Tegwyn shivered and shook her head, recalling the awful hours aboard the wrecked *Sea Dragon*. 'I should simply hate it.'

They heard the door and a few minutes later Pomeroy entered the room. 'Ah, Craven, good evening. Are you tormenting Tegwyn again?'

'I keep trying to seduce her, Pom, but she's depressingly faithful. I even offered to show her my winkle but she declined.'

'I've told you before she's a woman of discernment and taste. Tell me, have you come across any more of those Tasmanian carvings?' Pomeroy smiled up at Tegwyn as she put a glass into his hand.

'No. What d'you want more of the things for? They give me the willies.'

Pomeroy said nothing, but smiled as he sipped his cocktail. 'I bumped into Stanier today,' he said, addressing Tegwyn. 'He was full of himself, as usual.'

'I really don't know why you encourage him, Pom.'

Pomeroy shrugged. He had known Caroline since she was a girl, but his real motive for the friendship with the Staniers

129

was more obscure. He used Tegwyn's reaction to the occasional encounter with her former lover as a barometer of her own affection for himself. Perhaps, he thought, he ought to shift his focus to Lord Craven. The dilettante art dealer might prove more dangerous than Pomeroy supposed.

'Who?' asked Lord Craven.

'I don't think you know him, Roger,' Pomeroy said. 'He and Tegwyn used to know each other.'

'We were lovers,' Tegwyn admitted candidly, 'before I met Pom.'

'What's the lucky devil got that I haven't?'

'Charm,' riposted Tegwyn swiftly.

'Oh, *touché*, darling,' laughed Craven. 'Is he the fellow who married Caro Black-adder?'

'The same,' said Pomeroy.

'Well, he might have charm, but he certainly has no taste. She's clever, but cold. It must be rather like making love to liquid carbon dioxide; you get burnt, but the experience freezes you.'

'She's a very clever woman,' Pomeroy said. 'Uses her divine Jimmy up front, and pulls the strings from behind. He's a marionette.'

'Yes, I know the cove. He's a club member; isn't he Chairman of the Cambrian Steam Navigation Company? Pater had some dealings with him. Tried to get one of his ships to run to Ynyscraven to increase the visitors, but the ship was put on another service to those islands to the north, what are they called, Teggy?'

'Ynys Meini and the Bishop's Islands. You mean the *Kurnow* then. She runs out of Porth Ardur. I didn't know Cambrian Steam owned her, I thought—'

'Oh, it's some sort of fiddle,' said Craven, running his left hand through his long flax hair and throwing one leg over the arm of his chair. 'The *Kurnow*'s registered as a single ship in a discreet company, but she's beneficially owned by Stanier's lot ... What used to be Blackadder Holdings. I'd forgotten you came from Porth Ardur. Funny little place. I'm intending to call in with *Lyonesse* next month. Pity old Pom's not interested in shipping, isn't it, Pom?'

'I never want to see another ship in my life,' Pomeroy admitted. 'Surviving one shipwreck is enough for one lifetime.'

'Ah, but you floated out of it with Teggy, now didn't you, eh?'

'Now you're being impertinent, Roger, and I shall not be able to ask you to dine with us.'

'Oh, damn you, Pom, for an old spoilsport,' Craven said with a good-natured laugh, hauling himself out of his chair. 'In that case I shall have to dine at the club.'

After he had seen Lord Craven out, Pomeroy returned to his wife. 'You know, for all his light-hearted banter, I really believe he would take you from me if you ever gave him the chance,' he said.

She smiled up and stretched her arm out towards him. 'I know, darling,' Tegwyn said smiling, 'but I have no intention of ever giving him the chance.'

The club seemed to Lord Craven more than usually boring. An hour later he was seated alone, toying with a lamb cutlet and musing over the unkindness of a fate that allowed an old queen like Pomeroy to possess as lovely a wife as Tegwyn. The vivacious and spontaneous charm of her transcended anything he ever came across in the young women paraded by their greedy mothers for his own delectation. It was true Lord Craven kept a mistress in a small flat in the northern suburbs, but Nancy was a convenience, a good-time girl four years older than his lordship, who knew her fate even before she let his lordship into her bed. One day she would be dropped, but he would never quite forget her and, she knew in due course, he would be kind-hearted enough to make a small provision for her out of his fortune.

Musing on whether or not to stay in the club, seek out Nancy's bed, or wander to the family's town house, Craven was startled from his reverie by a greeting.

'May I join you, Lord Craven?'

Looking up, Craven evinced surprise. 'Good God, it's Stanier, isn't it?'

'Indeed it is, my lord. May I ...?' Stanier had the opposite chair half drawn out.

'Well yes. Yes, by all means.' Craven watched Stanier settle himself, trying to imagine him and Tegwyn making love.

'I wanted a word with you, Lord Craven—'

'Oh,' Craven said, surprised, as if Stanier had divined the impiety of his thoughts. 'What on earth about?'

'Your father once approached one of my companies with a view to our mail ship visiting Ynyscraven. We declined at the time, didn't have the capacity, d'you see, but I anticipate we might be able to accommodate his lordship in the near future. I'd not like to let an opportunity slip.'

'It's rather small beer for a chap of your, er, what-d'you-ma-call-it?—expanding enterprise, isn't it?'

'Oh, you've heard about Porth Ardur.' Stanier chuckled and sat back as the waiter handed him a menu and he quickly ordered. Craven thought it odd that not only Stanier but Porth Ardur had cropped up either in the flesh or in conversation twice in one evening and leaned forward, filling Stanier's glass from his own bottle.

'Oh, I heard something,' Craven admitted vaguely.

'From your father, I suppose.'

'Yes,' lied Craven. 'But he wasn't very specific. Pater's got this dreadful habit of thinking I'm about to take over everything before he's dead. Reads too much Shakespeare, I guess.'

His casually confidential tone fooled Stanier, who leaned forward, dropping his voice. 'Well, we're going to open a new export trade in coal from Porth Ardur. As you probably know I've recently been appointed a Commissioner of Celtic Lights and this has helped. We're taking over the whole port ...'

Craven spotted the lack of logic in the use of the pronoun and rightly concluded Stanier was drunk. 'You mean "we" as in Cambrian Steam, rather than the Lighthouse Authority, I take it?'

'Absolutely, old man. There won't be any Lighthouse Authority presence in Porth Ardur by the end of the year. It'll all be down to Old King Coal.'

'And where's this coal coming from? The nearest deep mine is thirty miles away and most of its output goes into power stations.'

'The coal, old man, will come out of the ground about five miles from the dock at Porth Ardur. New. Open cast. Hardly an overhead in sight. Stacks of it. Coal I mean. Piece of bloody wonderful cake.'

Craven frowned. 'I've seen no new flotation on the stock market.'

'Didn't need one. Old company own a quarry almost on the spot. It produces nothing now, only ever had a small vestigial strata of slate. Most of it's now covering the roofs of Porth Ardur. But the Ardurian Slate Company actually owned a substantial part of Mynydd Uchaf which, though it has no slate, covers a great deposit of coal.'

'I know the mountain,' Craven muttered, more to himself than to Stanier.

'The slate company cost us a mere one hundred pounds! Of course the purchase of two adjacent farms has set us back a bit more, but very little in real terms. It's an absolutely sure-fire project. We just can't go wrong.'

'Who's in with you?' asked Craven, with just that tone of breathless excitement that persuaded Stanier he too might be fired with investment fever.

'Oh, Dickie Angerstein and Julius Throgmore, along with David Smith—'

135

'The local MP?' Craven said surprised.

'Yes, but he's a sleeper, so that's confidential, old boy.'

'Of course, of course,' soothed Craven. 'By God, Stanier, you don't let the grass grow under your feet, do you?'

Stanier's smile was almost sickening. 'Nice of you to say so. What's more, the exporting company will be Cambrian Steam.'

'So you've got the whole thing sewn up. Well, well, nice work if you can get it, as the Yanks say.' Craven watched Stanier tuck into his meal. 'And you're a Commissioner of Lights too, eh. Haven't you got the annual inspection cruise coming up soon?' Craven deftly turned the subject and Stanier, his mouth full, nodded. 'I thought so,' Craven went on. 'Pater was saying something about it. He used to go down to Ynyscraven about this time of the year so that when the Commissioners arrived to inspect the lighthouse, he'd get an invitation to dinner aboard the lighthouse yacht. He used to say the Commissioners kept a better table than anyone else he knew and the only way to get at least one good meal on the island was to waylay them! I wouldn't be surprised if he tried the trick again this year; he's been reviving some of the worst habits of his youth as he enters his second childhood.'

'Well, old boy ...'

'For heaven's sake, do call me Roger.'

'Well, Roger, oh, please call me St John ...'

'I thought your name was Jimmy.'

'Ah, that's what my wife calls me,' Stanier said with a hint of sheepishness.

'Ah yes, Caro ...'

'You know her?'

'Not in the biblical sense, but yes, I am acquainted with her. Pater used to be quite friendly with her father. He had some investments with the old boy some time ago. He was killed when his yacht ran aground and broke up. All the fault of the yacht skipper, I believe ... You all right, Jimmy? Had a bit much of the old pig-swill, have you?'

Justine finished reading the letter out loud. It was Tegwyn's habit to write a fortnightly letter to her mother. These were more often than not filled with news and gossip about Tegwyn's new circle of friends, distant characters known to Justine only through Tegwyn's correspondence, but Tegwyn took her duty seriously and, when news of so overwhelming a nature cropped up, intimately affecting the place where her mother lived, she passed it on quickly.

Of course, Tegwyn's emphasis was quite different. First came the news of Craven's intention to ask Charlie and Sonia to take over from the Reeve. This was followed by the possibility of an increase in the island's tourist trade if a new ferry service was opened up. It was only then that Tegwyn informed her mother of the dissolution of the lighthouse depot at Porth Ardur. Both women saw the opportunity this might provide for Captain Macready to retire to the island. Tegwyn, long uneasy about her mother's current circumstances, wished only for her happiness as she grew older. Mother and daughter were very close, the long years of Justine's widowhood having dominated Tegwyn's childhood and adolescence.

It was a quite incidental postscript that mentioned the involvement of Mr David Smith MP, for Tegwyn hardly thought it worth adding until she suddenly recalled that, in the days when the voluptuous Mrs Morgan ran a small lingerie shop, it had received a visit from a young, prospective Tory candidate. Mr Smith had been canvassing and, in the hope of securing Mrs Morgan's vote, had bought some feminine items from her. They had afterwards laughed over the matter, since Betty Byford, Justine's assistant, had sworn they were for himself, not the wife he vaguely alluded to.

It was fortuitous, too, that Lord Craven

had discovered another Tasmanian wind mask and, opportunist that he was, had called upon Tegwyn late one afternoon, long before her husband was expected home, to leave the hideous thing for Pomeroy to see. He also brought her a present of red jade, a small figure of the sea-goddess Kuanyin which, he assured her, 'is at least five hundred years old'.

Craven, besotted by Tegwyn, used the news gleaned from his encounter with the bibulous Stanier, in tandem with his gift, to increase his standing in Tegwyn's eyes. To be in her presence was delightful enough, but his lordship enjoyed even further excitement at the prospect of seducing her. She had, after all, fallen for a twerp like Stanier and lived in some state and, as far as he could see, perfect harmony with her odd, strangely likeable but undeniably queer husband. Pomeroy *must* have acquired her on some sort of a rebound, Craven believed. Some time soon, he concluded, Tegwyn's natural desires would manifest themselves and he wanted to be the fortunate fellow who benefited from their re-emergence. He was therefore generous and attentive in dispensing as much gossip as Tegwyn's feminine curiosity wished for.

It was not long before the intelligence

had been passed by Justine to Captain Septimus Macready.

'I knew it!' exclaimed Macready, his eyes alight. 'The bastard! The festering bastard!'

'Septimus!' Justine had upbraided him. 'Is there anything you can do?' she asked.

He shrugged his broad shoulders and looked at her. 'D'you want me to do anything? I thought you wanted me to ditch Gwendolyn and come and live here in quiet retirement.'

'Of course that is what I want, my darling, but—'

'But what?'

'Life is never quite that simple, is it? You'll spend the rest of your life with a bad conscience on two accounts—your wife and your ship. One we could live with, but two ...' she shook her head, tears filling her eyes, 'I'm not so sure.'

Macready took her in his arms. 'The course of true love never runs smooth,' he observed. 'Shakespeare was right, the canny old devil. We are a pair of star-crossed lovers, all right.'

'You could expose Stanier. I mean his conduct is improper, so is that of the MP ...' She told Macready of her past meeting with David Smith and the conviction of Betty Byford that the prospective MP had purchased a basque, two garters and

140

some stockings for himself. Their laughter rescued them from depression and when Macready left her, he had decided to write in confidence to Captain Jesmond. Justine's tale had reminded him of an incident in his own past. It had been a very long time ago, he thought with a chuckle as he walked briskly down the path towards his rendezvous with Mr Farthing.

He saw Charlie blow the rain off the end of his nose as both men began the descent to the beach and the motor boat.

'Not so pleasant this morning, sir.'

'No. Remind's me of the morning we nearly lost old Jessie Jesmond. Have I told you the yarn, Charlie?'

'I don't believe you have, sir.'

'Oh, it was when I was mate of the old *Naiad*. Lovely old ship with a clipper bow, counter stern and auxiliary sails. We used to set them to steady the ship when the Board were dining. Old Jesmond refused to have fiddles set up on their table in bad weather and it was our job to keep the ship as steady as possible!' Macready chuckled. 'Silly buggers used to lose tons of glass and crockery and the pattern of the saloon carpet used to receive regular additions, but we'd get a message, brought up by one of their stewards, congratulating us on our fine seamanship if the losses were below a certain number of plates and glasses for the state of the sea!'

Charlie shook his head in wonder.

'Anyway, one day we were off the Buccabu light and the weather was terrible,' Macready went on. 'Rain and wind and plenty of both. Jesmond insisted on landing to inspect the place even though it was not just dangerous, but quite impossible. Old Captain Voss, whom you won't remember but who was the best seaman I've ever known, was in command of *Naiad* and took me to one side. "I can manoeuvre to lower a boat and pick you up," he said. "I want you to take the Commissioners in and give that fool Jesmond the fright of his bloody life. Can you do it?" So off I went. None of the other Commissioners wanted to go but once Jesmond had announced they were off, it was a matter of honour. They all mustered on the boat deck, putting on their life-preservers and going a pale shade of green. You know what the Buccabu reef is like, there's a powerful eddy on the last two hours of the ebb just off the southern rocks and outside it, about fifty yards away, are those standing waves you got caught in once, d'you recall?'

'How could I forget?'

'Anyway, I primed the boat's crew and while we were getting ready, Voss had the signaller send a semaphore message to the keepers not to leave the security

142

of the tower to rig the landing. Voss made a superb lee and we got the boat away, even though there was a hell of a sea running. Then we were on our own and it wasn't long before we were off the reef. It was almost low water, but even so the rise and fall of the swell was completely inundating the main rock at times. I thought the sight would put Jesmond off, but not a bit of it. He had commanded a wool-clipper and liked us all to know he was a real hard case. He used to tell a tale about amputating a seaman's crushed hand when off Kerguelen and I've no doubt it was true.

'Anyway, at this point the entrance door to the Buccabu tower, which, as you know, is about thirty feet above the rock, opens up and we could see two of the keepers staring at us.

' "Mr Macready," Jesmond sings out, "there are no keepers rigging the landing!" "No, sir," I replied, "it's too dangerous." "Well, we can't go alongside without the boat ropes being rigged for us," he glared up at the two faces, "and if they won't do it for us, we'll have to do it ourselves!"

'By now I realised it wasn't Jesmond who was going to get a fright, it was me! "We can't do that, sir," I shouted back above the roar of the wind and the breaking sea which was terrific. "Look, it's

143

like a bloody pond in there," he bellowed, pointing, as you will have guessed, at that small area just off the landing steps that is cut to a smooth by the effect of the ebbing tide. A seal had popped his head up and was looking at us in disbelief. Anyway, I tried to explain to Jesmond that this was deceptive and the rise and fall of the breaking waves and swell made the whole thing so dangerous that we would assuredly smash the boat if we approached any closer. The next thing I knew he's kicked off his boots and dropped his hat in the lap of one of the other Commissioners who had been regarding this whole farce with faces stark with terror, and jumped over the side!

'He made two or three strokes towards the landing before the tide got him. The next minute I saw him dashed against one of the rocks. I ordered the coxswain to get out of the way and to take the boat out south of the standing waves and went in after the silly bugger. I knew there was no chance of plucking him out of the sea before we were clear of the overfalls and fortunately I managed to grab hold of him and get him over on his back. He was out cold with blood running all down his face, but by good fortune we went into the smooth and I could see he was breathing. I remember seeing the lighthouse go round me, though of course it was us spinning in the eddy, but it was growing smaller and the next thing we went through the overfalls. Those standing waves must be six or eight feet tall, I was nearly sick with going up and down; had my guts in the sky one moment and God knows where the next. Anyway, we broke out into the regular waves to the south which, though it was still blowing hard, seemed like heaven. Then the boat loomed up and fished us out after a bit of a struggle.

'Old Voss picked us up and we got Jesmond down aft into the Commissioners' quarters. I'd just got myself dry and into clean gear when I was called down there. Jesmond had come round by then, declined a hot bath and sent for me. The other Commissioners had retired to their bunks and Jesmond was alone, sitting in the smoke room dressed in a magnificent silk dressing gown, his feet in a bowl of steaming hot water, smoking a cigar and drinking a large peg of whisky.

' "Mr Macready," he said, waving his cigar at his feet, "this bowl of water is slopping all over the deck! Kindly set the auxiliary sails!" "Aye, aye, sir," I said and turned to leave when Jesmond called me back. "Mr Macready," he said, "you were right and I was wrong. You saved my life. Don't come crawling to me with any trivial matter, but if there's ever anything I can do for you, don't hesitate to ask." '

'And did you, sir?' Charlie asked. The two men stood on the tideline as the motor boat's forefoot scrunched on the shingle. 'No, never. Not until now, that is.'

# The Obscure Decisions Of Fate

Macready's letter to Captain Jesmond reached its destination ten days later. It had had a curious genesis, originating in Stanier's bibulous admission, spurred on its way by Craven's self-centred lusty desire and, finally, by Tegwyn's familial duty. Idle gossip was in this way passed through the due processes of human motivation and analysis, augmented and presented to Captain Jesmond as matters of established fact. It was not so much that Macready had penned the letter with such certainty that the allegation was laid out in cold accusation, but the power of the allusion was taken as implicit by the reader. Captain Jesmond, who in his younger days had dismissed as mere cowardice the caution of a professional, was no less a man of certainty in his later days. Age had cemented the vigour of his prejudices and his powers of judgement were swift and stubborn.

Captain Jesmond dived into the maelstrom of capitalism with as little fear as he once, long ago, braved the broad bosom of the Atlantic. Besides, he could not abide

Stanier. The one almost objective faculty the old man still possessed undiminished by a hard life and rooted dislike, was his ability to tell a good seaman from a bad one. Stanier was not merely a bad seaman, he was a sham, a phoney, a man whom Jesmond could not even countenance as a master mariner, and admitted to the councils of the Commissioners only as a shipowner. And for Jesmond, who had grown up in the days when a sailing ship was not romantic but back-breakingly hard work and a constant concern for the man who occupied the berth of master, a shipowner represented the most extreme form of capitalist. Politically, Jesmond occupied that strange no man's land of a man who automatically and naturally assumed the mantle of tyrant whenever he was afloat, but who, in the more reasonable atmosphere of a drawing room, was the mildest of socialists, genuinely believing in the dignity of labour, but admitting the depravity of sailors and the divinely appointed divisions of rank. This came with a degree of contempt for money, which he regarded only as an adjunct to survival, not a reason for living. As any man knows who has driven a sailing ship round Cape Horn in all weathers, there are other things in life. With this philosophy, Captain Jesmond nevertheless dutifully turned in a

148

handsome profit for his owner and kept his crew in thrall, admired by both for his fair dealing, but disliking both parties himself, for their ignorance and weaknesses.

As well as intensely disliking Stanier, the old man greatly liked Macready; Macready was a similar soul to himself, not so much a seaman, as a man of the sea. It was therefore with a mounting sense of wrathful indignation that Jesmond read Macready's letter. Detained in his bed by rheumatics, the old shipmaster had been unable to attend the Board meeting at which the Commissioners had approved the entire shutting down of the buoy yard at Porth Ardur. Unfortunately, since he never read minutes, Macready's letter first acquainted him with what he considered as a perfidious act.

A telephone call to Mudge confirmed matters and his protest found only a partial sympathy. 'The motion was carried by a majority,' Mudge explained, 'and though I was against it, I was the only one. Even if you had been there, Jesmond, we should have been overwhelmed.'

'Damn it, Charlie, get rid of *Caryatid* by all means, old ships must go when they're ripe, but the whole of our depot at Porth Ardur ... what's the point of scrapping that as well?'

'Economics. We can run matters just

149

as well from Cavehaven; the place isn't tidal, *Waterwitch* is only five years old and the buoy yard there is a more up-to-date facility than the old place at Porth Ardur.'

'Yes, but the bloody *Waterwitch* will have to steam a lot more miles to get up into the Silurian Strait on a regular basis.'

'She doesn't steam anywhere, Jesmond, she *motors*. She's a motor ship and her bunkering costs are a fraction of *Caryatid*'s. To be frank, we should have thought of all this years ago. It's no consolation to have this young jackanapes Stanier pointing out so obvious a matter to us. It's rather embarrassing.'

'He's doing it all in his own interests, you know, Charlie. You're being made more of a fool than you know.'

'What d'you mean?'

'You wait and see.'

Jesmond came off the telephone chuckling. He was not going to reveal all and risk a tip-off being passed to Stanier, to rob himself of a dramatic moment at next month's Board meeting. Jesmond felt an anticipatory surge of blood in his old arteries. By God, he would show the young whipper-snapper that he could not abuse his position as a Commissioner of Celtic Lights! It was an almost sacred trust and safe in the hands of men like Jesmond, but the influence of a self-seeking worm like Stanier, a man who could buy the services of a Member of Parliament and wreck a whole community with his greed could not, *must not,* be allowed to get away with it! Such modern notions, Jesmond told himself, had no place within an ancient organisation dedicated to the sole purpose of serving the mariner where constancy, probity and, above all, reliability were the watchwords!

As he laboriously ascended the staircase at the Commissioners' Headquarters on the day of the next Board Meeting, Captain Jesmond felt his old heart thumping with suppressed excitement as much as the effort of climbing. He fetched his seat with a sigh and glanced round the assembled members. There was an empty seat.

'Captain Stanier sends his apologies, Sir Charles,' intoned the Secretary. 'He is unavoidably delayed in the West Country.'

It was a second before anyone present noticed the empurpled visage of Captain Jesmond. Only when he kicked his legs in a fury of frustration at the choking in his throat, did they sense something was wrong with the eccentric old man. His eyes had begun to start from his skull and then, with what seemed an impertinent and final act, his tongue stuck out at them. For horrified moments they all stared at the appalling sight and then Jesmond ceased to twitch.

In a rictus of startled horror Jesmond's head lolled sideways. He slowly fell from his chair onto the carpet, stone dead.

The signal arrived while *Caryatid* was at sea. The ship was ordered to haul her ensign down to half mast in honour of the deceased Commissioner. Macready, watching from the bridge as the quarter-master dropped the ensign its own depth below the truck of the staff, saw his own hopes descend with it. Turning forward he stared at the horizon. He wished a good gale would stir itself up and blow like blue blazes for a bloody week so that he could anchor *Caryatid* under the lee of Ynyscraven and he could disappear into the Craven Arms and get very, very drunk. But the day was fine and there was work to be done lifting and cleaning the fairway buoy at Aberogg, removing a sick man from the St Kenelm lightvessel and attending a fishing boat aground near Port Mary. Fat chance he had of drowning his sorrows! No, life went on and he had a job to do. Until they took it away from him, that was.

Gwendolyn Macready's hand shook as she

accepted the cheque. Her mouth was dry and the fur cape she had set her severe black suit off with seemed to be generating a tremendous heat. The partial shadowing of her face afforded by the hat's veil helped her dissimulate a little, but she was desperately uncomfortable and ill at ease.

'Five thousand is a most handsome settlement, Mrs Macready,' Mr Robertson, her solicitor, was saying. 'Why, at two and half per cent per annum the income will be most useful.'

'Yes, yes, Mr Robertson, I am sure you are right ...' But Gwendolyn was not sure at all. She could have stopped the sale, could have put the brake on the whole thing, if she had had the moral strength, but once the neighbouring farm had been sold—at half the price per acre she herself had been offered, Robertson had informed her—the mine was inevitable. A patch of land isolated by an open-cast mine would have been of depreciating value and fallen to this modern, unavoidable economic siege as surely as Monday followed Sunday. She would have ended up with nothing, not even the means of providing for the Evans brothers whom, she had been told only that morning, were quite unsuitable for even a labouring task on the mine.

'They are starting work almost immediately, I understand,' Robertson said matter-of-factly. 'A shipment of plant is expected within a day or two and then, well, a new era of prosperity for us all I hope.' He looked at his watch. It was almost one, time for Mr Robertson to make his daily journey the hundred yards to the Tory Club.

Gwendolyn rose. She held out a gloved hand and shook Robertson's pudgy paw. 'Mr Robertson,' she said formally.

'It is always a pleasure to do business with you, Mrs Macready. I should deposit that cheque without delay, if I were you.'

In the street the sea-breeze cooled her. She hesitated a moment and then walked quickly, almost furtively to her bank. Passing under its sign, the red Pendragon, she felt like a traitor. No native of Porth Ardur, she had nevertheless come to love the place for it had, in its way, provided her with all the consolations absent from her marriage. To her surprise she found the manager himself waiting for her.

'Robertson telephoned, Mrs Macready. I have delayed my lunch—'

'That is very good of you, Mr Sinclair.' She followed the manager into his office and sat down.

'Not at all, Mrs Macready. I did not suppose you would wish one of my tellers to become acquainted with the details of your recent business,' Sinclair said, sitting opposite her, behind the rampart of his desk.

'No. That is most thoughtful of you.' Gwendolyn found herself flushing again. She most certainly did not want Porth Ardur to know that she had been enriched by five thousand pounds. The sum, already shrinking in her own imagination, would conjure up fabulous wealth in that of the less fortunate. She pulled herself together and sought to regain the upper hand.

'Mr Sinclair, Mr Robertson said that a two and a half per cent investment would yield a reasonable sum. Is there not a better rate to be obtained somewhere?'

'Of course, Mrs Macready. There is always a better rate, depending upon the risk you wish to take. One could, if one was brave enough, attempt to secure twenty per cent, but one would have to accept the fact that there would be grave risks. One might lose that part of the capital sum one had put at risk. On the other hand, one can spread an investment in a portfolio, risking a little while holding some in a cast-iron fund with a low yield. The remainder one can juggle with, using one's fiscal judgement; it can be quite absorbing and many people actually enjoy playing the stock market. There are also,' went on Sinclair, waxing as lyrical as it is possible for a bank manager, 'means

155

by which we, the bank that is, can act as your agent and broker, taking a small commission on your profits. In addition,' he learned forward confidentially, 'you can attend to matters on your own behalf and I am quite willing to come to a private arrangement to act as your adviser, if you so wish.'

'Thank you, Mr Sinclair,' Gwendolyn said, feeling better at this small revelation of parochial venality. She took the cheque from her bag and passed it across Sinclair's desk.

He took it and stared at it for moment, then looked up smiling. 'You are fortunate, Mrs Macready. Most people have to work for their money. Some of us are lucky enough to possess money which can work for us.'

Sinclair's smile, Gwendolyn thought, possessed no charm and she wanted time to think. 'I should like to place it in a safe deposit account at your best rate of interest for the time being,' she said. 'I shall return to settle matters with you in a week's time, when I have made up my mind.' She stood up.

'Of course, Mrs Macready, that is most sensible. You will want to discuss the matter with your husband, I am sure.'

Walking home it occurred to her that she did not want to discuss matters with Septimus in the least. Whatever her previous misgivings, the deed was done and the money was hers. For a wicked moment Gwendolyn was overcome with a wave of pure, almost terrifying elation. It caught her so suddenly that she felt her knees buckle and had to pause, leaning against a lamp-post until she had mastered the emotion. When it came down to practicalities, she had a decision to make between two choices: invest sensibly or speculate?

For a moment she vacillated, suddenly wanting to see the reassuring bulk of her husband, and looked down into the harbour in sudden expectation, but the dock was empty of all but a few fishing trawlers. Then her resolve hardened again. No, he had repudiated her and it was her turn to repudiate him. The money was hers by due process of law; she had no need to be ashamed; she would put it to good use but she must not be like the woman with the talents, hiding them under a bushel. First, as Sinclair had pointed out, it had to be made to work.

She drew in a deep breath and stared at the horizon. The sun sparkled on the sea and in the very far distance she could make out, blue as a bruise, the undulating line of the southern shore of the strait. Between lay the small, blue-grey silhouette of a ship.

It was not *Caryatid,* that much she knew, and was probably a tramp passing along to one of the several ports to the eastwards of Porth Ardur.

Mrs Macready was proved wrong. Next morning the strange ship filled the enclosed dock in Porth Ardur and with her derricks swung out over the quay, disgorged some of the contents of her hold. The caravans, huge diggers and crane-grabs that were deposited so surprisingly, were accompanied by several score of rough-looking men who, having fired up these monstrous items of industrial plant, either drove them away, or swaggered off in their wake, winking at the young women of Porth Ardur as they marched in a loose and insolent column, like an impromptu army of invasion.

The men who worked on the docks reported the ship as being the SS *Lancelot,* belonging to the Cambrian Steam Navigation Company. They had had little notice of her arrival since their trade union had been hurriedly locked into discussing more important matters. Quite by chance one of the shop stewards had discovered the port had changed hands over the previous weekend and the dockers were eager to enter negotiations with the new owners. These turned out to be a company called

Celtic Ports Limited and the Chairman and chief negotiator was a man called Stanier. People remembered him in Porth Ardur for being not only their harbour master, but the man who had taken on Captain Septimus Macready of the Celtic Lighthouse Service. The name of his company seemed somehow to defy that of the lighthouse authority which was not without its enemies in Porth Ardur. Most of these comprised the casual labour erratically employed on the other side of the enclosed dock, who regarded everyone paid by the Commissioners for Celtic Lights as having well-paid sinecures for life.

In fact, many more of the townsfolk, those not intimately concerned with ships and especially the women of the town, remembered Stanier for his brave stand against Captain Macready and his filthy old ship whose black funnel-smoke besmirched their weekly washing. Among these people, the intelligence that *Caryatid* was to be scrapped caused unalloyed joy. To this good news could now be added more, for Stanier's company had offered Porth Ardur's small group of dockers a deal promising them a great future centred on a regular sailing by a Cambrian steamship. Moreover, until the new tips were constructed, the first cargoes would have to be handloaded. This would provide

159

a great deal of manual work.

'What happens when the tips are finished?' one man had queried from the back of the hall in which the meeting had taken place.

'By that time,' Stanier had said, 'the local economy will have picked up and our predictions show that a general import-export trade resourced from locally generated and regenerated trades will create a highly viable environment from which you will all be able to derive great benefit.'

'And what does all that mean?' the hectoring went on, though others in the hall were hushing the man to silence.

'It means more ships, more work and more money, my lads.' A modest cheer greeted this news. Stanier held up his hands for silence. 'Moreover,' he went on, 'we are a highly progressive organisation. We want to end the pointless and mutually destructive confrontation of capital and labour. The Celtic Ports Company wishes you all to participate in its success by becoming stakeholders. Your labour is as important as the capital invested by shareholders. We promise we will share our profits equitably with all of you who chose to work for us. Therefore, in addition to your contracted wage, we will pay you an annual bonus ...'

Stanier sat down to the gratifying ring

of genuine, heartfelt applause. He began to believe he had written the speech himself.

The SS *Lancelot* had sailed by the time Macready next brought *Caryatid* into Porth Ardur, but she left in her departing wake air thick with rumour and speculation. News had yet to break formally about the full dissolution of the Lighthouse Authority's depot, for Macready had not divulged it for fear of it causing too much trouble both on board *Caryatid* and ashore. He expected the matter would be revealed by the Commissioners themselves when they arrived in *Naiad* for their annual inspection. He therefore bent his neck to the haughty impositions of fate and awaited the dreadful moment. Meanwhile, as the weeks passed, the turf on the lower slopes of Mynydd Uchaf was torn up; the gangs of navvies laboured on the embankments of the new railway; granite boulders rent from the higher slopes of the mountain were crushed and spread along the levelled stretches and new tarred sleepers were placed in position, to be, in due course, overlaid by steel rails which gleamed like spear shafts, as they ran from the heart of Mynydd Uchaf straight into Porth Ardur. Amid all this seething change, the public houses of Porth Ardur benefited from the thirsty influx of navvies, while fights occasionally erupted between them and the young men who had expected jobs on the new mine and whose girlfriends were proving faithlessly fickle. About now the first unexpected conceptions were reported.

It was a kind of madness that settled on Porth Ardur. Captain Macready continued his business as though nothing was wrong, while his wife had privately turned her life upside down by investing heavily in the new companies which seemed to be running the town. Sinclair confessed he had himself ventured some capital and viewed Mrs Macready's decision with huge enthusiasm. The promised return was forecast as seventeen per cent and Gwendolyn would have been personally satisfied with half, but she was suddenly intoxicated with the prospect of so large a return that she happily agreed to allow Sinclair to handle the matter for her, his commission notwithstanding. She told her husband nothing of all this, beyond admitting that she had been pleased with the sale of the farm.

'I hope you got at least two thousand,' Macready had observed.

'I got a little more than that, dear,' Gwendolyn had replied, a self-satisfied little smirk playing around her lips, and Macready, pleased that she appeared happy

162

with the transaction, decided to leave her to enjoy her triumph.

'I am pleased to hear it,' he said, picking up the day's newspaper. Had Gwendolyn not had her own preoccupations, she would have noticed that something had knocked much of the stuffing out of Septimus Macready.

Lord Craven was not a wicked man, but indolence and intelligence had combined to make of him a mischievous one. His father, bowed with age and the growing uncertainties of keeping together a small, though undeniably aristocratic fortune, had done his heir the disservice of not soon enough involving the young man in his family's affairs. It is difficult for a man who has sired a son and seen him grow from infancy to manhood, to define the precise moment of maturity that permits admission of confidences and the discussion of private affairs. Sadly, Lord Dungarth's countess had died while the boy was still in preparatory school, so his lordship, who exercised his paternal responsibilities through the assorted agencies of schoolmasters and his Steward, was apt to regard his heir as locked into a permanent state of adolescent rebellion. Equally sadly, idleness had produced in Lord Craven a predisposition to act the fool in his father's presence. It might have been helpful to both of them, had they been sailing together for, notwithstanding Nancy and Tegwyn, Lord Craven's real passion was exercised in his ketch *Lyonesse,* while his father had once been a notable yachtsman and beaten the old king himself.

However, shortly after Parliament was prorogued that summer, Lord Dungarth ran into his son in the hall of their town house and the two men were more or less forced to dine in each other's company at their mutual club. Here, to Craven's dismay but his father's evident pleasure, they ran into Stanier. The conversation soon concentrated upon the possibility of a new steamer service to Ynyscraven and, as the matter now seemed certain, Craven sat back and let the other two formulate a loose, promisory agreement. As he smoked his cigar, Craven felt a great longing to see Tegwyn, but, just as he was seeking a convenient moment to extricate himself from his father's society, another man joined them. He was clearly known to both Lord Dungarth and Stanier, though Craven, beyond acknowledging a vague familiarity from newspaper pictures, failed to put a name to the man's face. Since no-one introduced them, on the pretext of visiting the lavatory Craven buttonholed one of the club stewards.

'That is Mr David Smith, m'lord, Junior Minister in the Ministry of Power and member for, er, I beg your lordship's pardon, but I cannot quite recall which constituency Mr Smith represents.'

'No matter, Hopkins. I don't know how you manage to remember us as well as you do. Thank you.'

As he returned to the table, Craven heard Stanier mention that he must leave and pick up his wife who was dining with the Pomeroys. The thought of Tegwyn stirred Craven with itchings of illicit desire.

'Should catch a nightcap,' Stanier was saying. 'Anyone coming?' he added expansively.

'Is Pomeroy that art collector fellow?' Lord Dungarth asked.

'Yes, Lord Dungarth. A true connoisseur—'

'D'you know him, Roger?' the Earl asked, turning to his son for the first time for over an hour.

'Quite well, Pater. He's interested in Tasmanian wind masks. Odious things. Why, are you still trying to get rid of that alleged Canaletto?'

'Taxes, my boy, damned taxes. Anyway, what d'you mean, *alleged* Canaletto. The picture has as good a pedigree as yourself.'

'Well, that's very reassuring, Pater, I'm

165

sure, but why don't you give me the thing to auction instead of trying to con Pomeroy?'

'No harm in asking him though, is there?' Dungarth turned to Stanier. 'Will he think we're intruding, Stanier?'

'I shouldn't think so,' Stanier said, pulling out his watch and looking at it. 'It's not quite nine yet.'

'Let's all go then ...'

And during this impromptu attempt by Lord Dungarth to sell a bad Canaletto, Mr David Smith MP first met Mr Pomeroy, though no-one at the time thought the casual encounter of any consequence whatsoever.

The final meeting of the Commissioners of Celtic Lighthouses before their annual inspection cruise was marked by one of the institution's traditions, specifically the formality observed when one of its members died.

Death was not actually admitted; the deceased was ritually said to have 'slipped his moorings and passed the last bar', a pronouncement made by the senior Commissioner, in the present case Sir Charles Mudge, while all those present sat, as though under the low deckheads of an ancient man-of-war, with their hats on. Sir Charles turned an old minute glass and all watched the grains of sand run from the top of the chamber to the bottom, a microcosmic representation of life itself. At the expiry of the minute, although all had been staring at the glass, its end was signalled by Sir Charles striking his gavel on the bruised table. The assembly then whipped off their hats and inclined their heads, immediately after which they rose and continued in conversation, as though nothing untoward had taken place, while wine and biscuits were brought in to symbolise the continuity of life and the stern business of the Lighthouse Authority.

This odd ceremony, seen for the first time by Captain Stanier, was also witnessed by a Captain Bernard Foster. Not being a Commissioner, Foster merely stood respectfully beside the table, his uniform hat tucked beneath his arm, watching in some wonderment what he had only hitherto heard of, despite his many years in the Commissioners' service. Once Macready's Chief Mate aboard *Caryatid*, Foster had risen to command the Commissioners' motor yacht, the *Naiad*. Properly, so prestigious a duty should have fallen upon the shoulders of the Senior Master, Captain Macready, but at the time the post fell vacant, Macready had no desire to leave Porth Ardur, *Caryatid*, or the isle of Ynyscraven.

When sufficient wine and biscuits had been consumed to persuade all present that they were still physically in the temporal world and capable of digestion, Sir Charles Mudge called them to order.

'Now, gentlemen, we are of course also to consider our various duties during the forthcoming Commissioners' Cruise of Inspection. Captain Foster is here to outline our itinerary ...'

An hour or so later the Board rose for lunch. All were acquainted with their proposed duties and the only matter they unfortunately had to leave until they reassembled at the end of the summer, was the election of a replacement for old Captain Jesmond.

From Captain Stanier's point of view, Foster had quite unintentionally done him an immense favour, for the cruise concluded in the Silurian Strait. This would give Stanier time to consolidate his position among the Board members and divine the best way of administering the *coup de grâce* to Septimus Macready. It would be like training for a race, gradually working up to a peak of performance, something upon which he could concentrate all his faculties. Stanier was confident, now that all was in place, that any small matters of business that cropped up in his absence could be handled by Caroline in concert with David Smith.

The first coal was gouged from the flank of Mynydd Uchaf the same day. A month later heaps of it were growing along the quayside of the enclosed dock at Porth Ardur. In a high wind the dust blew back over the town, besmirching the washing hung in gay lines to catch the breeze. The protesting women were hushed to silence by their menfolk who were anticipating good rates of pay as soon as the measuring clerks reckoned 10,000 tons was ready for shipping. After the first cargo had been cleared, the prefabricated coal tips would be erected, for the incoming cargo steamer would discharge the sections before loading the coal. The new port manager assured them that the inconvenience was only temporary.

# Coal And Coalitions

Disillusion came upon the townsfolk of Porth Ardur like the dawn, beginning with a first vague suggestion, sensed more than actually perceived by a few souls. Later, as convictions hardened, the matter became more certain, a twilit realisation, and while it was some time before real evidence rose like the sun itself, there remained a few weeks before the full extent of the deception was known and understood by all. Many men and women relinquish their dreams as reluctantly as they relinquish their beds, belatedly confronting the realities that daylight inevitably brings.

The first few weeks of intense and profitable labour promised much. Coal seemed to tumble down from Mynydd Uchaf in such quantities that chapel preachers quit their promises of hell fire to the eager, promiscuous and pregnant young women of Porth Ardur, choosing instead to descant upon the bounty of the Almighty, the dignity of work and the eternal benefits accruing to the charitable. The visible heaps of coal were scooped up by grabs operated from the derricks of the first pair of the Cambrian Steam Navigation Company's ships, the *Bedivere* and the returning *Lancelot*. As the second cargo was loaded, the tipping towers were speedily erected. Two of these curious structures of steel and wood, each intended to service the fore and after hatches of the visiting steamships, reared up to dominate the dock, throwing their austere shadows over the town and signalling the march of industrial progress to those far out at sea.

'Bloody ugly things,' Captain Macready pronounced as he made his approach, ringing the engine-room telegraph and reducing *Caryatid*'s speed as he prepared to swing round the end of the lighthouse pier and pass the open caisson into the enclosed dock.

Once the railway lines were connected, the laden coal trucks ceased depositing their cargoes on the quay and the great heaps of coal vanished forever. The waiting housewives sighed with relief, for now the coal was stockpiled at the mine where a mechanical loading system had become operational. This flung ton after ton of coal into the trucks just before the arrival of the ship was telegraphed. The trucks were then marshalled in sidings and trundled directly into the tipping towers where, one at a time, each was raised on the platform by a single operator, and up-ended. With a roar each truck flung its contents into a chute which was skilfully directed by a system of wires and pulleys, into the open hatches of the waiting steamship below.

In a stiff south-westerly breeze the dust produced swept in concentrated swathes directly across the backyards huddling behind the houses of Sudan and Egypt Road, soiling the washing hung out there. But, it was generally acknowledged, though it was a shame for the inhabitants of Sudan and Egypt Road, it could be avoided if they simply postponed their washing until the steamship had sailed. As for the rest, only the *Caryatid* still besmirched the sheets and pillow cases hung up behind the houses of Kitchener, Khartoum, Askari and Omdurman Roads, and she would soon be a thing of the past. Most people agreed that things were generally looking up.

Of course, once the tipping towers were established, the vast numbers of men employed to load the *Lancelot* and *Bedivere* were laid off. It would only be temporary, of course; once the generation of other trades got under way, the import and export of general cargo would mushroom and they would all have their jobs back. It was just a matter of time.

'Pie in the sky,' one or two disenchanted souls muttered into their beer, pointing

172

out that in addition to job losses on the docks, no more than two men had been employed as security guards at the mine. The remaining work at the mine was taken by the residue of the navvies who had arrived by ship to establish the eyesore in the first place. Most of them had now departed, no-one quite knew where, but those that remained were attracting an increasing hostility from the townsmen. The first marriage between a local girl and one of their number had very nearly been disrupted by the bride's brother who had had, it was generally acknowledged, more than he could comfortably drink. He had lost his job on the docks the previous day and the charitable considered this misfortune as his motive in mobilising his mates. Violence was fortunately averted at the last moment. Just as the vigilantes, led by the bride's brother and who had naturally boycotted the wedding, arrived at the church, the guard of honour appeared.

The happy couple emerged under an arch of turfing spades whose polished and honed blades gleamed in the fitful sunlight as the score of navvies waved them above their grinning colleague. The bride's brother, swearing vengeance, wisely ordered a retreat to The Feathers from where the landlord had trouble evicting them some three hours later.

Two weeks afterwards a more effective counter-blow was brewing in the sculleries of Sudan Road amid the damp washing now festooned indoors. It had been precipitated by a single, significant event. When the newlyweds returned from a brief honeymoon the bride bore a black eye.

'She fell out of bed,' her husband explained in The Feathers, laughing, as his colleagues laughed with him.

Some thirty miles to the south-south-west of the island of Ynyscraven, the ketch *Lyonesse* was on a broad reach, scudding along under the impulse of a fresh breeze, swooping and diving over the low swell. At the helm sat Lord Craven, his blond hair dishevelled by the wind, an expression of complete satisfaction upon his face. Seen thus for the first time, an observer, had one been present, would have found it impossible to reconcile the same young man with the indolent spark formerly drifting round the capital, squandering time and money. A sailing yacht possesses the quality, for those who seek it, of putting constant demands upon her crew. One cannot dodge tasks without compromising one's very existence and Craven found this knife-edge life so exhilarating, so contrasting with his normal aimless existence, that he usually sailed single-handed. Not for the first time he toyed with the idea of simply taking it up permanently and sailing off around the world.

It was such a sunny day that he could easily persuade himself that he was off the Azores, heading west for the Indies. An hour ago a school of bottle-nosed dolphins had raced in from the starboard side and frolicked under the *Lyonesse*'s spoon bow for ten or fifteen minutes, adding to this illusion. But such a passage would be a long one on his own, and he was still troubled by the image of Tegwyn Pomeroy. What a delight it would be to have her here!

The last time Craven had seen Tegwyn had been on the occasion he had accompanied his father, Stanier and David Smith to the Pomeroys' apartment. It was clear the visit had been an intrusion. Pomeroy was not interested in the Canaletto. Craven had not for a moment supposed he would be. Pomeroy's taste for Tasmanian wind masks might have been reprehensible, but he was not foolish enough to believe Dungarth had a Canaletto worth buying. Still, Pomeroy's desire to show off the bloody wind masks in which Smith had shown a surprising and, Craven suspected, impulsive interest, had given him a moment with Tegwyn while his father paid Caroline

Stanier flattering compliments.

'Sorry about this descent, Teggy,' he had said. 'This time it really wasn't my idea.'

'You're just awful,' she had said, but she had smiled when she said it, and he cherished the smile now. Had there been a hint of weary resignation in her face? He was sure he had noticed something like sadness in her expression. At this point a herring gull swept alongside him and, soaring close by for a moment, suddenly emitted such a raucous cry that it sounded like the gods laughing derisively at him. Craven chuckled at himself. What a self-deluding fool he was; if Tegwyn seemed weary it was due to their ill-mannered intrusion and not boredom with Pomeroy. An hour later Craven was frantically tucking a reef in his mainsail as a dark cloud began to brew to windward.

*Lyonesse* lay down under the assault when the squall hit her. It came with heavy rain which knocked the sea flat and the ketch seethed through the suddenly dark and cold sea. Dolphins and gulls had vanished and Craven strained at the tiller as the weather helm increased. Twenty minutes later the yacht emerged into sunshine as the cloud drove downwind. He shook his head, sending the raindrops flying and stared ahead. Craven caught his first sight of the Buccabu lighthouse as it broke the sharp line of the horizon.

Captain Macready spread his legs against *Caryatid*'s lazy roll and looked through his glasses at the Buccabu lighthouse at the same time, but from the opposite direction. He briefly recalled telling Charlie Farthing the story of Captain Jesmond and then dismissed the memory. Why on earth did his mind keep coming back to the mad old shipmaster? Jesmond was dead, and with him went the only hope Septimus Macready had of averting what he had come to think of as a great tragedy. That he had a central role in this drama was a natural assumption by the man who was, after all, the commander of *Caryatid*, the guardian of the ship's soul, the man whose will transformed her inert form into a moving entity and made of her a useful, almost sentient thing. It was something that one could only explain to another commander; a chief engineer for instance, was incapable of comprehending such a thing. It was something of this that had prompted the remark he had made to the Chief as the steamroller ploughed into the Mermaid Bakery.

Macready reached for the brass handle of the engine-room telegraph, wondering if that public display of hubris had precipitated the intervention of the fates. The notion perplexed and unnerved him.

He swung the handle to Stand-by, and then, a few minutes later, to Half Ahead. 'Starboard easy, Quartermaster ...'

Macready raised his glasses again and shook off the metaphysical nonsense. He was depressed because he had lost Charlie. The mate had packed his traps and left the ship two days earlier, just before they had sailed from Porth Ardur on their present tour of sea-duty. He would have liked to have taken Charlie out to Ynyscraven aboard *Caryatid*, but the ship was not due at the island's lighthouse for a fortnight and, in any case, strictly speaking it would be contrary to service regulations.

His new mate, Mr Watson, was a decent and experienced officer, the temporarily promoted Second Officer of *Waterwitch*, who came aboard in the full knowledge that it would not be long before he returned to his old ship and reverted to his former rank. Macready manoeuvred *Caryatid* into a position to lower her boat and effect the relief of the keepers of the Buccabu light. When the boat returned the senior keeper coming off duty reported to Macready on *Caryatid*'s bridge.

'All well on the Buccabu light, Mister?' Macready asked formally, acknowledging the man's salute.

'Fine, Captain, except that the station could do with some oil fuel. We're well below half-tanks.'

'Yes, I've seen the figures,' Macready replied, indicating the board on the after bulkhead upon which the fuel and water states of all the lightvessels and lighthouses in the Area were recorded.

'I was just thinking that, as it's a nice day,' the keeper hinted, 'you might consider making a delivery.'

Macready sighed. He had the St Kenelm lightvessel to relieve before dark and she was very low on oil fuel *and* fresh water. 'We'll be back in a week,' he said. 'You go off and enjoy your leave. The station will be full up by the time you come back.'

'Very well, Captain.'

It was the first time in his career as a shipmaster that Septimus Macready simply could not be bothered. Nor did he feel guilty about it.

Charlie Farthing *was* feeling guilty. Arriving after a long and tedious train journey at Aberogg, a journey which had followed the anti-climactic business of leaving the service of the Commissioners for Celtic Lights and amounted to a tedious hour or so of paperwork in Mr Dale's office and an uncomfortable night in the Station Hotel. Now he was consequently

179

experiencing an undeniable sensation of freedom. An efficient and conscientious officer, Charlie had always carried out his duties assiduously. Since his marriage, however, his life had been full of compromises. He saw too little of his beloved wife who had refused to move from Ynyscraven to Porth Ardur. Yet *Caryatid*'s routines were based upon the assumption that their ship's company were domiciled in their base port and the Commissioners for Celtic Lights were parsimonious with both the officers' salaries and their leave. His original expectation of soon becoming the Reeve of Ynyscraven, which had initially suggested that his continued employment aboard *Caryatid* would be short-lived, had not materialised. Charlie and his wife had had to bite the bitter bullet of separation. The course of true love, as Septimus Macready had sagely quoted to Justine some weeks earlier, never did run smooth.

But now, poised thus between one existence which was doomed, and another which was full of sweet promise, Charlie Farthing felt an intense surge of joy and unsullied happiness.

This received a blow when he discovered the island's supply ship, a small coaster named *Plover*, leaning against the small quay wall of Aberogg with engine trouble.

All passages, it was announced on a blackboard lying against the wheelhouse, were postponed for at least five days.

'Bugger!' said Charlie, wondering if he could afford the lodgings and deciding that he was hot and thirsty. He headed for the open door of a public house on the quay named after the Buccabu Lighthouse above which hung a painted representation of the light tower offshore. It was an understandably popular name for public houses.

It was about this time that Lord Craven and *Lyonesse* swept past the lonely tower. A keeper on the gallery waved at the passing yacht; Craven waved back. Once clear of the reef, he ducked down into the chart space and picked up the dividers. Ahead of him opened the Silurian Strait; on the port bow the etched outline of Ynyscraven, to starboard and nearer, just past the great headland known to countless generations of seaman as Landfall Point, nestled the small, tidal port of Aberogg. He stepped off the distances and consulted the tidal atlas. He could just make Aberogg before dark. What was more, he could carry the flood and get alongside on top of the tide to enjoy a pint of ale and a star-gazey pie at the Buccabu Light.

'Right,' he said out loud, climbing back

out into the cockpit, 'from the Buccabu Light to the Buccabu Light. That'll do us, won't it?' and he patted the tiller as he cast off the lashing and took it again. 'Yes,' he added, speaking for the yacht, 'that'll do us very well indeed.'

The following morning Charlie woke with a slightly sore head and the feeling that all was not well. Confused for a second by his unfamiliar surroundings, he staggered to the window and remembered everything: he was marooned in Aberogg for at least four more days and with a rather depressingly finite sum of money. Across the estuary he could see the pine-clad hills rise rapidly to the scree-covered slopes of Cefn Mawr. The long ridge lay like a great sleeping dinosaur along the far side of the estuary of the River Ogg. It was low water, but the tide had turned. The silver stream running between gleaming sandbanks was imperceptibly swelling, inching out laterally over the sands upon which the oystercatchers fed. Immediately below the window of Mrs Gatcombe's guest house spread the quay with its litter of fish crates among which strutting gulls industriously foraged. The masts and superstructure of the immobilised *Plover* kept company with three smaller fishing vessels. More gulls wheeled and shrieked, perching and launching themselves in an endless circuit of flight and rest on the masts and dan-buoy spars of the fishing boats. Charlie yawned. How the hell was he going to spend the long hours of the day?

Shaving and dressing, he partook of one of Mrs Gatcombe's full breakfasts. The mass of eggs, bacon, mushrooms, tomatoes, black pudding and sausage, accompanied by buttered toast and a pot of tea, put him in better humour. At about nine o'clock he strode out onto the quay and, in the manner of seamen, started at one end and conducted a private review of the craft moored alongside. He passed the *Plover*, from the engine room of which came the dull ring of a hammer but which was otherwise deserted, and stared with a modicum of interest at the fishing boats. It was then that he spied the two masts of the ketch. The main mast towered over the quay and Charlie strode to the edge of the coping to stare down upon the deck of the elegant, teak-decked yacht.

The doghouse hatch was open and the smell of bacon wafted up into the clear morning air. He caught a glimpse of someone moving about below and felt himself impertinent in thus staring, as it were, into another's private life. He walked idly away and for an hour lost himself in a second-hand bookshop near the church. After impulsively spending a pound on a slim, illustrated volume entitled *The Raptors of the Celtic Uplands,* Charlie drifted into the church, read all the tablets erected to the various worthies of Aberogg over the previous three centuries and then emerged into the sunshine again, just as the clock in the tower above his head struck half past ten.

He toyed with the idea of getting a message through to Sonia, but the difficulties of obtaining a telephone connection with Ynyscraven discouraged him. Besides, as yet he had no clear idea when he would arrive. It was this thought that drove him back to the quay. Perhaps someone would be more forthcoming with information about the *Plover.* All Mrs Gatcombe had been able to tell him was that the coaster would leave when the engine was repaired. This might be good news for her, but it was small comfort to Charlie.

The tide was making swiftly now, and had already reached the grounded keels of the vessels alongside the quay. The white-hulled ketch, whose name he could see was *Lyonesse,* was no longer deserted. One of the crew was up forward fiddling with the halliards at the base of the mainmast and looking up along the mast. Charlie saw a tall, slim, blond-haired young man a few years younger than himself. He followed the young man's glance aloft and at once located the fouled halliard.

'It's caught round a shackle pin at the hounds,' he said.

'Ah, yes,' said the young man, 'I see it now, it's a bit difficult against the sky. You're a lot nearer.'

'If you pass me a boat-hook I reckon I can clear it from here.'

'Right. Thanks.'

It was the matter of only a moment's effort to clear the halliard and, as he passed the boat-hook back, Charlie said, 'If you turned the shackle the other way, that pin wouldn't foul the halliard.'

The young man looked at Charlie and then at the shackle. 'I don't suppose ... No, silly of me.'

'D'you want a hand? I've nothing better to do.'

'I'm single-handed, so it's a bit awkward on my own.'

'Have you got a bosun's chair? I'll hoist you up if you like.'

The offer was accepted and Charlie clambered down on the yacht's deck while the young man disappeared below, to reappear a moment later with a short plank slung in a rope bridle. 'You know about boats, I suppose, being from round

185

here?' the younger man asked.

'Oh, I'm not from round here, but yes, I know a bit about boats,' Charlie replied, smiling. 'Have you got a spike? I'll slacken the bottle-screw.'

As Charlie eased the tension in the shroud, the young man shackled the chair onto the main halliard and slipped his legs inside the rope. When Charlie was ready he sat on the plank as Charlie took the weight up on the halliard and then hauled him aloft. Ten minutes later, the job was done, the bosun's chair was thrown back down the fore hatch and the young man turned to Charlie.

'Thanks very much.'

'That's all right. I'll be off then.'

'Stay and have a cup of tea. I've another hour before the tide floats me off. If you're not in a hurry, that is.'

'No,' Charlie admitted ruefully, 'I'm killing time. I'd be delighted to accept.'

'Right. I'll put the kettle on. Come below.'

'I'll just set up the shroud again,' Charlie said, gesturing at the slack bottle-screw.

'Right. Thanks.'

Going below, where the gas burner hissed under the copper kettle, Charlie passed the spike back to its owner. Taking it in his left hand the young man held out the right. 'I'm Roger Craven.'

'Charlie Farthing.'

For a moment Lord Craven stared at his new acquaintance. 'Did you say Charlie *Farthing?*'

'Yes,' said Charlie, frowning, then he in turn recognised his host's surname. 'Did you say *Craven?* Are you Lord Craven?'

Craven laughed. 'Yes, I am, but don't let that worry you. Please call me Roger.'

'I, er, I ...' Charlie bumbled awkwardly. He could cope with knowing a peer by his Christian name, but when the chap was his prospective employer matters were less straightforward.

'Oh look,' said Craven, 'please feel free to dispense with formalities. I understand now why you're at a loose end. I heard when I got here last night that the *Plover* had coughed a head gasket or something technical. I had a star-gazey pie in the Buccabu Light,' he added.

'I'm sorry, I didn't see you. I was drowning my sorrows there.'

'Well, it doesn't matter, it was pretty crowded. The important thing is that you are here now and as one good turn deserves another, I can run you across to Ynyscraven when we float.'

'That would be marvellous.'

'Well, it gives us a chance to become better acquainted.'

'Yes ...'

187

Craven grinned as he put leaves in the teapot and poured in the boiling water from the kettle. He sensed Farthing's awkwardness and, having taken an instant liking to Charlie, sought to prevent the instinctive barriers of social diffidence from choking all prospects of friendship. 'Make yourself at home, Charlie. Sit down.'

Charlie squeezed along the settee and leaned his elbows on the fiddled tables. He recalled Macready's story of the old *Naiad*, Captain Jesmond and the lack of table fiddles.

'You're married to Sonia, aren't you?' Craven asked.

'Yes.'

'When I was a small boy I used to spend some of my summer holidays on Ynyscraven. She was the first girl I ever tried to show my penis to. She had the good sense to decline the offer.' Craven laughed with such self-deprecating enthusiasm that it broke Charlie's reserve.

'I'm glad to hear it,' he responded quickly. 'It might have put mine in the shade!'

They laughed together as Craven stirred quantities of sugar into the brew. 'You come highly recommended,' he said as their laughter subsided.

'I do?' Charlie frowned.

'D'you know Tegwyn Pomeroy?'

'Justine's daughter; yes. Not very well, but I know of her. My wife's a close friend of her mother.'

'A sort of surrogate daughter, I hear.'

'Well, I don't know about that—'

'I tell you what, Charlie,' said Lord Craven, leaning across the table on his elbows and betraying the consequences of the loneliness inherent in sailing single-handed, 'I'm absolutely enchanted by Tegwyn Pomeroy.'

The effect of the deliberation in the sculleries and back kitchens of Sudan Road took some time to implement and a little longer to take effect. A reign of terror needs teeth to frighten and while no actual bodily malice was intended by the conspirators, its fortuitous appearance was not unwelcome to them.

The plan was as ancient as tragedy itself but, thought up as it was by women for whom its application was unlikely, the convincing of their younger, unattached sisters, daughters, nieces and cousins was a difficult matter. It is never easy to ask others to selflessly sacrifice what one has access to oneself. That those asked to give it up lacked the legal title that those who would continue to enjoy it possessed, did not help, for into the cogent arguments of logic was poured the bile of emotion. Once the plan of the matrons of Sudan Road was made known, it gained support not only with their sisters in Egypt, Khartoum, Kitchener and Omdurman Roads, but found allies up the hill towards the headier altitudes of Aspen Way and Acacia Avenue.

The transformation of this alliance into reality required several hundred private battles, battles held behind closed doors, when menfolk were at work, in the pub, or the lavatory. The arguments were hissed insistently between mothers and daughters. Tales of unnaturalness and beastliness, long known among the women to haunt the dark imaginings of men, gained new credibility and were added to whispers of bigamous conduct and the general infamy of foreigners. All boiled down to the Lysistratan admonition: 'Don't give the buggers the slightest chance to impregnate you!'

There were mild threats added to this instruction which were largely toothless until the unfortunate young woman who had been the first to marry one of the navvies, was found dead in a ditch. She had a deep head wound, and while the police were quite unable to find sufficient evidence that her husband was in any way responsible, for he had a cast-iron and apparently genuine alibi, the

190

power of circumstantial evidence fanned by oblique suggestion and pure invented fiction was immense. Although a post-mortem showed her to have consumed a considerable quantity of raw potato spirit and an adjacent rock still bore traces of her blood, it was clear other marks upon her fair body were due to the intimate attentions of her husband. Mention was made of her earlier black eye. Morally, even the police considered a degree of guilt lay at her husband's door. Enough was known of his brutality to add weight to the story and lend it all the force of absolute truth.

The news passed quickly among the women, young and old. There was no need of more; chastity clamped its firm grip on Porth Ardur as formerly as the thighs of its peccant women had held the loins of their lovers.

# The Inspection

It was long after midnight when Captain Foster dropped anchor off Ynyscraven and waited while *Naiad* brought up to her anchor. It had been a tediously long day. That morning *Naiad* had lain off Porth Neigwl and, in defiance of Foster's carefully planned itinerary, Captain Stanier had persuaded Sir Charles Mudge, who was naturally inclined to leave the matter alone, to call upon Mr Ifor Davis of the Mermaid Bakery.

'It will demonstrate that we care about what happened, Sir Charles. To simply sail into the bay then out again might put us in a bad light,' Stanier had argued.

The Commissioners therefore left in their barge after breakfast next morning and landed ahead of the *Kurnow* which had just berthed and whose crew lined the rail and cat-called *Naiad*'s seamen and their strange passengers. The group of Commissioners, attired in formal blazers and flannels, and wearing straw boaters, moved through the disembarking crowd of visitors led by Captain Stanier who testily waved the mass of peasantry out of his way with his walking cane.

The repairs to the bakery had been completed long ago, but when he learned of the strangers standing outside his property, Mr Davis joined them, the marks of his honest trade covering his person.

Half an hour later as they returned to their barge, the Commissioners were soothed by Mr Davis's complimentary remarks. They were, he had assured them, gentlemen with whom it was a pleasure to do business. The only drawback to this effusion were the two floury loaves of fresh bread which Davis pressed upon them. Sir Charles insisted that Stanier accepted these on behalf of them all. Relinquishing the two loaves as quickly as possible to the boat's crew, Stanier brushed down his blazer while the barge headed back towards *Naiad*.

'Lucky Macready hasn't got a photograph of you, Stanier,' Sir Charles joked, causing a ripple of amusement among his fellow Commissioners. Stanier mustered a thin smile, harbouring increased resentment towards the man he now considered an implacable enemy.

The delay had cost them the tide at Mitre Rock. Foster was adamant that they were too late, the schedule was tight enough. To land too near high water was highly dangerous. A few years ago a keeper had been carried to his death with only a

193

couple of inches of water sweeping the flat plateau upon which the tower was built. The thin layer of weed which covered it dried out within minutes of its exposure by a falling tide, but once wet it was as slippery as ice. They would have to steam instead directly to the St Kenelm's lightvessel, carry out the inspection there and then return to Mitre Rock and land after high water, as the tide fell away. It would mean additional fuel costs, but that could not be helped. They would just be that much later anchoring that night at Ynyscraven.

'You will have to eat dinner under way, gentlemen,' Foster explained, 'rather than in the security of the anchorage.'

'That doesn't matter,' Stanier said.

'Not to you, Stanier, maybe,' grumbled Sir Charles Mudge, 'but I've eaten too many meals at sea. A dinner in tranquil waters is always welcome.'

'Oh, I'm sure, Sir Charles—'

'You're always *sure*, Stanier, that's your bloody trouble,' grumbled Sir Charles. 'By the way, what happened to that fresh bread?'

'I, er, I've no idea, Sir Charles, I passed it to the boat's crew.'

'That's the last we'll see of that, then. I think I could swallow a whisky and soda.'

Stanier felt better after the inspection of the St Kenelm's lightvessel. Sir Charles had deputed Stanier, Blake and Gostling to carry out the duty.

'No point in arriving mob-handed, damn it,' he had decided, calling for another whisky and soda.

The inspecting party arrived back with Stanier in gleeful mood. They had discovered what he reported to Sir Charles as 'irregularities'. These turned out to be a seaman with hair of excessive length, the master's top reefer button undone, an ullage in the station's rum bottle for which there was no documented reason, a spillage of oil in the oil store and a coil of fire hose stretched along the deck, rather than nestling coiled in its box.

The Master accepted the hair length of his crew member as being a little untidy, but he was unable to explain the lack of rum, viewing the revelation with some surprise, even though the bottle was locked in his cabin. He hung his head shamefully at the oil spillage, but explained that they had washed the decks down in honour of the occasion with the fire hose and it was against regulations to stow damp hoses.

Stanier pooh-poohed all these excuses and inscribed the station's deficiency in the station order book. This leather-bound document dated back 128 years, recording every visit of the Commissioners since the establishment of the station. In all that time Stanier's opprobrious comments were only matched on two previous occasions. When the unfortunate skipper read what Stanier had written on the Commissioners' behalf, he was mortified. He was most personally hurt by the comment that he himself 'seemed incapable of wearing the service uniform correctly'.

It was only on the way back to *Naiad* that the bearded Gostling turned to Blake and asked, 'Isn't there some tradition that if a lightvessel skipper has been in the rank for more than twenty years he's allowed to leave his top reefer button undone?'

Blake frowned and nodded sleepily. 'Yes, yes, I think there is, old boy.'

Both men looked at Stanier who stood staring astern with a stopwatch in his hand. He was timing the light and fog signal that now suddenly blasted its diaphone through the clear air of the afternoon.

'Are they all right, Stanier?' asked Blake.

'They'll time them from the ship too,' Gostling said. 'Sit down, Stanier. No point in keeping a kennel of dogs and doing all the barking ourselves now, is there?'

'Well, there wouldn't be if they were reliable,' Stanier said obscurely, 'but that fog signal's slow.'

As Stanier climbed up to *Naiad*'s bridge after the barge had been recovered he had intended to complain the fog signal was slightly slow, but was met by Foster reporting it correct.

'I made it a little slow, Captain Foster,' Stanier said sharply.

'The barge makes eight knots under full power, Captain Stanier,' Foster said.

'I don't follow you.'

'Eight knots introduces a period of delay between the arrival of the first signal and the second due to the increased distance the sound has to travel to reach you in the barge as you speed away from it.'

'I see ... Oh yes, of course, you mentioned that to me before.' Stanier flushed, irritated.

'I did, sir, yes. And the position of the lightvessel is correct. We have just verified it.'

'I see.'

'I believe your steward is serving tea, Captain Stanier, if you'll excuse me, we have to set course back for Mitre Rock.'

Stanier fulminated under Foster's withering politeness. As he reached the after smoke room Gostling met him with a broad grin. 'Got caught with that old time and distance nonsense again, did we, Stanier?' Gostling's laughter followed him below to his cabin. Caught or not, Stanier told himself, that fog signal was slow and Foster was covering for his colleague. The truth was that Macready's Area was a bloody mess!

On the bridge Captain Foster handed over *Naiad* to his Second Officer and went into the radio room. He switched on the transmitter and let it warm up. When, on pressing the handset, the tell-tale neon attached to the aerial glowed bright orange, he began to call *Caryatid* on 2241 kilocycles.

'*Caryatid, Caryatid,* this is *Naiad,* come in, please. Over.'

Unsurprisingly, with the whole Board of Commissioners in his Area, Macready's radio watch was efficient and the response of his ship almost immediate.

'*Naiad,* this is *Caryatid.* All attention. Over.'

'Request Captain to Captain. Over.'

'Very good, sir. Stand by one.' There was a pause, then Macready's deep bass boomed over the airwaves, making Foster smile. '*Caryatid* to *Naiad.* Macready here.'

'Hullo, Septimus, Bernard here, who was that on the blower? Over.'

'My new Mate, young Watson on loan from *Waterwitch.* Charlie's gone, settling at last on Ynyscraven. We've had the bad news. Over.'

'Yes, we heard, sorry about that. I've got

some more for you. We've just cleared the Kenelm. I think there's an anchor problem. Over.' It was a euphemism, just in case one of the Commissioners rumbled their conversation.

'Oh, right. Thanks, Bernard. Not much of one I hope. Over.'

'Middling, I'd say. Over.'

'Got it. See you off the island. Over and out.'

'*Naiad* out.'

'Bugger,' swore Macready as he emerged back on the bridge and met Mr Watson.

'Something the matter, sir?'

'Yes. Bloody St Kenelm's off station.'

'Oh, shit.'

'We must have dragged her when we were oiling the other day.'

'Yes, quite possibly.'

Macready reproached himself. He had not bothered to make a final check. It was unforgivable. The problem was he found his mind wandering these days. It was too stuffed full of uncertainties.

The Commissioners' inspection of Mitre Rock was similar to that of the lightvessel. It was sunset as they completed it and they decided to let the keepers light up before they concluded their business. The lighthouse was actually in first-class order, but a pedant seeking for dust could find it if he put his mind to the task and Stanier was in a bristlingly pedantic frame of mind. On their departure, above the Commissioners' signatures, the order book bore in Stanier's handwriting the comment that 'this station is covered in dust ...'

It was a quite unnecessary sophistry, for in fact one of the keepers provided Stanier with exactly what he wanted, a direct accusation aimed at Macready. When asked if anyone had any complaints, the man stepped forward and said he had been denied compassionate leave when his wife had been expecting a baby.

'The regulations state compassionate leave is automatic, sir, if due notice is given, and I got a doctor's letter to be sent to Porth Ardur with all the details.'

'And?' prompted Gostling.

'I got a message that my wife had gone into labour, sir—'

'At the time expected?' asked Blake.

'No sir, a week early. But it was our first, sir, so it wasn't *that* unexpected.'

'Go on. You were out here, I suppose?'

'No sir, I was on the Buccabu light then, sir, last March it were, sir, I've only been here since the twelfth of May, sir, haven't I, Chief?'

The senior keeper confirmed the fact and the supplicant continued. 'As soon as I got the signal, sir, I asked the Senior to call up *Caryatid* and let Captain Macready know. The message I got back was in the negative, sir.' The keeper drew himself up and added, 'And I wish to make a formal complaint, sir.'

'Of course, my man,' said Stanier, taking his name and entering it into his notebook. He suppressed any sense of triumph with great care, but his heart was singing.

It was almost completely dark by the time the barge edged its way out of the gut between the dark fangs of the complex geological formation that made up Mitre Rock. Foster was fuming at the delay, but was mollified when at last the barge emerged and headed back to the ship, a touch of phosphorescence in her bow wave. Then they had had a five-hour passage to Ynyscraven.

It was now gone 0200 and by the time the Carpenter called from the forecastle that the anchor had brought the ship up, Foster was drooping with fatigue. He would have to be up by 0700. No wonder old Septimus had declined the command. It might be the most prestigious in the Service, but it was also the most wearying!

Foster was in fact woken shortly before 0600 by the Commissioner's senior steward, Sudbrook.

201

'I'm sorry to bother you, sir, but it's Captain Stanier.'

'What?' said Foster, trying to clear his head of the fog of sleep. 'What's the matter with him? Is he ill?'

'Oh no, sir,' the Steward said, smiling. 'He's asking where the *Caryatid* is, sir.'

'He's *what?*' Foster's tone of incredulity startled Sudbrook. 'Did you wake me to ask that?'

'Yes, sir. Captain Stanier told me to call you and ask you where the *Caryatid* is.'

'Look, Sudbrook, go and tell Captain Stanier to ... *Oh, blast it!*' Foster threw aside his bedding and got up.

Sudbrook fell back. 'I'm sorry, sir—'

'Oh, it's not your fault, Sudbrook.'

'I think Captain Stanier expected to find *Caryatid* at anchor in the bay, sir.'

So did Foster, knowing of old Macready's arrangement with his lovely mistress, but if *Caryatid* was late arriving it did not matter. Her inspection was not scheduled until the afternoon and Macready was quite capable of arriving at the very last moment. Besides, inspection or not, the business of the Lighthouse Authority came first and Foster guessed that at that very moment, *Caryatid* was probably alongside the St Kenelm lightvessel, weighing the huge anchor which had dragged from its officially assigned position. Foster knew

202

Macready well enough to know not even his mistress would divert him from his duty.

Foster shaved and dressed and then went aft. On the quarterdeck Captain Stanier was pacing up and down in a silk dressing gown with a telescope under his arm. To the south and west, the cliffs of Ynyscraven beetled down upon them. Although it was broad daylight, the two lighthouses at each end of the island were still flashing. Then, as if acknowledging Foster's appearance on the *Naiad*'s quarterdeck, they went out.

'I understand, Captain Stanier, you wish to know where the *Caryatid* is?'

'Indeed I do, Captain Foster. She is due to be inspected today.'

'She is due to be inspected this afternoon, to be precise, Captain Stanier. I am confident that, unless some duty has unavoidably delayed her, Captain Macready will honour his obligation and turn up on time.'

'I hope you are not being insolent, Captain Foster.'

'So do I, Captain Stanier, but I resent being woken unnecessarily.'

'That *is* insolent, Captain Foster,' said Stanier, raising the telescope to his eye and laying it upon a yacht anchored close in, under the cliffs, not far from where a slim silver freshet fell down the precipitous rock.

'Then please feel free to report it to Captain Sir Charles Mudge.'

'Oh, I shall, Captain Foster, I shall,' remarked Stanier, still staring through his glass as Foster turned on his heel and angrily stumped forward.

Lord Craven woke to the steady roar of a boat engine passing close. A moment later he was almost tossed from his bunk as the Commissioners' barge surged past and *Lyonesse* rolled deeply in her wake. Indignantly he leapt into the cockpit stark naked waving his fist at the barge's stern.

'What's the bloody idea, you damned idiots!'

No-one in the boat noticed him, they were all deafened by the roaring engine and looking forward as they approached the beach where a uniformed keeper, the Senior from the south light, stood waiting to meet them.

Swearing fluently, Craven went below and put the kettle on. He knew the boat, and the ship lying offshore. Stanier would have been in the barge, of that there was little doubt and he would get even with Stanier later. He sat in the cockpit and drank his tea. Afterwards he jumped over the side and swam four times round *Lyonesse*, then hauled himself back on board by way of the bobstay. He had been invited to lunch with Sonia and Charlie Farthing and was looking forward to the occasion. He really felt the chance meeting with Charlie was fated far more than fortuitous.

They had enjoyed an exciting passage across from Aberogg, a brisk sail during which Charlie had demonstrated his ability as a yachtsman.

'You're a natural,' Craven had said admiringly, 'we must do this again. D'you think your wife will come with us?'

'Not if you ask her to cook, she won't,' Charlie had laughed.

'I wouldn't dream of such a thing. I enjoy cooking myself. It's the only chance I get. We could sail round the island.'

'She'd love that.'

'We must do it then.'

'Give me a day or two to settle in, then. How long are you staying?'

'How long's a piece of string?'

'Ahhh,' Charlie had laughed again, *'that* long.'

'You're implying the length of string on Ynyscraven may be considerable.'

'No. Only that anything on Ynyscraven tends to be more complicated than one imagines.'

Charlie watched the motor barge leave *Naiad*'s side from the window of his bedroom. It gave him a queer, disjointed sense of *déjà vu*. It was the wrong ship and he had no need to rush down any more and catch a boat, yet the sight was tinged with a strange sadness. He must have sighed audibly, for Sonia called from the bed.

'Are you all right, Charlie?'

'Of course I am,' he said, turning.

She let her gaze trail down him. 'Come here.'

'Is it better than Roger Craven's?' he asked smiling, feeling it had a sense of its own importance.

'I never saw Roger Craven's. That one,' she said, kicking aside the bedding and spreading herself, 'is just fine.'

As Charlie and Sonia drove each other to their climaxes, Captain Macready, with the St Kenelm lightvessel grinding the fenders between herself and the *Caryatid* to a flattened disfigurement, nudged the inert craft a few hundred feet back to the westward. On the monkey island above his head Watson and the Second Mate wielded their sextants and sought the crucial angles on the distant land that would refix the correct position for the lightvessel's anchor. The offending killick swung beneath the bluff bow of the lightvessel, a clod of shell-encrusted mud clinging to its flukes.

Patiently a seaman on *Caryatid*'s foredeck played a hose on the anchor disturbing clods of the mud, which fell away with loud plops as Macready neared the correct position.

'Left-hand angle coming on, sir,' called Watson.

'Right-hand angle almost there, sir,' added Wentworth.

Macready rang the ship's engines to stop and she lost way.

'On, sir!'

'On, sir!'

Macready gave a double ring for full astern. 'Let go!' Macready roared and the lightvessel's anchor dropped from the hawse pipe with a roar and clatter of veering cable.

Twenty minutes later *Caryatid* and the St Kenelm lightvessel lay back to a scope of ninety fathoms of heavy cable. Shortly afterwards *Caryatid* detached herself from the lightvessel's side and headed south, bound for Ynyscraven at full speed.

'Oh well,' mused Macready who really could not give a damn what the Commissioners said about a ship they had already condemned to the scrapyard, 'better late than never.'

He suddenly felt exposed and alone.

Having inspected the south lighthouse, the

Commissioners bumped across Ynyscraven to and from the north light by tractor. To be accurate, they were actually accommodated in a small trailer which towed behind the tractor, an odd cargo with their sticks and straw hats who recovered their joint composure after a short stay at the Craven Arms where they were served by Sonia. It was clear they would have stayed and lunched at the inn had it not been for Captain Stanier who was anxious to get back to *Naiad*, to prepare himself for the afternoon.

They trooped out and made for the path to the beach while Sonia gave Charlie the all clear. He had no desire to run into his recent employers, but watched them retire down the cliff path.

'I recognised Stanier,' Sonia said, clasping her husband's arm and laying her head upon his shoulder. 'But I don't think he recognised me.'

At the bend in the path the group met a solitary figure coming up from the beach. They saw the Commissioners halt and Stanier addressed the blond-headed young man.

'Here comes our lunch guest,' said Charlie.

At the bend in the path overlooking the bay, Craven almost bumped into the gaggle

208

of dusty and oddly assorted gentlemen confronting him.

'Good heavens, Lord Craven ...' Stanier held out his hand.

Craven ignored Stanier's outstretched hand and regarded the lot of them with an extreme air of truculence, his hands upon his hips. 'Don't you buggers have any consideration for others?' he asked accusingly.

Stanier's face crumpled into a sheepish grin. 'Craven, I don't think you've met Sir Charles Mud—'

'Met him? I don't need an introduction, the bugger tossed me out of my bunk this morning! What speed does that barge of yours do, Stanier?'

'About, er, eight knots ...' responded the flustered Stanier, embarrassed at having revealed his acquaintance with this rude young man and confused as to Craven's line of reasoning.

'Eight?' roared Craven. 'Eight? You shouldn't exceed four in Ynyscraven road—'

'Excuse me, young man, but there's no speed limit in the anchorage—' put in Gostling.

'There is now,' Craven said. 'Four knots!'

'What authority do you invoke?' asked Gostling.

'By mine, you damned fools. Don't you know who you chucked out of his bunk this morning? Stanier'll tell you. Good day to you!'

And Lord Craven all but ran until he was round the corner, out of sight of the blazered gentlemen, where he collapsed laughing. He was still chuckling when he reached the Farthings' cottage. Soon the walls of the place rang with it, so much so that Justine came in from next door, joined in when she heard the reason for their mirth and stayed for lunch.

As for the senior Commissioners, they agreed the young man must have been drunk and, metaphorically pulling their tattered dignity about them, they continued their descent to the beach.

'You and that young fellow seemed to be acquainted, Stanier,' Sir Charles Mudge said.

'I am acquainted with him, Sir Charles, somewhat regrettably, I think,' Stanier added awkwardly.

'Well, who the devil is he?' asked Blake.

'Lord Roger Craven, heir to the Earl of Dungarth, the owner of this island.'

'Then the bugger *can* make a local bye-law governing a speed limit within the island's inshore waters,' observed Captain Blake, addressing Gostling who was famous among them for his recondite

210

grasp of the most arcane facts of maritime law.

'Oh yes, yes indeed. And by ancient statute he still has the right to hang pirates caught in waters under his jurisdiction.'

'Well, we're not pirates,' said Stanier, attracting glances of withering contempt from his fellow Commissioners.

When they reached the beach the motor barge was awaiting them. Stanier suddenly recollected the business of the afternoon. Apart from Lord Craven's white ketch and the black, white and buff splendour of *Naiad*, the bay was still empty.

The lighthouse tender *Caryatid* steamed into the anchorage of Ynyscraven at 1355, just as the Commissioners emerged onto *Naiad*'s quarterdeck after their lunch. As they went forward to board the barge, Sir Charles Mudge went up onto the bridge.

'Ah, Captain Foster, please extend dinner invitations to Lord Craven and ... what's the official name of the chap who helps run the tractor up to the lighthouses?'

'The Reeve, Sir Charles.'

'That's the fellow. I suppose he's married?'

'He certainly was when I was last here.'

'Very well, we'd better include his wife.

211

And get Macready and his Chief Engineer over here ... Oh, and I suppose you'd better come.'

'Thank you, Sir Charles,' Foster said dryly, adding, 'that leaves the Reeve's wife rather on her own, Sir Charles.'

'Any bright ideas?'

'There's a rather attractive widow, er, Captain Macready knows her quite well. I'm sure he'd be pleased to act as escort, or, if you wished, I could ask her.'

'If you can rustle up another lady, that'll be fine. Oh, and Craven's on his yacht, I understand. Must be that ketch inshore. I haven't seen another boat about.'

'I'll see to it, Sir Charles.'

'Very well. Now let's go and give poor old Macready the bad news.'

Foster was about to say that Macready already knew, but decided against it. Idly he watched the barge leave *Naiad*'s side then quickly went to his cabin, wrote several notes and, after instructing his Second Officer what to do with them, he folded himself in his armchair and went to sleep.

Aboard *Caryatid* the Commissioners rooted into every compartment in the ship. They were attended by Macready and his senior officers who picked up various key personnel as they progressed, such

212

as the Second Engineer at the engine-room door, the Bosun in the hold and the Carpenter forward in the stores. By now Mudge and his colleagues were so used to Stanier fussing and complaining about every misplaced item, every smear of grease and scar of rust, that they discounted most of his diatribe as he tut-tutted his way through the ship. For those personally responsible for these various workaday blemishes that inevitably marred an old ship like *Caryatid*, this tooth-sucking disapproval was demoralising in the extreme. Finally, when Stanier, leading the posse like a bloodhound, discovered a small pile of paint scrapings and a scraper leaning against a bulkhead, he pointed and asked what on earth these things meant.

'I've a seaman working on scraping this bulkhead, sir,' said Watson.

'But this is an inspection, Mister. All this stuff should be squared away before we come aboard.'

'I'm sorry, sir, I had intended this should be finished, but it isn't and I thought it better to continue the work until it is.'

'Then where is the man now?' Stanier persisted with warped logic.

'I expect he's taken himself off until you gentlemen have all passed through, sir.'

'You mean you don't know where the dickens he is, Mister?'

'Not exactly,' admitted Watson, wearying of the farce.

'An officer who doesn't know exactly where his men are is incompetent.'

'Let's move on,' said Sir Charles, taking Stanier's elbow.

'Incompetent, Mister, d'you hear me ...'

The inspection completed its round of the ship on the bridge. Here Sir Charles took the *Caryatid*'s order book from Stanier's hands and wrote briefly in it before handing it to Macready. 'I regret having to write what I have, Captain Macready, but ...' Mudge shrugged, 'these things cannot be avoided.'

Taking the book Macready read the senior Commissioner's remarks and then repeated them out loud.

'*The final inspection of the SS* Caryatid *took place off the island of Ynyscraven. The ship was found in good, serviceable order, reflecting credit on Captain Macready, his officers and ratings. The vessel has acquitted herself very well during her long years of service and has always maintained the high standards of the Celtic Lighthouse Service.* Thank you, Sir Charles.'

'Sorry, Macready. You'll retire with the ship, of course. We've no plans to replace

214

her, I'm afraid. *Waterwitch* will take over her work.'

'And the base at Porth Ardur, Sir Charles?'

Mudge shook his head. 'We're shutting up the whole shop. You'll get your orders in the next few days. But it seemed proper that I should let you know officially.'

'That's kind of you, Sir Charles.'

'It's unfortunate, Captain Macready, but duty compels me to raise the matter of a formal complaint laid against you by Assistant Keeper Macleod on the Mitre Rock light. He was formerly on the Buccabu—'

'I take it this is about his aborted compassionate leave, Captain Stanier,' Macready broke in.

'Er, yes.'

'The night his wife went into labour, it was blowing a sou' westerly nine. The following day it had veered westerly and increased to storm force ten. It dropped to an eight the next day, backed sou' westerly and blew like that for a week. By the time the sea conditions enabled us anywhere near the Buccabu reef, Macleod was due for normal leave. We took him off as a matter of routine. I think even the good Lord Himself would have found walking on the water difficult that particular night, Captain Stanier. That is the reason why

215

Junior Keeper Macleod could not be with his wife the night her baby was born.'

'Well, that settles that matter then,' said Sir Charles hurriedly. 'I think it's time we returned to *Naiad*.'

The Commissioners' barge ran alongside *Naiad* and they disembarked. On deck a fuming and frustrated Stanier ran into the Second Mate who was about to leave with the letters of invitation. From the casual conversation of Sir Charles and Captain Gostling, Stanier had heard Macready's name mentioned as a dinner guest.

'D'you have an invitation there for Captain Macready?'

'Yes sir, and his Chief Engineer. They're the last to be delivered. I was waiting for you to finish your inspection before taking them across to *Caryatid*.'

Stanier smiled. 'Don't bother. They won't have the opportunity. Give them to me.' He took the two envelopes and, stuffing them into his pocket, motioned the Second Mate to follow him up to *Naiad*'s bridge.

'I want you to send *Caryatid* a signal,' Stanier said, waiting while the young officer reached for the message pad. *'Prefix: priority, stop,'* he dictated. *'Proceed and verify position of St Kenelm lightvessel, stop. Reported off station, stop.* That's all, get that transmitted right away.'

The Second Mate looked from the message to Stanier. 'We haven't received ... I'll send it by semaphore, sir.'

'At once, Mister!' Stanier commanded, waiting while the Second Mate called up the *Caryatid*. When the answering flutter of red and yellow flags indicated her readiness to receive, he went aft chuckling to himself.

'What's *Caryatid* signalling about?' Sir Charles asked as he took tea on the quarterdeck, having noticed the flutter of the flags.

'Oh, something's out of position, Sir Charles, I guess he's sending his apologies about dinner tonight.'

'You were damned hard on him, Stanier.'

'Got to maintain standards, Sir Charles, you know that. It's not our business to go about making ourselves popular,' and he swung the older man away from the fluttering flags for fear he might actually read the message. 'And it's particularly important,' he added with a flash of uncharacteristic genius, 'to keep up the pressure, particularly as we enter this period of change.'

'Well, you do have a point there, I suppose, Stanier.'

'Thank you, Sir Charles.'

After the Commissioners had gone, Macready stared across the water until their barge had disappeared behind the low hull of *Naiad*. He felt a profound sense of anti-climax. Although he had long known the truth, it hurt him to have been officially told the news of *Caryatid*'s demise under the cliffs of Ynyscraven. It was for him a place invested with enormous charm, a personal private place with which the Commissioners had only the most tenuous connection. The lighthouses were not theirs, they belonged, morally at least, to their keepers and the officers and men of the *Caryatid* who collectively maintained them with devotion for the benefit of the passing mariner. Those remote, unknown ships, bound outward or inward, each upon her own lawful occasions, moved him with their innate dignity. Yes, it was the essential dignity of ships with which he, Septimus Macready, identified. They inherently possessed something majestic, even, he ruefully admitted, the rust buckets owned by Cambrian Steam. He had not thought of it quite like that before. Perhaps it was only at this moment of realisation that his long connection with ships was coming to an end, that he was capable of formulating such a thought, but he felt it justified his hubris.

No-one saw the solitary tear that rolled down his cheek. He dashed it to one side as *Naiad* began semaphoring.

# Invitations To Dinner And Other Intrigues

Captain Foster's invitations to dine aboard *Naiad* arrived at the Farthings' cottage as they finished lunch. It had been a happily relaxed occasion, with Lord Craven obviously charmed by Justine. She in turn enjoyed the young man's attentiveness. Even the intrusion of *Naiad*'s Second Officer failed to puncture the mood and he was invited to enjoy a glass of wine, happy to have found the elusive Lord Craven in the company of the new Reeve.

'Well, well,' said Craven on reading the note. 'I clearly did not insult them enough.'

'Perhaps they want you to revise the speed limit,' Charlie said laughing.

'I'm sorry about that,' said the *Naiad*'s Second Mate. 'I was in the boat this morning. They were muttering about your rights to impose it on the way back to the ship.'

'If you can prove them to be pirates, I think I can hang them, too,' Craven said, smiling.

'Yes,' agreed the officer, 'I overheard

220

them mention that too.'

'I'm glad they know about it.'

'Well,' said Justine, 'it would certainly solve some of our problems.'

'I don't think we've a tree tall enough on the island,' chuckled Craven.

'Oh, there are some lovely old oaks in the coombe,' protested Sonia, who would defend all criticisms of Ynyscraven.

'Well, we could always use the gallery rails of the lighthouses and string 'em up like pheasants after a shoot,' suggested Charlie.

'What a delicious prospect,' Craven agreed.

'I must go,' said *Naiad*'s Second Officer, tossing off his glass.

'Just one thing,' Charlie had said as the officer rose to leave. 'I'd be obliged if you didn't let on to anyone that the new Reeve is a former officer in the Lighthouse Service.'

'No, of course not,' the fellow said, grinning conspiratorially.

'My God!' exclaimed Craven, slapping his forehead in mock horror after the officer's departure, 'what the dickens will I wear? I suppose they'll all be dolled up in mess kit or something?' he looked enquiringly at Charlie.

'Yes, I'm afraid so.'

'I've a plain reefer on board, but I'm

221

damned if I'm going to wear that. What are you ladies going to wear?' he asked, winking at Charlie and precipitating a discussion that rambled on for almost half an hour during which Charlie and Craven made serious inroads into another bottle of Sonia's excellent gorse wine.

Justine felt strangely excited. Although she loved her new life on the island, she was undeniably attracted by the touch of glamour suggested by a formal dinner in the splendid surroundings she had heard prevailed aboard the Commissioners' yacht. As a former ballroom dancer she had a love of clothes and display, small vices she had no chance of indulging on Ynyscraven. Of course, she would have to be circumspect regarding Captain Macready, for in the invitation the tactful Foster had indicated Macready would be present, but he had underlined the fact that she was to be partnered by Foster himself. By such a diplomatic device, Foster could rob the occasion of any whiff of scandal. Justine chided herself; she had always thought of Bernard Foster as a dull man!

When the lunch party broke up amid yawns and protestations that it might be a good idea to lie down for an hour or two, Sonia cast a look out through the window as she began to carry the dirty dishes to the sink.

'*Caryatid*'s steaming away,' she said, staring through the glass. 'I wonder why.'

Justine and Charlie crowded round her. The old ship was half a mile north of the anchorage, running up the eastern shore of the island, the white vee of her wash and the coiling black smoke that she trailed astern showing she was already at full speed. Clearly she was not just popping up to the north light.

'Any idea, Charlie?' Justine asked, her low voice vibrant with emotion.

Charlie frowned. 'No.'

He paused and Justine said, 'If they're off somewhere, Septimus won't be there this evening.'

'But you said Bernard Foster said he would be,' Sonia put in.

'It must be an emergency,' said Justine, used to disappointment.

'The weather's good,' mused Charlie.

'Someone sick?' suggested Craven.

Charlie nodded. 'Yes, it could be that.'

'Well, there must be a logical reason,' Craven said, uncertain exactly why the departure of *Caryatid* should so interest these people until he recalled they were islanders, and obsessed with the small things that loomed large in their lives. 'It doesn't really affect us—'

'It affects me, Roger,' Justine began.

'Oh yes. You and the Captain. I'd

forgotten. I'm sorry ... But look,' Craven added brightly, 'you can come as my guest.'

'Officially, I'm already going as Captain Foster's.'

'Captain Foster—' frowned Craven.

'The commander of *Naiad*,' Charlie explained quickly, something occurring to him. 'This could be deliberate, you know.'

'You mean a snub to Septimus?' Justine asked.

'Stanier could have a hand in it,' Charlie suggested.

Macready strode his bridge in a towering rage. He did not often lose his temper, but to be kicked out of the anchorage of Ynyscraven was a further affront and he wanted to believe that Stanier was behind the alleged signal claiming the St Kenelm lightvessel was out of position. But the knowledge that he attended to the very matter only hours earlier that same day and restored the lightvessel to her precise position, did nothing for Macready's equanimity. The fact was that once a lightvessel's mooring anchor had been broken out of the ground it was sometimes difficult to rebed it. Even digging it into the bottom by running the *Caryatid*'s engine astern at the end of a generous scope of cable might not

224

entirely bury the anchor securely. It was therefore *just* possible that after they had left this morning, the strength of the tide had moved the lightvessel again. The uncertainty nagged at Macready, increasing his fury, until Mr Watson, his own competence affected by the apparent failure of the morning's operation, asked to have a word with him.

'What the devil is it, Mister?' growled Macready, following the Mate out onto the bridge wing out of earshot of the Quartermaster on the wheel.

'I took the liberty of going through to Porth Ardur on the radio, sir, by way of the coastguard.'

'What?' Macready frowned. Strictly speaking, Watson had exceeded his authority in making a radio transmission through the coastguard without the permission of *Caryatid*'s master. But Macready sensed the moment was inappropriate for raising any objection. Besides, he had a vague feeling that he knew why Watson had done it and that he should have thought of it himself.

'The Nelson spirit, sir,' Watson said by way of exculpation.

'Go on, Mr Watson,' prompted Macready, feeling his temper subside.

'I asked the coastguard to query the time and origin of the signal that reported the St

Kenelm out of position. He said he had not received one, so I asked him to check with Mr Dale at the base. Since we know that it was *Naiad* that discovered the matter yesterday and by so small an amount that a passing ship would only have thought it meant the lightvessel had a lot of cable out and not reported it, we could not get this report, if it existed, confused with another—'

'Yes, yes, I understand. Go on.'

'Well, that's it really, sir ...' said Watson.

He was a nice lad, Macready thought, he had used his initiative, but he was not of Charlie's calibre. 'So what you're saying is that no-one, not the coastguard nor Mr Dale, has received a message stating the St Kenelm was out of position. Have I got that right?'

'Yes, sir. Didn't I make that clear?'

'Not entirely,' Macready said dryly.

'Sorry, sir. You see it occurred to me that it was a bit odd that *Naiad* knew but that we didn't. Then I thought that with the Commissioners onboard, their bloody radio watches will be closed up all the time and nothing would please them more than to intercept a message for us and pass it on.'

'Makes them look smart, eh?' Macready ruminated.

'Just so, sir.'

226

Macready stood for a moment, then with a, 'Thank you, Mr Watson, thank you very much,' he headed for the radio room.

Captain Foster woke from his snooze and, after a quick wash and a brush of his teeth, felt himself a new man. He strolled out of his cabin and onto *Naiad*'s bridge. One of the few compensations of commanding her, he reflected, was that occasionally the day's work finished early and one had only to attend a dinner by way of duty. And then he recalled Justine. He had met her, of course, known her quite well when she and Macready had been ballroom dancing partners in Porth Ardur. A sexually unadventurous man, Foster was scrupulously loyal to his wife, but even he used to marvel at Justine's bosom, the complementary waspishness of her waist and the fine line of her legs. Though always slightly overblown for his own taste, it was impossible for any man not to be affected by Justine Morgan. The prospect of being in her company this evening gave him a small, delightful sense of anticipation. That he would be able to gently guy his former commander, only increased this rather unfamiliarly lubricious sense of anticipation. He emerged onto the port bridge wing smiling, sucking in fresh

227

air with the enthusiasm of a man who takes some joy in his life.

The Second Mate straightened up from the rail. 'Afternoon, sir.'

'Afternoon.' Foster stared round the anchorage. 'Where's *Caryatid?*' he asked suddenly.

'Oh, she got under weigh, sir. Apparently a report had come in that the St Kenelm lightvessel was off station.'

Foster frowned. 'Oh ... have you a copy?' He wanted to check the time of origin. If the report had originated before he had passed word to Macready yesterday then Macready was on a fool's errand and was reacting for nothing.

'Oh, there's no copy, sir. Captain Stanier passed the message.'

'Stanier? Where did he get it?'

The Second Officer shrugged. 'I have no idea, sir, I only—'

'Yes, yes, I understand—'

'Sir?' Both men turned as the quarter-master called from the wheelhouse door. 'I've Captain Macready on the radio.'

'Very well.' Foster ducked back into the wheelhouse and passed quickly through to the wireless office.

'*Naiad* to *Caryatid*, Foster here. Over.'

'Bernard, I'm going back to the St Kenelm. Received a message from your ship that she was off station. There's no

228

corroboration that it was reported by any other ship. You'll appreciate my position. Can you confirm accuracy of origin, please? Over.'

'Yes. I suspect mischief, Septimus. Report originates from, er, a Sea Dragon. Said dragon knew nothing of our conversation of yesterday. Over.'

The veiled reference to Stanier concealed in Foster's reference to his first, wrecked command, was what Macready already suspected. Now Foster also confirmed it had nothing to do with what he and his officers had found out and passed covertly to Macready the previous day.

'Do you concur that a whiff of malice is involved?' Macready asked. 'Over.'

Foster did not want to make much of the matter. If the Commissioners had their radio receiver on and were listening to some light music, they would pick up his transmissions on almost any frequency as they blasted out from *Naiad*'s aerial.

'More than a whiff. Over.'

'Perhaps one too many to dinner tonight, eh? Over.' Macready was being persistent, Foster thought.

'Something of that order. Over and out.'

'Wait one, Bernard. Anyone going that I know? Over.'

'Affirmative. Don't worry. I'll look after it.'

'I trust you, Bernard. Over and out.'
'Thank you. *Naiad* out.'

The decision of what Justine and Sonia were to wear was influenced by the necessity for them to clamber aboard the Commissioners' barge. This ruled out long dresses, but both looked, as Charlie remarked with ironic gallantry, 'a huge credit to the fashion houses of Ynyscraven'.

Their embarkation was facilitated by a small brow the barge crew lowered and there was no lack of strong arms to see them to the padded settles that lined the luxurious cuddy of the barge. On her return to *Naiad,* the barge ran carefully alongside *Lyonesse* where Lord Craven awaited them.

'I hope I shall not out-peacock you, ladies,' his lordship said, stepping down and ducking under the cuddy.

'Oh, my word!' exclaimed Justine while Sonia giggled.

It was not that Lord Craven's attire was gaudy, for his resources were limited, but it was scarcely suitable dress for a formal dinner. He was in the habit of keeping an old set of cricket whites aboard *Lyonesse* which, with the addition of a tie or cravat and his blazer, could quickly provide him with the sort of dress in which he could attend a party. However, his lordship had eschewed the blazer and wore about his neck what appeared to be a bright scarlet sail tie knotted unconventionally in a loose and vapid bow. His shirt sleeves were rolled up and about his waist was a gaudy roll of yellow and black silk which Charlie guessed was Craven's personal yacht-racing flag, though in fact it was his father's. This improvised cummerbund gave the outfit a piratical, rather than a formal air, and this impression was heightened by his lordship's lack of footwear.

'Please do not tread on my toes this evening,' he said.

'D'you mean metaphorically as well as literally?' Charlie asked as the barge chugged across the bay at a steady four knots.

'Are you meditating mischief?' Sonia asked.

'I'm *always* meditating mischief, Mrs Farthing.' Craven laughed as the barge drew alongside *Naiad*'s accommodation ladder.

Caroline Stanier sat back in the taxi and lit a cigarette as the damp and crowded pavements of the capital flashed past. She was too self-possessed a woman to betray any sign of self-satisfaction, but she was confident her dinner with David

Smith would go well, for she had done the groundwork too carefully. Her dinner partner was, she was compelled to concede, a man who, when he wished, could deploy a compelling charm. Moreover, though she admitted it only in the deepest recesses of her heart, she found him more than a little attractive. He exuded a powerful air of success, of being a man capable of thrusting himself at the very heart of things, unlike her poor, dear, silly and quite stupid Jimmy.

At the thought of her husband she exhaled cigarette smoke through slightly viciously pursed lips. Sometimes the thought of him ... Well, she had privately sworn not to dwell on such matters. He was useful ...

No. He *had been* useful, Caroline mused, leaning forward, stubbing her cigarette out and calling to the driver, 'Set me down here, please!'

Tegwyn and her husband dined at home. She was aware that all was not well with Pomeroy. He was occasionally susceptible to prolonged bouts of silent introspection which customarily ended in the purchase of an *objet d'art,* after which he became his old, considerate and attentive self again.

'Darling,' Tegwyn said gently, tentatively seeking to prod Pomeroy into a more

232

sociable frame of mind by inducing him to consider a purchase, 'did you ever actually *see* the Canaletto Lord Dungarth is offering for sale?'

'Mmm?' Pomeroy looked up abstractedly. 'What did you say?'

Tegwyn repeated her question and Pomeroy stirred himself. 'No, no I didn't, but it's almost certainly not by Canaletto,' he said kindly. 'Frankly it isn't worth bothering with.'

'Oh, I just thought that you might be considering another purchase.'

'No, no I wasn't.' He smiled wanly at her. 'Look, my dear, I'm sorry if I'm a bit withdrawn. Truth is, I feel a bit off colour.'

'Why don't you go to bed?' Tegwyn looked at her watch. 'It's already quite late.'

Pomeroy shook his head, looking at his own watch. 'No,' he said with what appeared to be sudden resolution, 'I think I need some fresh air. Mind if I take a turn round the square?'

'Not at all,' she replied brightening and smiling back at him. 'I'll probably be in bed when you get back.'

'Sweet dreams, my dear.'

And Tegwyn held up her face for Pomeroy to kiss as he went out.

The Commissioners' dinner ended convivially. It had not been an unpleasant evening at all. Justine, although intensely disappointed at Macready's absence, found herself reconciled by the splendour of her surroundings. The opulent dining room fitted for the exclusive use of the Commissioners, occupied the beam of *Naiad*, a grand, rococo room which seemed out of place aboard ship and oddly at variance with the black and gold of the Commissioners bedecked in their evening finery. Sir Charles Mudge wore the ribbon and star of his order, while Gostling and Blake sported miniature medals and decorations, evidence of gallantry in the late war.

To have had Macready present but tantalisingly remote, separated by not only the conventions of staid morality, but those of the Commissioners' pomp, would have been well nigh intolerable, Justine thought. Dear Septimus would have been ponderously awkward in such surroundings, though Bernard Foster, who had greeted her with a kiss, had, it seemed, come into his own. Slowly Justine saw her lover's absence as perhaps a blessing in disguise.

She found herself seated between Captains Gostling and Blake, both of whom were overwhelmed by her and vied with each other in the extravagance of their flattery. Thus distracted, mellowed by wine and sated by rich food, Justine found she enjoyed being the cynosure of all eyes. Even the smoothly confident ogling of James Stanier only added to her pleasure and she purred under the compliments showered upon her by the two shipmasters.

Sonia, between Blake and Sir Charles Mudge, was less well equipped than her older friend to enjoy such an occasion. Island-born and island-bred, Sonia claimed the paternity of a Russian *émigré* nobleman, but in her case nurture rather than nature dominated her personality. Untutored in the matter of small talk, she was a young woman of simple pleasures. The gilt and pastel decoration, the false, fluted columns and brocade drapery seemed quite ridiculously superfluous. There was, she thus concluded, a tedium about the evening, set, as it was, amid the pomps and etiquette of a strict formality.

Charlie had had a difficult moment, for Stanier had inevitably recognised him. While the party was still being introduced, Stanier confronted him.

'What the hell are *you* doing here?' he had hissed into Charlie's face.

Though somewhat affronted, Charlie had responded with considerable dignity. 'I am now the Reeve of this island. You

235

invited me.' And with that Stanier had to be content, though it was clear that, completing the circle between Foster and Charlie, Stanier found himself isolated, disdaining to talk to Charlie and ignored by Gostling who was too occupied in fawning over Justine's bosom.

To his own left, Charlie became absorbed in conversation with Mudge and his lordship who, by virtue of his rank sat on Mudge's right. Craven had apparently been forgiven his morning impertinence, for no allusions were made to the encounter and it was as if it had never occurred. The eccentricities of his dress were similarly accepted without comment. Mudge, moreover, seemed equally unaffected by the identity of Mr Farthing as the recently resigned chief mate of *Caryatid,* courteously acknowledging that Charlie was free to decide these matters for himself.

'My wife was born on Ynyscraven, d'you see, Sir Charles,' he explained, 'so it seemed the most logical thing to do.'

'Quite so, Mr Farthing. I drink to your good fortune.'

'You've lost a good man, Sir Charles,' remarked Craven, smiling at Charlie, 'but that's my gain, wouldn't you say?'

Mudge sighed. 'It is going to be our misfortune to lose a good many more,

Lord Craven, once we close down the operation at Porth Ardur.'

'Well, I must confess I'm surprised, Sir Charles. But I'm sure you know your own business best and my own nautical experience is confined to that of a common yachtsman. However, I have always considered the Silurian Strait, with its strong tides, to be one of the most dangerous places, fully justifying the retention of its own tender. Yet along the extent of its shores lie some of the country's most important harbours and it will always support a lively trade.'

'It's economics—' Stanier leaned across and tried to break in.

'It's a matter of economics,' Sir Charles remarked, ignoring Stanier, 'and the fact that *Caryatid*'s an old ship.'

They then became absorbed in an analysis of the pros and contras pertaining to the provision of seamarks in the Silurian Strait. From time to time, Charlie contributed a technical detail, but mostly he was content to listen, exchanging the occasional, furtive wink with Sonia.

It was after they left the table and retired to the smoke room on the upper deck above that the first sign of awkwardness occurred. There was no provision for the ladies to withdraw, so they moved *en masse* and, while those who wished to smoke stepped out onto the now moonlit quarterdeck, the ladies and their eager admirers remained inside the warmly lit, oak-panelled smoke-room, sipping their liqueurs.

The movement broke up the symmetry of the seating arrangements. Blake and Gostling had exhausted their vocabulary of superlatives and the predatory Stanier, fuelled by a swiftly swallowed cognac, moved in upon Justine, seating himself beside her and handing her a brandy. She looked in vain for Foster, but Sir Charles Mudge had buttonholed him. He cast a despairing glance towards Justine, but she smiled back reassuringly and turned to the importunate Stanier as he bent over her décolletage.

'I am delighted to see you again, my dear Mrs Morgan,' he said, as if addressing a woman of equal age to himself instead of the mother of his former mistress. 'The last time we met was in most unfortunate circumstances.'

'You have done very well for yourself, James,' she said coolly. 'I understand from Tegwyn that you and Caroline sometimes visit her and her husband.'

'Yes indeed. I wouldn't say we were intimate any longer—'

'That's just as well, seeing that you are married to Caroline,' Justine said sharply,

238

her antennae warning her that Stanier was drunk and had his own, sinister agenda.

'Marriage is just a convention, Mrs Morgan. I should like you to know that is how I view it.'

'And why should you like me to know that?' she asked quietly.

'Because,' Stanier said, dropping his voice and hurrying on as the knot of men clustered about Sonia burst into cheery laughter, 'because I enjoyed your daughter and she enjoyed me,' he breathed, 'and because I wish to pleasure her mother.'

It took a moment for Justine to grasp the extent of the man's meaning and when she did, she had lost the reflexive urge to strike his face, remembering her surroundings. Instead she took another tack. Keeping her voice deliberately, even seductively low, she leaned slightly towards Stanier, dangerously closing the distance between his nose and her breasts.

'Oh James, is that why you banished poor Septimus?' And when he nodded, she added breathlessly, 'I scarcely dared hope so. You see, James, dear ...' and here she put her warm palm upon his left thigh, 'I am almost ashamed to say so, but I was always a little jealous of Tegwyn ...'

She saw the gleam of triumph in Stanier's eyes. 'My dear ...' he breathed, so close to her that she smelled the alcohol on his breath.

'But what about Caroline?' she whispered.

Stanier, not the brightest of men sober, frowned. 'What about her?'

'You threw Tegwyn over for Caroline. I imagine she is wonderful in bed.'

Stanier shook his head and Justine saw a slight welling in his eyes. 'She's cold, so cold—'

'My poor, poor boy,' Justine said, almost moved now she had touched the core of Stanier's unhappiness.

'Don't monopolise Mrs Morgan, Stanier!'

Justine and Stanier both looked up as Craven bent over them. 'Would you take the night air with me, Justine?' Craven asked, offering his arm.

'Of course. Excuse me, James,' Justine said, rising as Stanier fell back in confusion.

As they emerged on the quarterdeck, Justine said, 'Thank heavens you arrived when you did, I was on the verge of humiliating that creature.'

'Well, I felt *he* needed *his* toes trodden on,' Craven said. They chuckled, then Craven asked urbanely, 'D'you find it odd that he was once your daughter's lover?'

'Well, he had a certain charm when he arrived in Porth Ardur all that time ago and my daughter's head was easily turned.'

'I'm in love with Tegwyn, you know,' Craven admitted simply.

'Good heavens!' Justine exclaimed, genuinely surprised, stopping and staring at him. 'I had no idea.'

'She can't be happy with Pomeroy.'

'Why not?'

'Because she can't. He's a queen ...'

David Smith threw away the butt of the cigar and put both hands in his pockets. His dinner with Caroline had been most enjoyable and they had concluded their business to a nicety. It was stimulating working with someone who was as straightforward as Caroline Stanier. If more women were like her, Smith thought, there would be fewer of them having nervous breakdowns.

The frisson that business stirred in him also aroused other passions and when he had said goodnight to Caroline, he had decided the night remained young and he was ripe for adventure. As he turned into the square a clock somewhere nearby chimed midnight: he had been walking for about three quarters of an hour. For a moment he stopped to consider the wisdom of his intentions. It was late and he did not want scandal. It was one of the joys of working with Caroline. Her sense of discretion was almost painfully watertight.

He wondered if she ever submitted to the sheer abandon of passion and decided it was unlikely. He was too little of an expert in the ways of women to wonder whether the quality was unique to her, or was to be found in a particular type. Anyway, her example was admirable. He must be careful, he warned himself, and hesitated.

But it was at this moment that he caught sight of a familiar and half-expected figure. Smith started forward again and quickly overtook the idling Pomeroy.

Captain Macready stood on for the St Kenelm lightvessel and, having taken a further check on its position, headed *Caryatid* for Porth Ardur. He knew it was the next port of call for the *Naiad* and anticipated that Sir Charles would make an announcement to the staff of the base and buoy yard about their imminent and collective redundancy.

For himself, the sheer stupid malice of Stanier stripped away the last shreds of his own sentimentality. He trusted Foster to watch over Justine and entertained no doubts as to her own loyalty. He was in a sense also glad that he had not had to pay court aboard *Naiad* that night. And he was touchingly sorry for old Mudge and the others. It was odd that they allowed themselves to be bamboozled by the likes of Stanier, but Macready had always remained uninterested in the higher politics of the Lighthouse Service. They somehow seemed too remote from the everyday realities he had to deal with.

As the shipowners' representative Stanier, Macready assumed, would naturally possess enormous clout at the Board. Nor would it help that while Mudge, Blake and Gostling were former shipmasters, they were all so much older than the ambitious Stanier.

'Damn the man!' Macready thought as he settled himself to sleep. 'Damn him to perdition.'

The barge rumbled across the anchorage towards *Lyonesse* at four knots. To starboard the great dark bulk of the island reared up into the night sky silhouetted against the moonlight. To the south the lighthouse gleamed dully, the light bright within the lantern. They could see the great lens revolving and the three fingers of gathered and concentrated brilliance revolve above their heads, periodically sweeping them. From a distance the group of three flashes would show to any passing ship every twenty seconds. Over to their left a low swell broke upon the extension of the island's shore, the rocks of the Hound's Teeth. At low water a few rusty remains of what had once been the engine of the motor yacht *Sea Dragon* could still be seen.

Yawning, the Coxswain conned the boat alongside the ketch.

'Are you sure ...?' Craven said, bending over Justine.

'Quite,' she reassured him.

Craven hopped nimbly across the narrow gap onto the yacht's deck. 'Good night and thank you, Coxswain.'

'Pleasure, m'lord,' said the young seamen grinning, delighted to have his overtime acknowledged. The barge drew away from the pale waving figure and headed towards the beach in silence.

It was unfortunate that Stanier insisted on accompanying them. Both Charlie and Craven had tried to dissuade him, but he had followed them down into the boat and now sat slumped opposite Justine. She found herself silently praying that he would fall asleep in the short period it took to close the shingle beach, but as the barge slowed and the crew prepared the wooden brow he stirred.

'Now, m'dear.'

'I'm really quite all right, James,' Justine said, making one last attempt to dissuade Stanier from rising.

'No, no, we must see our guests safely ashore ...'

244

But once on the beach, Stanier began to walk up towards the path with them.

'Charlie,' Justine hissed, 'please try and get rid of him.'

'Yes, of course. Walk on with Sonia,' Charlie said quickly and turned, confronting Stanier. 'Look, Captain Stanier, it's very kind of you, but I see no point in you coming any further. You don't want to keep the boat's crew up too long, I'm sure.'

'I'll see Mrs Morgan home, damn it. It's no business of yours ...' Stanier tried to push past Charlie, but Charlie kept moving in front of him, conscious that the ladies were beating a hasty retreat.

'Look, I'd hate to seem ungrateful after your splendid hospitality tonight, Stanier, but actually it is. You see, I'm the Reeve and, it may come as something of a surprise, but I combine the powers of police, magistracy and, er, the keeper of the Bridewell. I don't think the Commissioners would really appreciate having to bail you out tomorrow morning, do you?'

'You cheeky bugger! Are you threatening me?'

'No, Stanier,' Charlie said with weary resignation, 'I'm actually cautioning you. In my judgement, you are drunk and potentially disorderly.'

Stanier's blow caught Charlie squarely

and he felt his head snap back, but the effort cost Stanier his balance and he staggered forward, so that Charlie, recovering, caught Stanier's chin with his knee. The Commissioner fell with a scrunch on the shingle and lay groaning.

'Bowman!' Charlie called. 'I think Captain Stanier could do with a hand.'

The seaman loomed out of the darkness and swore. 'There's always one of them,' he said as both men got hold of Stanier and began to half drag him down the beach.

'Yes,' said Charlie between clenched teeth as they manhandled Stanier towards the boat, 'isn't there just.'

By the time he reached the cottage the women had lit the lamps and were pouring tea.

'Oh Charlie!' Sonia exclaimed, 'what on earth happened?'

'You've a black eye, I think,' explained Justine when she saw Charlie's lack of comprehension.

'Well, it was worth it,' Charlie said grinning. 'I think I came off best.'

# Porth Ardur

It was afterwards said that the air had been full of portents, for those who knew how to recognise such things. At the time, however, the first of these was remarked upon as being funny, an event of appealing poetic justice with more than a hint of irony in it.

It was a meteorological curiosity of the Silurian Strait that, if the centre of a depression passed eastwards between fifty and sixty miles to the south, and that this coincided with a spring ebb tide, an exceptionally strong easterly gale was induced in the Strait itself. Fortunately the conditions necessary for this phenomena synchronised relatively rarely, since the prevailing wind over the whole area blew in from the Atlantic from the west, or south-west, but when it happened, a strong easterly came as a highly disruptive event. Lying in the direct path of such a wind was the island of Ynyscraven, where an easterly gale was still known as 'an invader's wind', since such a gale had long ago brought the first conquerors to subjugate the indigenous Celtic inhabitants.

However, any meteorological analysis after the event shortly to be described would fail to associate this initial easterly breeze with any depression anywhere. Indeed it was this completely anomalous origin which gave this wind and the consequent incident the quality of a portent, like the quick, fleeting appearance of a scouting patrol, far ahead of the assault of the main war host.

Captain Macready had berthed *Caryatid* alongside that part of the lighthouse pier that lay inside the enclosed dock. On the opposite, landward side reared the monstrous coal-tipping towers, beneath which lay the dingy chocolate brown hull of the Cambrian Steam Navigation Company's 5,000-ton tramp steamer *Galahad*. Squeezed in ahead of the tramp, lay the *Kurnow* loading her passengers and cargo for the Bishop's Islands. Advertisements on the quay announced a new, twice-weekly service to Ynyscraven. Passengers could land upon this 'wonderfully remote, romantic island and meet the isolated inhabitants who carried on a tranquil way of life undisturbed by the worries of modern life'. Though not bound for the island this morning, bookings were available for the Friday service. At present only half a dozen people had shown any curiosity about the 'isolated inhabitants', while the local opinion in Porth Ardur was that the enterprise would founder, as seemed to be happening to so much of the promised expansion of Porth Ardur.

At high water the following morning, the caisson was drawn back and *Kurnow* slipped out to sea while into the already crowded dock edged the *Naiad*. Foster brought her in and laid her neatly alongside *Caryatid*, making the huge frattan fenders between the two vessels creak. Lying secured some four feet apart, a distance soon bridged by a short brow, the two lighthouse tenders made a curious sight, almost completely filling the dock. A moment or two later a bag of mail was brought aboard *Naiad*, passed over from *Caryatid*, most of which was for the Commissioners and included a note for Stanier.

At exactly half past nine o'clock that Thursday morning, saluted off *Naiad* by her officers and led by Sir Charles Mudge, the Commissioners for Celtic Lighthouses crossed the deck of *Caryatid*, where a similar side party led by First Mate Watson formally acknowledged their passage with their own salutes. Above their heads and at the sterns of the two ships, the flags strained at their halliards in a freshening easterly breeze.

Once ashore by way of *Caryatid*'s own

brow and in the rear of which marched Macready and Foster, the little procession turned right and made for the whitewashed buoy yard. Here Mr Dale, immaculate in striped trousers, dark jacket and Eton collar, had assembled the entire workforce. In a huddle surrounding Mr Dale, as though unused to the bruising effects of fresh air, were the wages clerks, the stores clerk and his two storemen, Miss Gaynor Penfold the shorthand typist, and Cyrus Jones, a former seaman who had lost an arm in an accident on the foredeck of *Caryatid* and was employed as a telephone operator and messenger. In a darker, more truculent phalanx, stood the blacksmith, the carpenter and his two mates, the three stone-masons, two painters and two dozen workmen who by their labour attended to the harsher end of the Commissioner's business. It was these men who complemented *Caryatid*'s crew, for they cleaned off the rusty buoys that she landed, then scaled, serviced, repaired and painted them, finally preparing them for a further three years at sea. They also ranged worn lengths of chain, cut out weak sections and assembled new moorings by forging new links and joining up existing runs. Stores, engine spares, diesel and lamp oil were ordered and held until loaded aboard *Caryatid* for carriage to the lighthouses and lightvessels in the Silurian Strait and adjacent sea area. In fact, everything from heavy spare anchor cable, to small, light rolls of blue and white lamp wick was prepared for despatch, each item carefully parcelled in accordance with the station requisition order. Marked with its destination these disparate stores were loaded aboard *Caryatid* until her boats delivered them as the tender effected the period reliefs of the crews of each lightvessel and lighthouse.

It was a ceaseless routine that had run for years with the oiled precision of near perfection and it was this very seamless, unglamorous ordinariness of its business that seemed now to be somehow in question. To those men waiting the arrival of Sir Charles Mudge, the air seemed pregnant with foreboding, so charged with rumour had the atmosphere of Porth Ardur become in recent weeks. Men for whom politics was a venal trade with which they wanted no contact, and which they regarded as the improper occupation of public school boys and the sons of miners whose mothers affected exaggerated airs, found themselves arguing about the irreconcilable nature of capital and labour. These men grew eloquent and passionate in expressing half-grasped opinions about the fundamentals of economics as the promised wealth of Porth Ardur failed to materialise. The previous day, when the *Galahad* had arrived, the dockers had mounted a protest and sat down on the railway track to the mine in protest at the loss of jobs, now that the loading of the coal had become fully mechanised. No general cargo trade had materialised, though the management claimed that increased passengers aboard the *Kurnow* had meant that two extra boys had been taken on, and no bonuses were forecast. A noisy meeting had been held the previous evening between labour and management and a compromise had been announced, the port manager guaranteeing that six men would be engaged on every shift as trimmers.

The uncertainty of this industrial unrest was infectious, spilling over into the staid ranks of the stolid labour force who had given their lives to the service of Sir Charles Mudge, his antecedents and, it had been assumed, his successors. Mudge was ignorant of this local dispute, but he was no fool. Despite the confidential nature of the news he and his colleagues were about to reveal, Mudge considered it likely word had leaked out that in the wake of the scrapping of *Caryatid,* more changes would follow. He was not a coward and fully accepted the responsibilities of his high office, but what was easily resolved

252

in the remote fastness of the capital's board room, was less easily argued in the windswept buoy yard while standing on a wooden crate thoughtfully provided by the yard's carpenter.

'My men,' he began, clapping his hand on his hat to restrain it in a sudden gust of wind as the Commissioners and the two ships' commanders fell in behind him.

'We aren't *your* men, mate!' an unidentifiable voice called out from the rear, to be ignored by Sir Charles, who may not even have heard it.

'As you know the government has taken a very hard line with all of us in the public service. The Celtic Lighthouse Service has a record to be proud of ...'

The clatter of shunting came downwind as a load of coal trucks arrived from the Mynydd Uchaf mine to coincide with the resumption of the *Galahad*'s loading. Some of Mudge's words were lost in the racket.

'... And of course that means many of us will have to work harder. It also means we will all have to make sacrifices—'

'What sacrifices will you make then, mate?' the anonymous heckler asked, stirring a chorus of assent from the workforce and prompting a low chuckle from Macready. Foster shot his former commander a nervous sideways glance.

'Give up your eight-course dinners, will you?'

Mudge ploughed on, suddenly wishing that Stanier was delivering this unpleasant homily instead of standing behind him, half hidden from the expectant faces staring up at Mudge himself. The heckling in front of, and the distracting racket behind him, had cost Mudge the thread of his logic. He drew a deep breath and plunged on.

'Unfortunately in order to make the necessary economies, the Board have been compelled to retire the *Caryatid* from active service—'

'If you're going to scrap the old rust-bucket, just bloody say so, for God's sake, man.' A chorus of affirmative exclamations greeted this unsurprising news and several men relaxed, thinking this was all Sir Charles Mudge had to say.

Mudge detected this softening and hurried on. 'She will not be replaced ...'

The crowd suddenly seemed to stiffen. He was aware that he now had their full attention. Behind him, his heart beating, Stanier was watching the reaction of the men, wishing he was somewhere else, but aware that he had no option but to stand shoulder to shoulder with his fellow Commissioners.

'There will be no replacement for the

254

old ship and ...' Mudge looked round and waited while the crash, clunk and roar of the first upended coal truck shot its contents down the chute into the after hold of *Galahad*. As the roar subsided, he concluded his speech as hurriedly as possible.

'And this entire facility will be shut down.'

There was a moment of silence. Definition of the word 'facility' spread from the startled Dale, through the ranks of the salaried office staff to move among the dismally clad members of the yard labour force.

'Does that mean we've lost our jobs?' a voice called in the wake of the clatter and roar of the second truck depositing ten tons of coal down the much nearer chute into *Galahad*'s forward hold.

'It means you are redundant ...'

It was at this moment that Foster felt his sleeve insistently plucked by Macready.

'Move back, Bernard! Full astern,' Macready whispered as he shuffled back into the shelter of the buoy-yard wall behind them. Then the storm of wind-blown coal dust swept across the yard, scouring the neck of Captain Sir Charles Mudge and his colleagues and blowing full into the faces of the entire staff of the base at Porth Ardur.

As hands went up to faces and the ranks wavered, cries of 'Oh, bugger!' and 'Filthy shit!' and 'Fuck the mine!' mingled with 'Redundant, by God!' 'You bunch of bastards!' and 'What does Jimmy Stanier have to say?'

Then the dust cleared and before the next truck reached the top of the tower, Mudge was waving them away with a dismissive gesture.

'That's all I have to say, men.'

But Mr Dale, his face pale with shock, had already turned on his heel and led his stunned staff off towards the office door, while the tradesmen and labourers, less intimidated by a cloud of coal dust, surged menacingly forward.

'Why don't you all come back when you've thought up something worse, you bloody pigs!'

'Where's Stanier?

'Aye, what's he got to say?'

Mudge was off his box now as, with a sigh, Macready detached himself from the shelter of the wall and with a 'Come on, Bernard,' walked forward through the retreating ranks of the Commissioners.

Macready held up his hands, the sunlight sparkling on the four gold rings on his sleeves.

'Keep order, men! Don't bugger everything up! We've all lost our jobs, me included, but don't put yourselves in the wrong.'

Macready's standing was such that his sudden appearance checked the impulsive forward movement. The men surged round him until he was directly confronting the base blacksmith, a huge bear of a man whose heavily muscled, scarred and tattooed forearms were crossed over his leather apron.

'What are you going to do?' Macready asked the scowling blacksmith. 'Throw them into the dock and get yourselves assault charges? They're not worth it and it will prejudice any chance of fighting this whole idea.'

The blacksmith and those about him hesitated. 'Are you for us, Captain Macready?'

'Aye,' said another. 'Are you with us in fighting this then, Captain?'

A brief image of Justine waiting for him on Ynyscraven flashed across his mind, but then he was caught up in the mood of the men. He had been part of the Celtic Lighthouse Service all his working life; it was a part of him. It would moreover do no harm to try and help where he could. He had known the fathers of the younger lads and many of the older had served at sea, in *Caryatid* or the lightvessels ...

'Yes, I'll do what I can.'

And then they cheered him. It was quite stupid and the noise brought no comfort to Mudge and his party hurrying back to the sanctuary of *Naiad* through the gritty air, wiping their eyes. For as Macready waved them to silence with the remark that they should all disperse to avoid the next lot of coal dust, the black cloud coming from the after hold struck the retreating Commissioners as they were fully exposed on the quay.

'Damn and blast it!' Sir Charles swore as he blew his congested nose and the impassive Sudbrook handed him a cup of tea. The roar and rattle of another emptying truck came from the far side of the dock and a cloud of black dust trailed across the immaculate teak planking of *Naiad*'s quarterdeck.

'Shut that bloody door!'

The steward obliged as the sooty Commissioners restored their equanimity.

'Ah,' said Blake who had regarded the whole proceedings not without a certain humour. He nursed a private envy that he, not Mudge, should have been knighted for his services to safety at sea and Mudge's predicament had amused him. 'Ah, the cup that cheers, but doth not inebriate. How very welcome it is.'

'I don't think it went too badly,

Sir Charles, all things considered and excepting the coal dust.' Stanier's smooth smug face mooned over the rim of the porcelain cup and Mudge found it difficult to conceal his growing dislike of Stanier.

'That is one of your festering ships, Stanier!' Mudge nodded beyond the smoke-room windows. 'Now far be it from me to interfere with the trade of our great nation, but you might have had the wit to have ordered the loading suspended while we attended to our business. When she wasn't working cargo this morning, I thought for one indulgent and clearly misplaced moment, that you had actually had some foresight '

'Sir Charles!' Stanier protested, secretly pleased that the industrial dispute, of which he had been notified by the port manager in the mail arriving earlier that morning, was now over. The slight dusting of coal dust that he had received, while extremely irksome and ironic, had nevertheless arrived like a tactical smokescreen, enabling the Commissioners in general and Stanier in particular, to beat a timely retreat.

'Inconvenient though the coal dust was,' Stanier said, 'it rather conveniently got us off the hook, don't you think?' The grim silence following this announcement was broken by a grunt of agreement from Blake.

'Stanier's got a point, Sir Charles. The men's mood was turning decidedly ugly—'

'It was old Macready that pacified them,' Gostling said and Mudge agreed.

'That's true, Sir Charles,' said Stanier, quite willing to give Macready his due if the man was out of earshot and it suited his own purposes.

'I shall have to thank him,' Mudge grumbled.

'I entirely agree,' said Stanier, reaching new heights of pomposity. 'Where we chastise when it is due, we should also praise when it is timely to do so.'

Mudge looked at Stanier and grunted. The man was impossible!

The wives of Sudan Road were in raptures when they learned that the two lighthouse ships, *Naiad* and *Caryatid* had been liberally covered with coal dust throughout the day. Held captive by the tides, they were subject to a ceaseless deposit of sulphurous filth and were forced to secure all ports, hatches and companionways to keep the pernicious dust at bay.

The first sign of the success of their own grand plan was whispered up and down Sudan Road, rapidly spreading throughout the town as it emerged that same day. It was another factor, it was afterwards claimed, which showed the workings of

260

fate quite clearly. News came in from the mine that three of the men working there, one of whom was known for his skill with the largest of the grab-cranes, had packed their hands in and moved on. Production, it was said, was drastically affected, an embarrassment to the management who were in the very act of loading a ship.

The actual impact of the defection of the three men was somewhat exaggerated, and the precise cause was uncertain, but since the three young women who had enjoyed the favours of these men swore blind that they had refused their beaux the smallest favours, the Lysistratan plan seemed to be working. In fact the men had been summoned to the capital while their three girlfriends, two of whom had recently fallen pregnant, had covered their humiliation by a story of abandonment.

The three women were later mentioned in chapel by a pastor who did not known them, except by hearsay. His sermon, based upon the repudiation of temptation and repentance for sin, was long held to have been an inspiration and was afterwards published in an anthology of original sermons and homilies. For this reason, it was fortunate that he did not know the ladies' reputations, which it would be salacious to expand upon further.

A lady whose sensibilities are more closely associated with the grander events in Porth Ardur was actually that same morning more than two hundred miles away in the distant capital. Tegwyn Pomeroy woke with a vague sense of unease, touched perhaps by ancient, inherited Druidic instincts or by half-dreamed disturbances in the night. It was not unusual that she woke alone, for her husband often slept in his own room, being an insomniac, but something prompted her to get up. Thinking Pomeroy might be unwell, she was about to enter his bedroom when the door opened and the figure of David Smith emerged.

In the split second of mutual surprise, Tegwyn saw—and never forgot—the face of her husband lying on his pillow, his hands behind his head, the look of satisfaction frozen in the terrible rictus of discovery.

The presence of the coal dust persuaded Captain Foster to sail from Porth Ardur as soon as possible. Having announced the closure of the base, Captain Sir Charles Mudge had no desire to stay either. But that afternoon, Mr Dale had sent aboard, by the single hand of Cyrus Jones, a note stating that Lord Dungarth, on his way to Ynyscraven by way of the new service run by the *Kurnow*, had just arrived at the Station Hotel and sought a meeting with Stanier.

The information was, of course, an attempt by his lordship to enjoy a lavish dinner at the expense of the Commissioners, but Stanier took the bait and, pleading that his lordship was both the owner of an island upon which the Commissioners maintained establishments and a member of the upper House whose influence might at any time come in useful, prevailed upon Mudge to send Mr Jones on to the Station Hotel with an invitation to dine aboard *Naiad* that evening.

Captain Foster's plans to sail were therefore postponed to the next morning and he slipped ashore to join Macready and dine with his old commander and Gwendolyn, whom he had not seen for some time.

Curious about the state of the Macreadys' marriage, Foster noticed a change in Gwendolyn. Her bird-like frame seemed to possess even greater energy than the formidable reserves he remembered, as if she had, as it were, taken a new lease on life. This seemed to Foster in direct proportion to the growing indifference evident in her husband who, despite his rhetoric of that very morning, appeared

263

uncharacteristically reconciled to his forth-coming retirement, premature though it was.

While Septimus did not wish him to, he felt obliged to regale Gwendolyn with an appropriately doctored tale of her husband's suppression of the incipient mutiny of the base labour force. Without actually saying so, Bernard Foster managed to convey an impression that Macready had averted bloodshed. Mrs Macready seemed much impressed, particularly when Foster told of how he had stated publicly his intention to fight the closure of the base. This, too, was somehow embellished to give it the gloss of a sacred vow, so that Gwendolyn, apparently moved by Bernard's account, patted her husband on the hand in what seemed a gesture of admiration. Bernard found this touching and averted his gaze, not noticing the unfeigned astonishment clear in Mac-ready's face. Gwendolyn herself scarcely noticed what she had done.

Mrs Macready was in truth hardly listening to Foster. It was only later that night, as she lay sleepless and hardly knowing what to do with her good fortune, that it occurred to her that Macready's actions of the morning seemed destined to be cast in so favourable a light and that the town might forgive her, her own perfidy.

For Gwendolyn was troubled, hating disruption in the well-organised mechanism of her life, but tempted beyond endurance by the news that had arrived that morning when she had received a letter and an interim prospectus from the directors of the Ardurian Slate Company. It announced their success in securing a highly advantageous contract to supply the navy of the Central American republic of Costa Maya with a regular supply of 5,000 tons of coal a month. The republic's warships, an elderly fleet of laid-up dreadnoughts, had been hastily recommissioned and it was predicted that the state of emergency would last for a period of at least a year. Share prices in Ardurian Slate had rocketed, increased investment was invited from 'esteemed and farsighted investors who were able to see the magnificent, but short-term opportunity thus offered'. In short, Gwendolyn reflected as she stared at the ceiling, the logic of it was incontrovertible: the more coal that could be shipped to Costa Maya, the greater the profit accruing to the Ardurian Slate Company. By the same token, the swifter the insurrection would be suppressed and thus human suffering minimised. There was, incidentally, no doubt about these facts, or so Mr Sinclair had assured her as she considered the matter in his office, her trembling hand holding both letter and prospectus.

'My dear Mrs Macready,' Sinclair had said, scarcely able to suppress his own excitement. *'Carpe diem!* Seize the day!'

'But what,' she had sensibly prevaricated, 'about the stoppage at the docks.'

Sinclair had smiled. 'It is already as good as over. A small concession is even now being made to keep the workers happy. You will hear those new coal chutes sending the black diamonds, and that is really what they are, Mrs Macready,' Sinclair said with unfeigned and surprising enthusiasm, 'tumbling into that dirty old ship!'

'But—' She hesitated. How did one explain doubts about accruing wealth? How did one make excuses for greed?

'My dear Mrs Macready, I understand your misgivings.'

'You do?'

'Of course, it is natural in one of your probity, but please be assured that nothing but good can come of such an investment, not least to the population of ...' he looked at his own copy of the letter on his desk, 'of Costa Maya who will not long have to labour under the misfortunes of anarchy.'

And so she had agreed to substantially increase her shareholding in the company, following his example and assisted by an additional loan secured against the deeds of the house which, many years earlier and against the unexpected death of himself, Septimus had made wholly over to his wife.

Lying sleepless, Gwendolyn was wickedly excited by the prospect of augmenting her windfall, increasingly convinced that she might soon cease to depend upon her husband in any way. Not that she sought divorce, she thought suddenly, only the upper hand.

She might have been even less inclined to sleep had she known that Captain James St John Stanier knew nothing whatsoever of either the news from Central America or the additional flotation of shares.

At the same hour that Gwendolyn Macready lay unsleeping, Tegwyn Pomeroy lay awake on the uncomfortably jolting bed of a first-class sleeper on the Western Night Mail. Having spent a miserable day tramping the streets of the capital, unable to locate the only women with whom she might claim an intimate friendship, she had left her husband. It was as though, at this desperate and unhappy moment in her life, Caroline Stanier had chosen to disappear.

By an odd coincidence, Caroline Stanier

was also settling aboard an overnight train. The Pullman express was leaving the capital heading for a Channel port, scheduled to connect with a ferry and sweep her in due course to a new life on the shores of the Mediterranean. David Smith had seen her tucked into her sleeping compartment after they had enjoyed a cocktail together in the station lounge bar. He had also paid off the three men who, in a matter of less than an hour, had cleared her belongings out of her flat, carried much of her own furniture and private effects to a furniture store and taken her personal baggage to the station. As she smoked a last cigarette, Caroline smiled at the curved and fluted ceiling of the Pullman carriage.

The Commissioners and their noble guest lingered for some time over their brandies. The conviviality of the evening had made up for the earlier part of the day. Mudge had not previously met the Earl Dungarth and, knowing him to be an hereditary knight of his own order, found his faith in the ancient institutions of the country restored. He even managed to forgive Stanier much of his stupidity, reflecting that the man's intentions were probably no worse than anyone else's. Moreover, Mudge reflected, as Stanier was so much younger it was not to be wondered at if he embraced some of the more incomprehensible enthusiasms of the modern age. Mudge remembered with a private chuckle that he had himself once argued with a shipmaster who insisted steam would never replace sail. And that had been only thirty years earlier!

That evening, Stanier himself behaved with unassuming propriety. He seemed to have abandoned much of the overbearing pushiness that had characterised his conduct during the last few final days of the Commissioners' cruise. He looked, thought Mudge as he regarded the smooth, urbane young man chatting to Dungarth, rather like a cat who had got the cream.

'Well, gentlemen,' Lord Dungarth said, rising somewhat unsteadily and noisily venting wind. 'I think it might be time for us to call it a day—'

'Nonsense, my lord. You must have one for the road while we summon a taxi,' Stanier pressed, taking the Earl's glass and refilling it.

'Oh, well, if you insist ... Good of you to get me a cab, though. Save the old pins.'

'Of course.' Stanier picked up the telephone to the bridge and looked at his watch. It was three minutes to two in the morning. Behind him Dungarth belched.

But Stanier never ordered the taxi, for at that moment Lord Dungarth rose to his feet and, swaying slightly, announced with a faint air of surprise, 'Damn me, gentlemen, but the old Queen has just sent for me to form a government!'

And as they all stared at him dumbfounded, he fell dead at their feet.

# Moments Of Decision

The death of Lord Dungarth further delayed the sailing of *Naiad*, drawing a gloomy pall over the end of the cruise of the Commissioners. Stanier had intended to remain in Porth Ardur and he now undertook to attend to the formalities of registering the death and making a deposition to the coroner's office. Mudge and the other Commissioners, pleading the delay would compromise the work of the Board, fell in with Stanier's suggestion and left the ship next morning, bound for the station and the long railway journey up to town.

'I shall see to all relevant matters here, Sir Charles,' Stanier reassured the Chairman of the Commissioners, 'before I leave.'

'Very well,' muttered Sir Charles, who was not looking forward to the journey and had a hangover.

'You have no objection?'

'Uh?' Mudge shook his head. 'No, no, do what you suggested.'

'What we all suggested, Sir Charles,' Stanier said, smilingly reminding Sir

Charles that the Commissioners' decisions were all made jointly.

'Yes, yes,' Mudge said, increasingly testy.

'Well, you need not concern yourself further, Sir Charles.'

Mudge grunted and it was only an hour later when Captain Blake remarked, 'I hope we've done the right thing leaving Stanier to sort matters out,' that Mudge felt a vague sense of unease.

'It's not that difficult to report a death, is it?'

Blake gave the Chairman an odd look, then shrugged. They had dined too well and too late. If he could not snooze in his cabin, he would have to make the best of the first-class seat. To hell with Stanier. To hell with Sir Charles Mudge, for that matter.

The Earl's death was one more circumstance afterwards indicated as causal in the chain of events now about to engulf Porth Ardur. When his lordship's booking aboard *Kurnow* was cancelled, the clerk shook his head. The new service was not exactly popular, but half an hour later he cheered up when a beautiful young woman, her face pale and her eyes shadowed, arrived to enquire about a passage to Ynyscraven. The *Kurnow,* which had returned to Porth

272

Ardur overnight, was already loading and, taking a cabin, the young woman half-ran, half-stumbled towards the gangway.

Scratching his head, the booking clerk thought the tragic figure looked vaguely familiar, but it was not until after the little ship had sailed that it suddenly struck him.

'By damn!' he exclaimed out loud, 'that was Tegwyn Morgan! Her mother used to run that brassiere shop in Chapel Street ... My word, she had lovely tits though ...' The astonished baggage boy who had just conducted the beautiful but obviously distressed lady aboard, overhearing this recollection, was uncertain who it was who possessed attributes he was much fascinated by of late. But noticing his boss's introspective air, he decided his own services would not be required for a while, and retired to consider the matter at greater length in private.

Aboard *Kurnow*, Tegwyn flung herself upon the bunk and, in due course, fell into a fitful doze.

Two days later *Naiad* finally sailed. It was a calm day of beautiful sunshine. The lack of wind meant that the instant her ship's company could draw clean sea water into the ship's fire main, every hose in the ship was employed in flushing out the

273

last offending grain of coal dust from the remotest corner of the Commissioners' yacht. She sailed down the bay, watched over the sea wall by Captain Macready from his viewpoint on *Caryatid*'s bridge. He could guess the activity upon her decks, for *Naiad* was enveloped in a fine cloud of spray which, catching the sun, made her radiate brilliant rainbows, so that she seemed a faery thing as she diminished with distance and headed for the horizon.

Macready turned away from the ineffable sight, his throat choked by a feeling of overwhelming sadness. He stared down across the filthy decks of his own ship. Across the dock the clatter and roar went on as *Galahad* sank her huge chocolate bulk imperceptibly lower and lower in the water. As each truck spewed its contents into her capacious hull, the black dust rose on the still air in a great cloud, to fall, with a soft patter all over the dock area, even on this calm day.

Macready swore under his breath. Somehow the presence of the tramp ship, almost too big for the dock itself, marked the unavoidable march of progress. Its dominating, juggernaut proportions seemed to Macready to be the very agent of change, sweeping him from his hitherto pre-eminent position as the foremost seaman in Porth

Ardur. Macready remembered his hubris at Porth Neigwl and knew the gods, having swept him up to the heights in his love for Justine, now intended to humble him. He sighed again. Well, at least Justine had no need to witness this sad end.

He felt the deck cant slightly under his feet and peered over the front of the bridge. The main derrick was lifting a clean buoy aboard. The brilliant red and white of its chequer-work was in odd contrast to the grimy, down-at-heel appearance of *Caryatid*. Oh well, Macready consoled himself and thinking a cup of tea might prove beneficial, there was still some work to be done.

He was sitting in his cabin, the teacup and saucer on his desk as he toyed with some paperwork, when the fateful knock came at the cabin door. It was the base messenger, Cyrus Jones.

'Morning, Cap'n.'

Macready turned and, recognising the man, smiled. 'Morning, Jones. How are you?'

'Better for knowing you're on our side, Cap'n Macready.'

'Oh yes. That.' He looked at Jones's expectant face. Jones was a messenger—perhaps he should be sent off with a message. 'To be candid, Mr Jones, I don't hold out much hope.' Macready watched the man's face fall.

'I couldn't get another job, sir ...' Jones waved the stump of his missing right arm and Macready recalled the circumstances of the accident. The buoy had been swinging across the deck, dragging its mooring chain as the derrick picked it up and the chain-gang ran in to hook the links. It was a wet day with a miserably persistent westerly wind making life as wretched as possible. *Caryatid* had been rising and falling in the swell, a common enough motion and certainly not one to intimidate either the ship's company or their commander. Then the nose iron by which the lifting gear hooked and handled the buoy, failed. The buoy dropped from a height of about six feet, four tons of riveted steel plate drawn swiftly back to the ship's side as the weight of the mooring took over.

One man jumped clear but Cyrus Jones, his boots slipping on the deck, was caught by the inert mass of metal and, as it leapt clear over the lip of the foredeck, it caught the after end of the starboard bulwark with a savage crash. Unfortunately Cyrus was carried across the deck with it, and his arm was crushed in the impact.

He had never complained; never whined that the Lighthouse Authority owed him a thing. Of course he had received the usual compensation, but this was little enough, quite inadequate to keep his wife and three growing sons. The job of messenger had come up within two months and Jones had been offered it; he was a bright man and made the best of a bad job. Most pleasing was his continuing association with the work he loved and the sight of him standing in the doorway hardened Macready's resolve. He simply could not abandon men like Jones, to go off and spend the remainder of his days living in sin with Justine Morgan!

Macready coughed awkwardly and smiled. 'We'll do what we can, ch, Cyrus?' he said. 'Never say die until you're dead, eh? You're a good example of that!' and the two men laughed with the black, gallows humour of seamen.

'I'm glad to hear you talking like that, sir, I really am!' Jones suddenly remembered his job. 'Oh, there's me almost forgettin', sir, I've a message from Mr Dale, sir. Would you mind very much steppin' across to the office?'

Dale rose as Macready entered the Area Clerks' office. It was a large room upon one wall of which a fine painting of *Caryatid*'s predecessor, a pretty steam paddle schooner named *Mermaid,* thrashed her way past Mitre Rock light with a distant prospect of the Bishop's Islands in the background.

The painting always pleased Macready and, with the sunlight falling almost directly upon it, he failed to see another figure in the room until Dale indicated the presence of Captain Stanier. The Commissioner was slumped in the single armchair that stood to one side of a large filing cabinet. He inclined his head, but made no attempt to rise, still less to shake Macready's hand.

'Captain Stanier has some instructions for us, Captain Macready.' Dale's tone of diplomatic distaste was eloquent of disapproval, dislike and disdain. Macready looked at Stanier as Dale sat at his desk and, picking up a pencil, began turning it in his fingers. The Commissioner's sprawled form bespoke utter contempt and Macready felt his colour rising with anger, humiliation and a dreadful embarrassment. He felt damnably awkward standing there like a schoolboy brought into the headmaster's study. It was unfortunate that Dale's detachment added to his own feeling of isolation, but it was not Dale's fault. Macready knew Dale enough to know the clerk would resent Stanier's presence in his office as much as he did himself. But there was an air of defiance in Dale, a hint of frosty spirit engendered by the revelations of yesterday morning. Emboldened, Macready went to the window and, with his back to it, he turned and confronted Stanier. With no chair to sit on, it was a not unnatural thing to do, but the silhouette of the bulky Macready against brilliant sunshine made Stanier squint. The small inconvenience gratified Macready as he looked at Dale.

'Well, Mr Dale,' he said pleasantly. 'I gather you wanted a word yourself.'

'Actually it was Captain Stanier who insisted on summoning you.' Dale smiled thinly, neatly emphasising the subtleties of cause and effect and the capsizing of the normal, civilised rituals of the base at Porth Ardur where Captain Macready was not usually summoned anywhere.

'I quite understand, Mr Dale,' he responded, turning to Stanier. 'And what can I do for you, Commissioner?'

Stanier sat up. 'Well, Macready, you can stop loading those buoys for a start—'

'We are due to lay them this week, Commissioner. We may be about to be decommissioned, but we must tidy the Area up before we hand it over. Besides, you have to give us all one month's notice.'

'*Waterwitch* is currently under orders to sail for Porth Ardur in three days. I think matters can wait that long. As for notice, Macready, you will require two weeks to

279

destore your ship, no doubt, and a week to proceed to the breakers. No doubt you and many of the ship's company have leave due ...'

Macready experienced a sudden, awful pain. It was clear Stanier did not intend that he should ever take *Caryatid* to sea on her proper business again. The whole game was up! He was finished. He was thankful that his stance in front of the window concealed the terrible, overwhelming sense of panic as he felt his whole reason for existence being torn from him.

'I have the authority of the Board in this matter, Macready ...' Stanier went on.

This was not the right way to end matters, Macready thought, trying desperately to find some reason for persuading Stanier to allow him one last trip to sea, even if for purely personal, sentimental reasons. That he would never, ever again anchor *Caryatid* under the great lee of Ynyscraven seemed a denial of the most dreadful cruelty. Surely his ship's company should be allowed one last fling in the Craven Arms, one last, valedictory roister back down the cliff path to the waiting boat. Even the sad, dawn partings from Justine's bed seemed full of a beautiful poetic sadness which he must experience for one last, lingering time, before such departures came, at last, to an end.

'You should discharge those buoys you have loaded this morning, Macready ...'

Mr Dale, sitting watching to one side of Macready did not have the sunshine in his eyes. Long association with Macready told him that the Captain would not wish to leave any business in his parish open to criticism and there was one matter which concerned him. He too had noticed a falling off of Macready's devotion to duty, ascribing it to worry and the prospect of unwanted retirement. He had intended to mention the matter to Macready in as discreet a manner as possible, but the Captain's obvious loss of initiative needed immediate prompting.

'Captain Macready, I have the station fuel figures here.' Dale held out a sheet of paper. It was a copy of the figures posted on the after bulkhead of *Caryatid*'s wheelhouse and, to Dale's relief, it triggered off Macready's memory. The Captain grasped at the half-forgotten fact like a drowning man seizes a passing straw.

'There is an urgent requirement for oil fuel at the Buccabu lighthouse, Commissioner,' Macready began, his argument gaining momentum as his mind abandoned its personal preoccupations and shifted into professional gear. 'The matter had to be deferred due to the programmed inspection at Ynyscraven and the subsequent problems at the St Kenelm lightvessel. We shall have to attend to that before we decommission.'

'That will not be necessary, Macready. I shall signal *Waterwitch* to attend to it. She has to pass the station on her way north.'

'The matter is increasingly urgent, Captain Stanier,' urged Dale. 'Any delay might result in the light being extinguished, sir.'

'And the weather at present is ideal,' added Macready, gesturing to the window behind him.

But Stanier ignored both Dale and the weather. He rose and drew himself up to his full height. 'The matter is not open to discussion, gentlemen. It is an order!' He paused and glared at both men. 'Do you understand?' he asked, but Macready had made for the door.

'What a damnably rude man,' Stanier said. 'Have a signal passed to *Waterwitch* to refuel and water the Buccabu light on her way here,' Stanier ordered Dale as he picked up his briefcase. 'If you want me, I shall be aboard *Galahad.*'

Dale nodded his head in assent. He wondered what Macready would do, for there had been a dangerous gleam in the Captain's eye as he had stalked out.

Back aboard *Caryatid* Macready penned a short note and went down to the saloon for lunch. Sitting down he ordered the steward out and stared at the officers, quickly outlining the gist of his encounter with Stanier. He then passed the note to the Second Officer. 'Take off your uniform jacket and pull on a sweater, Mr Wentworth, then take this to the harbour master's office after lunch.' He turned to Watson. 'Put that load of buoys ashore, but cancel shore leave. Don't tell the men until six o'clock, I want all this kept under wraps until the last possible moment. D'you understand?'

'Aye, aye, sir.'

Macready turned to the Chief Engineer. 'I want steam kept up, don't blow the boilers down even if Stanier comes aboard and personally orders it. Tell him we need steam to discharge our stores tomorrow. Just to keep up the fiction, Mr Watson, we'll land some slings of chain from the lower hold and leave the derrick hanging over the side when the men go to tea. I want it to look as if we're staying alongside all night.'

'So we're not, Captain?' the Chief said, frowning uncertainly.

'No, Chief, we most certainly are not. The Buccabu light needs refuelling and it is our job to do it.'

'Our last trip then—' the Chief said, a frog in his throat.

'Sadly yes. I'm asking the harbour master to open the caisson at about 0345 tomorrow morning. We'll slip out on top of the tide.'

'I see ...'

'No disrespect to you, Mr Watson, or your colleagues aboard *Waterwitch.*'

'I quite understand, sir. No-one hands the watch over without completing the log, as it were.'

'Quite so, Mr Watson.'

'Besides,' Watson added, 'I'm not sure that *Waterwitch* will be able to do the job, sir. The radio news this morning said there's a ship in trouble in the Atlantic. Her cargo of grain has shifted in very heavy weather. It may not be so pleasant in two days' time.'

'I had a revision of the figures this morning, sir,' put in Wentworth who seemed to have wanted an opportunity to speak for some moments. 'They are getting pretty desperate. We've really left the matter a bit too long.'

'All the more reason for us to get on with it then,' said Macready briskly, suddenly alarmed by the reproach in the young Second Officer's voice. He had lost his air of conspiratorial bravado. This was no longer a matter of defying Stanier. This was a matter of real urgency, for the gods were surely going to make him pay for his indifference. If the Buccabu light went out his own career would be eclipsed ingloriously.

Septimus Macready did not want that thought to mar the rest of his life.

On Ynyscraven Charlie Farthing had completed his daily round of the island. Sonia had insisted he accomplished this on one of the sure-footed ponies which formed the chief export of the place. It was a day of outstanding beauty and as the two of them had come back across the rough upper pasture of the high ground, having called on the two shepherds who had cottages in the remote northern part of Ynyscraven, they had stopped and made love in the grass.

Craven met them with the tempting invitation to circumnavigate the island that afternoon in *Lyonesse*.

'The breeze is perfect,' he said, 'I have a lunch aboard and you and I, Charlie, can play with the kites while you, my lady, can sunbathe.'

Sonia smiled. Craven delighted in flattering her and she adored his attentions.

Charlie just laughed, never doubting for a moment that Sonia was devoted to him while Craven's obsession with Tegwyn manifested itself from time to time in references he made to her.

They sailed swiftly up the eastern side of the island, standing about three miles offshore to the north to avoid the rocks and skerries which littered the north point, broken off remnants of a larger island which, Craven averred, was once part of the mystical land after which his yacht was named. The afternoon sun shone on the forbidding cliffs of the western coast which rose precipitously to a height in places of 500 feet. They watched a pair of peregrine falcons hawk among the auks, puffins, guillemots, kittiwakes and herring gulls which filled the air with their clamour.

The brilliance and warmth of the sun filled them with an indolent happiness. While Craven and Charlie pulled up a huge balloon jib, Sonia lay upon the deck, smiling at the gangling form of her husband as he tugged at halliard and sheet. It was five hours later that they doubled the eastern extremity of the Hound's Teeth. The reef looked full of chocolate box charm, a frill of white water which completely concealed the deadly rocks below. It was hard to believe it was the same place upon which they had seen *Sea Dragon* pounded to pieces.

Hardening in the sheets, the ketch stood back towards the anchorage; already the westering sun threw the east coast of the island into shade. The repaired *Plover* lay in the bay ahead of them.

'About time too,' remarked Charlie, relaxed after the undemanding sail.

'Oh look,' said Sonia suddenly sitting up and pointing to the north. 'We've got more company.'

'Ah, here comes the new arrival,' remarked Craven as *Kurnow*, inbound after a brief call at Porth Neigwl, steamed down the east coast towards them. 'I'm expecting my father any day,' he added.

'Does that mean you'll get all serious?' Sonia asked.

'But of course, my lady. You don't think that I can continue to live this life of hedonism with my old Pater cracking the whip, do you?'

'I'll have to have a word with him,' Sonia said, smiling.

They ran in and doused the sails. Craven went forward and eased the anchor over the bow, waiting until he could see down through the clear water, the chain stretching out ahead of them. He watched the curve ease and waved at Charlie who remained aft. 'She's brought up, Charlie. Let's put a harbour stow in.'

'I'll do that, Roger. Sonia's gone below to put the kettle on.'

'Then I shall take my ease,' Craven declared, 'as befits the skipper ...'

He sat in the cockpit and picked up the

binoculars, focusing them on the *Kurnow* as the mail steamer glided into the bay, her First Officer and Carpenter on her forecastle, ready to let her own anchor go.

'Tea's up.' Sonia appeared in the companionway with a tray, but Craven had stood up and was staring intently at the approaching *Kurnow*.

'Good God ... I don't believe it ... It is! It is!' He lowered the glasses and gestured with them at a lone figure standing on *Kurnow*'s deck. 'It's Tegwyn Pomeroy!'

'Are you sure, Roger?' Sonia asked putting down the tea tray. 'I'd hate you to be disappointed.'

Craven handed her the glasses. 'See for yourself,' he said happily.

Sonia put the glasses to her eyes and fiddled for a moment while Charlie joined Craven in staring across the water as the *Kurnow*'s anchor dropped from the hawse pipe with a splash.

'It *is* Tegwyn,' said Sonia, lowering the glasses. 'I wonder what on earth she's doing here?'

'Well,' said Charlie dryly, 'it's just possible she's come to see her mother.'

'Never mind about that. I'm taking the dinghy,' said Craven and Sonia and Charlie were left to their tea in the cockpit of *Lyonesse*, while Craven rowed frantically across to the steamer where they saw him attract Tegwyn's attention, saw her bend over the rail and shake her head. The two seemed to talk for a few moments, then Tegwyn straightened up and Craven began to row back. Sonia and Charlie looked at one another.

'He's pushing his luck,' Charlie remarked.

'I still feel sorry for him—'

'Well, he shouldn't fall for another bloke's wife. I daresay he could have the pick of plenty of lovely young women.' Charlie bent forward and kissed his wife.

'It's all right for you two blasted lovebirds,' said his lordship, climbing back over the rail and distracting them from their self-absorption. 'Any tea left in the pot?'

Sonia poured him a cup. She and Charlie stared at Craven.

'What are you two staring at? Don't you know curiosity killed the cat.'

'Oh, come on, Roger,' said Sonia, 'you haven't stopped talking about Tegwyn, she arrives like Venus in a machine, you row across and speak to her and then you come back and ask for a cup of tea.'

Craven held out his cup for a refill and looked at Charlie. 'Why is it, Charlie, that women are so insatiably curious about the lives of others?'

'I have no idea, Roger. But there are occasions when men share the same vice.'

Craven grinned. 'She's come to see her mother. She won't tell me how long she's staying, nor whether she will have dinner with me. She refused to come aboard and cruise up to Porth Neigwl, but she did say that she would call upon you this evening. So, if you have no objection, I shall join you for dinner. If you refuse, I shall declare you to have piratically seized my vessel and have you hanged.'

Sonia turned to her husband with an exaggerated gesture. 'I wondered when he would show his beastly side and claim a *droit de seigneur.*'

'I think he needs cooling off,' and immediately springing to his feet, Charlie made a grab for his lordship. Craven rolled onto his back and bent his legs, thrusting them at Charlie's belly. Charlie began to fall backward, but grabbed Craven's feet and, with a drenching splash, both men fell overboard.

Tegwyn landed by way of *Kurnow*'s launch. Twenty minutes later, after a punishing climb with her suitcase, she surprised her mother. A few minutes later, the extent of her shame exposed, she was sobbing in Justine's embrace.

'I am so glad you came here,' Justine

said, crying herself as she stroked her daughter's hair. 'You will feel better after a few days of rest with nothing to concern you.'

'I'm going to divorce him—'

'Of course, but in good time. When you feel better.'

'I left him a note.'

'Then so be it.' Justine was sure Pomeroy, queer fish that he was, would make a generous provision for his wife.

They had only just landed on the beach and were in the act of dragging the dinghy above the high water mark, when the master of the *Kurnow* approached them.

'Excuse me, but is one of you two gentlemen Lord Craven?'

'Yes,' said Craven, 'that's me. Don't tell me Pater missed the boat?'

The master of the *Kurnow* looked rather non-plussed. 'Well, in a manner of speaking, I suppose he did, my lord, though not quite in the manner you imagine.'

Craven saw the serious demeanour of the man, awkward in his gold-laced reefer, his shiny black shoes out of place on the shingle.

'What is it, Captain?'

'I'm afraid your father died last night, sir, at Porth Ardur. I was asked to keep a lookout for you, and let you know. I'm afraid he collapsed aboard the *Naiad,* the Commissioners' yacht—'

'Oh dear,' said Sonia, 'poor Roger.' She put her hand on Craven's arm as he turned away.

'I'm very sorry, my lord—'

'I'm so sorry, Roger,' Charlie added.

Craven sniffed and turned back to them, his eyes bright. 'Just when we were having a perfect day, too.' He paused then swore, apologised and pulled himself together. 'Captain, can you hold sailing for half an hour?'

'Of course, my lord. We aren't due to weigh for an hour.'

'Charlie,' Craven swung round, 'take me back to *Lyonesse.* I must pack a bag. Sonia, my dear, you know my situation. Speak to Tegwyn. Tell her I'll be back as soon as I can and that I forbid her to leave the island until I do. You do understand how important this is to me?'

Sonia shook her head, her eyes sad and serious. 'Yes, yes of course, Roger, but she's married—'

He leaned forward and took her by both shoulders. Speaking with an intense vehemence, he said, 'I don't care. Tell her not to go. Not to go until I get back.' Then he turned and grabbed the dinghy. 'Come on, Charlie,' adding to the *Kurnow*'s master, 'I'll go straight aboard,

292

Captain. May I see you on the bridge?'

'Yes, my lord, of course.'

Sonia sat on a rock and waited while the two men rowed back to the ketch. Craven leapt aboard, telling Charlie to remain in the dinghy. A few moments later, dressed in blazer and flannels, Craven stepped down into the stern of the dinghy.

Charlie plied the oars and quickly closed the distance between *Lyonesse* and *Kurnow*. As he drew under the stern in search of the accommodation ladder on the far side, Craven looked up at the sky.

'Bugger it. The weather's on the change. Just my festering luck!'

Charlie manoeuvred alongside the foot of the ladder. Craven stood up and handed his bag to a sailor who had nipped down to meet them.

'Goodbye, Charlie. I'll be back as soon as I can. Try and keep Teggy on the island.'

'We'll do our best, Roger.'

'Yes, I know you will.' Craven heaved himself up on the ladder while Charlie trimmed the rocking dinghy. 'Oh, by the way, Charlie ...'

'Yes?'

'Keep an eye on *Lyonesse* for me. Feel free to take her out if you wish. It'll keep the weed off her bottom.'

'Yes, of course. Thanks. I hope it all

goes as well as it can.'

Craven waved, turned, ran up the accommodation ladder and disappeared from sight. Charlie pulled back to the shore where Sonia helped him drag the dinghy up the beach.

'What on earth are we going to do, Charlie?'

'What he asks, I suppose. He is the gaffer, after all.'

# Fatal Errors

There was an easterly breeze blowing as Captain Macready walked out onto the starboard bridge wing of *Caryatid* at 0300 the following morning. Across the dock the deck lights of *Galahad* burned brightly, but the loading had ceased for the night earlier the previous evening. The stiff breeze on his face gave Macready the first sensation of alarm. Were they already too late to refuel the Buccabu lighthouse?

Within a few seconds he had another problem. Thomas Jones from the harbour master's office was on the bridge asking to see him.

'What's the trouble, Mr Jones?'

'The easterly, sir. It's getting up all the time. I'm going to have to boom the caisson before much longer. I thought I'd let you know, if you're after changing your mind about sailing.'

Macready shook his head. 'No, Mr Jones, I'm sorry, but we're going out, come hell or high water.'

'Very well, Cap'n, but you know what these easterlies can be like, it being a spring tide, like.'

'You're thinking it may be that bad?' Macready frowned.

Jones nodded. 'Reckon. Once you're out, you'll be boomed out. The *Galahad*'s due to sail later, but I thought I should warn you, especially as you seem to be sailing rather secretly—'

'Well, never mind that. We're sailing and that's that!'

'All right. Give me ten minutes. *Kurnow*'s going to come in after you've sailed. I've told him to let you get clear first.'

'Very well, Mr Jones.'

'We'll see you when we see you then, Cap'n Macready.'

'Yes, Mr Jones.'

Watson sent the ship's company to their stations quietly and Macready was thankful he commanded an old steamship with silent, reciprocating engines. The only noise would be from the jangle of the telegraphs and he could keep their movements to a minimum.

The word came up from forward and aft that the mooring ropes were singled up to bights, easily loosed from the ship, and, at the expiry of Jones's ten minutes, as Macready saw the caisson move slowly across the entrance and the popple on the dockwater where it was exposed to the wind, he ordered, 'Let go fore and aft,' and jangled the telegraphs from

Stand-by, to Slow Astern Port, then Slow Astern together. *Caryatid* gathered sternway, seeking the wind, and proceeded stern first out of the dock.

Once clear of the extremity of the lighthouse pier, Macready began to swing his ship and he felt the rising force of the wind properly as it blew on the beam. Then he was ringing the engines ahead and *Caryatid* steamed down the bay.

'It's blowing up a bit and clouding over,' remarked Watson, coming up onto the bridge to take over the watch after securing both anchors. He raised his glasses and followed Macready's example, staring at the pale white hull of the approaching *Kurnow*.

'Yes.'

'I hope we're not too late,' mused Watson.

'So do I,' snapped Macready.

Both officers stood and watched *Kurnow* pass, then they lowered their glasses. 'Coursc Sou' West by South, full speed away.'

'Aye, aye, sir.'

By sunrise, the wind had dropped a touch and Macready was feeling more cheerful as he returned to the bridge, unable to do more than doze in his cabin. He noticed the barometer had steadied and, going out onto the bridge wing, studied the sea and sky. It was cloudy, but bright patches of sunshine blotched the sea with their brilliance and the day seemed full of life and light. Perhaps it was not going to be so bad after all. Macready tended to think the gloomy prognostications of Jones and Watson belonged to the fearful hours of the night. In daylight the reality was not so terrible. He turned his mind to the more practical aspects of the coming day.

With the ebb tide out of the strait, they would be at the Buccabu light at about three in the afternoon. The tide, approaching high water at Porth Ardur, would already be falling at the lighthouse. If the wind stayed in the east they would be able to land a party on what was normally the windward side of the rocks. It was unorthodox, but they had done it before and he guessed his men would rise to the challenge. He could, if he had the nerve, get the ship quite close and pump oil fuel directly ashore. He had done that before and it would give him a hell of a kick to retire on a high point like that. It would be something they would all remember, by damn! Well, he would have to see. It would be stupid to take a foolish risk on this last occasion. He went below in search of breakfast.

By mid-morning Ynyscraven was dropping astern to the north-north-east. Macready stared at the fading and insubstantial-looking island. It seemed impossible that it was actually inhabited by the only soul in the world who made his life worthwhile.

Stanier arrived at the docks to see the loading of *Galahad* completed and her hatches battened down. From the windows of the port manager's office, he could see the derricks being lowered and it was then that he discovered *Caryatid* missing from her berth. He was about to leave and walk across to the Lighthouse Authority base and demand an explanation from Dale, when the port manager put down the telephone.

'The harbour master boomed the dock gate this morning, he doesn't want to drop the booms and let *Galahad* out at high water.'

'Why not?'

'He's unhappy about the easterly wind.'

Stanier looked out of the window and up at the sky. 'Well, it's a stiff breeze, but hardly a gale. Here, give it to me ...' Stanier took the phone. 'Is that you, Jones? Well, it's Captain Stanier here. Now listen, you can't pull the wool over *my* eyes. Remember I know as much about that bloody dock gate as you. Now I know you buggers have let Macready out in defiance of my orders ... What? All right, that may have nothing to do with you, but it's got a good deal to do with me. So has the sailing of *Galahad*. Her fortunes mean a lot to this town and don't you forget it. I want her out at high water. You see to it, Mister, that that bloody caisson is open.'

Stanier slammed the phone down and looked at the port manager. 'She'll be trimmed and ready by then, I hope.'

The port manager smiled. 'No question about it, Captain Stanier. Those extra coal trimmers make all the difference.'

Both men laughed, then the telephone rang again. The port manager held it out towards him. 'It's for you.'

Stanier took the phone again. 'It's Mr Dale, sir—'

'Yes, Mr Dale. D'you have a message for me from Captain Macready?'

'No, sir, I don't, though I can tell you that *Caryatid* sailed at 0300 this morning—'

'In defiance of my orders, Dale.'

'May I caution you before you take a stand too heavily upon that point, Captain Stanier—'

'What the devil d'you mean?'

'Well, I'm ringing you to let you know I've had a message from Cavehaven. *Waterwitch* has cancelled her trip up

300

here for the time being. She's gone to the assistance of a ship in the Atlantic. Apparently the vessel's cargo of grain has shifted and there's a danger she'll capsize. Perhaps it's just as well that *Caryatid* has sailed to look after the Buccabu light.'

Stanier spent a moment digesting this fact. He could not stop *Waterwitch* going to the assistance of a vessel in distress, nor would he be wise to compromise Macready's chances of refuelling the Buccabu lighthouse. Then a thought struck him.

'Tell me, Mr Dale, how desperate *is* the Buccabu light?' Had Dale and Stanier been in the same room, the clerk might have seen the look not of concern, but of cunning, in Stanier's eyes. But as the Commissioner was on the telephone, it was impossible to gauge Stanier's motive and Dale responded directly to the question.

'It's a matter of *extreme* urgency, sir,' he said.

'In other words it should have been attended to some time ago.'

Dale perceived the trap too late. He hesitated for a revealing moment before admitting, 'Well, yes, sir.'

'Thank you, Mr Dale.' Stanier came off the phone smiling and handed it back to the port manager. 'Got him!' he breathed.

Stanier had lunch in the Station Hotel where he unexpectedly bumped into Roger Craven. He had almost forgotten the sad business of the previous day and the telegram he had sent to the capital.

'Please accept my sincere condolences, my lord.'

'Thank you, Stanier. I gather from my enquiries this morning that you attended to most of the paperwork.'

'Yes. You got my telegram, obviously—'

'No, I was on Ynyscraven. The master of the *Kurnow* let me know. How was he told?'

'I'm not exactly certain, but the whole town knew during the morning ...' Stanier went on to recount the conviviality of the dinner and Dungarth's last words.

'Rum old bugger,' his lordship said affectionately. 'I've just made arrangements to have the body taken home. I'm getting the afternoon train. It means a long wait for a connection, but I need to attend to a few things in town.'

'Yes. Yes of course,' said Stanier, who had no idea what protocol had to be followed when one became the umpteenth Earl of Dungarth.

'Well, I'll be seeing you.'

'Yes. Yes of course, and my condolences, my lord.' Stanier watched him go, looked at his watch and then hurried back to the docks to watch *Galahad* unberth and sail.

The town of Porth Ardur still lay under sunshine, but a curtain of grey cloud was welling up from the eastwards in a great curve, clearly visible from the railings that skirted the descent towards the lower town. Stanier could already feel the thrust of the wind. Behind him, the villas of the better-off stretched up the incline. Somewhere up there in Glyndwr Avenue Stanier had once rented a house and enjoyed the delights of making love to an eager Tegwyn Morgan. The thought stopped him in his tracks and, at the same time, he recalled he had not rung his wife for several days. He paused, he could see a telephone box further down the road and began walking again. As he descended he stared out to sea. It was clearly blowing quite hard offshore. Macready was going to have a job to refuel the Buccabu lighthouse, Stanier thought happily.

'Got him on two counts!' Stanier muttered. Not only would the old charlatan retire and have no job, Stanier would see he lost his reputation as well!

He could not get through to Caroline from the telephone box and walked on. Down at the dockside, Stanier boarded the *Galahad*. Going directly to the bridge he announced he would sail with the ship and come ashore with the harbour pilot.

'I'm not taking one, sir,' the master told his owner. 'It could be tricky disembarking him outside and pilotage isn't compulsory. I've had some warps run across the dock. We'll heave her off and line her up and then go astern. Piece of cake. Besides,' the master said with a grin, 'it'll save you a few bob.'

'Yes. Oh, quite, yes. Very well, Captain ...' Stanier held out his hand. 'Good voyage.'

From the quayside, Stanier watched the tramp slip her moorings and heave herself into the middle of the dock. Suddenly he saw the dark swirl of water under her counter from her deep propeller. She was full to her marks, he observed with satisfaction as she drew astern and her master waved from her bridge.

'Good voyage!' he called out again.

'No problems,' the master shouted back.

Stanier stood for some moments until the chocolate brown stern had withdrawn beyond the entrance and Jones's men were sliding the caisson back as he had once ordered them too, in the days when he first seduced Tegwyn Morgan and knew the lubricious delights of her body. With that he turned back towards the port manager's office, resolved to call Caroline. At the end of the dock Jones's men boomed the gates again.

'There's no doubt,' Jones told them as they grumbled about the necessity of having to do the task twice in one day, 'there's no doubt that there's going to be a bloody hard blow before too long, my lads.'

It was Charlie who first noticed the increasing wind on Ynyscraven. He was making his rounds alone, leaving Sonia to keep Justine and Tegwyn company, shying away from what seemed to be a female occasion. From the high pasture, he caught a glimpse of a distant smudge of smoke on the horizon and, reining in his mount, he stared at it for some time, conjuring up in his mind's eye a picture of *Caryatid*'s bridge, imagining old Macready, his glasses about his neck on their sennit-work lanyard.

He smiled to himself, guessing the ship was off to the Buccabu light. It was amazing how quickly one got out of touch. He felt the pony beneath him twitch and remembered what Sonia had told him about their habit of turning their backsides into the wind. The sensation made him want to look the other way and he saw then the increased number of white horses heaping up to windward and the great swirl of grey cloud which was already covering half the sky. It was

305

this point that he remembered *Lyonesse,* lying at her single anchor, exposed to the increasing wind and tailing back on her cable, with the shore under her lee.

'Oh shit!' he swore and, kicking the pony into a canter, he tugged its head round.

He found Sonia in the cottage, preparing lunch. 'She's much better,' Sonia announced and it took Charlie a minute to recall Tegwyn's misery. He began to throw some items of clothing into a bag.

'What are you doing?' Sonia asked. 'Lunch is almost ready.'

'Never mind. Go outside and tell me what you think of the weather.' Sonia looked at him as though he had asked her to fly to the moon, then she suddenly caught the tone of alarm in his voice and went to the door. She was back in a moment her eyes wide.

'Well?' Charlie demanded. 'You think it looks bad, don't you?'

Sonia nodded. 'It looks like an Invaders' Wind.'

Charlie nodded. 'That's what I thought. Look, I'm going to have to get *Lyonesse* offshore, or she'll be wrecked.'

'You can't do that on your own—'

'I'm going to have to, darling, otherwise she'll be smashed to pieces. I haven't time to argue.'

'I'm coming with you—'

'No!'

'You haven't time to argue, remember? I'll get some food and some clothes. Give me five minutes. Let Justine know.'

Charlie did as he was bid and five minutes later the two of them were scrambling down the cliff path, shooting glances at the breakers already rolling into the bay.

Stanier was unable to reach Caroline on the dock manager's telephone. It was the middle of the afternoon, so perhaps that was not surprising. He set off to walk back to the Station Hotel and on the long uphill haul he was approached by a small, energetic woman. He recognised her and she him.

'Good afternoon, Captain Stanier,' Mrs Macready said. 'Have you just come up from the docks?'

'Mrs Macready,' he said awkwardly, 'er, yes, I have.'

'The *Caryatid* has sailed, I believe. It is most unusual for my husband not to let me know when he's going out—'

'Oh, there's an, er, an emergency, Mrs Macready—'

'Ah, that explains it, then.' She smiled and seemed to want to chat. Stanier tried to disentangle himself but before he could do so, she said, 'I suppose I ought to thank you, Captain Stanier. As a benefactor of the town.'

'Oh,' Stanier said with a self-deprecating shrug, 'well, one does what one can for the less fortunate—'

'I'm personally grateful as well, Captain. This new flotation on behalf of Ardurian Slate ...' She smiled again, seeing the expression on his face. 'Surely you've heard? Oh no, of course not, you've been at sea on the *Naiad*, haven't you. Well, you see ...' and she went on to explain the good news.

When they parted, Stanier hurried back to the hotel and picked up the telephone. Caroline would be having her bath about now, he thought, drumming his fingers impatiently. After several minutes he put the phone down, then after a moment's reflection he telephoned David Smith's number.

'Mr Smith's not here, sir,' Smith's manservant said. 'Would you like to leave a message?'

'Er, no, no, thank you.'

'Would you like me to say who called, sir?'

'Er, no, no, don't worry.'

He put the phone down and swore. Then he rang Tegwyn. Pomeroy answered the telephone. 'It's James Stanier here, Pom. Is Caroline with Tegwyn?'

'I haven't a bloody clue, Stanier,' said Pomeroy with uncharacteristic brusqueness. 'Where the hell are you?'

'Me? I'm in Porth Ardur.'

'Oh, that dreadful little place. If you see Tegwyn down there tell her she can have the divorce.'

'Divorce? What on earth's the matter, Pom? Why should I be running in to Tegwyn?'

'I've really no idea, Stanier, old boy—'

'You're drunk.'

'How very perceptive of you, Stanier. You always were brilliantly quick on the uptake.'

'You haven't seen Caroline, then.'

'You do catch on, old boy, don't you. Quite amazing.'

Stanier hesitated before discussing business matters with Pomeroy and in the end decided against it. He was panicking. Caroline would be home by now.

'Well thanks, Pom.'

'My pleasure, Stanier, old boy. Any time you like.'

# All At Sea

Even as the tall finger of the Buccabu lighthouse broke the regularity of the horizon, Macready realised he had run out of luck. The sea was humping up astern of the ship and the wind was blowing past them with considerable force. If one added to it the speed of the ship and that of the favourable tide, one arrived at the conclusion that, if the wind was not already at gale force, it was perilously close to it. Macready swore. He felt the jaws of fate close inexorably round him. This was the final payoff for his hubris, this was nemesis, the final humiliation that wrecked his reputation with his career. The sea, he reflected bitterly, always won in the end.

He was left with no alternative, for he could not run for shelter. He would have to heave-to and await a moderation, seizing the moment when it came. Fortunately an easterly gale tended not to persist. Although there would be no lingering ground swell, as occurred after a westerly blow, nevertheless the next few hours would be uncomfortable enough, requiring a degree of fortitude. While they were still running downwind it would be as well to make sure all was secure on deck.

Charlie and Sonia were soaked through by the time they got the dinghy launched and pushed it through the breakers. Charlie had a stiff pull out to the ketch and, when at last they clambered aboard, he took a few moments to catch his breath while Sonia stowed things below.

*Lyonesse* was pitching wildly, snatching at her anchor in such a manner as to make it obvious that they had arrived not a moment too soon. Once she broke its flukes out of the sandy seabed, the yacht would fall to leeward in a matter of moments to dash herself to pieces upon the cliffs of Ynyscraven which rose sheer from the sea astern of them.

Pulling himself together, Charlie went below and roused the spitfire jib out of the locker and dragged it forward. Shackling it onto the halliard, he indicated where Sonia should bend on the sheets.

'Use a bowline,' he shouted.

'I know.'

When the jib was ready for hoisting, they went aft, pulled the mizzen sheet in hard and threw off the sail ties. Then Charlie hoisted the mizzen and, leaving Sonia on the helm, turned to her before going forward again.

'I can't tell which way her head will fall when I get the anchor off the bottom, but get the jib sheeted home as soon as it becomes obvious, all right?'

Sonia nodded, biting her lip. Charlie smiled. 'Once we get away we'll be all right. Then we can get some dry gear on. Don't worry.'

'I'm not worried, except that you're standing there talking when you should be getting that anchor up before it drags.'

As if to add to Sonia's logic, *Lyonesse*'s bow rose and she tugged viciously at her cable. 'I'm off.' Charlie made his way forward, fighting the wind on the wildly plunging deck.

He hoisted the jib and got the halliard as tight as he could on the small winch. Then shipping the handle in the windlass and trying to dodge the wildly flogging jib clew above his head, he began to crank in the anchor cable. It was hard work. Despite the mechanical advantage of the windlass, he had to bodily haul the whole weight of the ketch, with the drag of wind in her rigging, against the force of the gale and the constant knocking back of the breakers now rolling into the bay, steepening with every moment that the tide fell.

Suddenly he felt the chain snag as *Lyonesse* began to rise to an incoming wave. The chain drew taut, restraining her

312

buoyant bow and a sea crashed inboard, rolling past Charlie and sweeping aft along the side decks and pouring overboard on either side of Sonia in the cockpit. Then the ketch shook herself, parted her anchor chain with a bang and began to fall astern. For a terrifying moment it seemed she would drive directly astern under the beetling cliffs, but then she fell off the wind.

Sensing the moment, Sonia quickly hove in the starboard jib sheet, belayed it and seized the helm. Veering as a wave struck her port bow in an explosion of spray and spent energy, *Lyonesse* began to gather forward way. A moment later she was moving ahead, crabbing across the wind. Pulling the loose end of broken cable in, Charlie scrambled aft. He was shivering with cold, but frantically hauled in another foot on the lee jib sheet as Sonia called out a warning.

'It's no good, Charlie! We'll have to go about, she won't weather the Hounds Teeth on this tack!'

He looked up and saw the foaming maelstrom of the tide rushing southwards through the black fangs of the reef. 'It's the bloody ebb tide! Keep her going for a moment or two. We can't afford to risk not staying properly! We must have enough momentum to get her bow through the

313

wind, otherwise ...' He left the shouted sentence unfinished. Sonia understood.

They stood on for one and a half minutes, then Sonia shouted, 'Tell me when, Charlie!'

He watched the crabbing motion of the boat, then at the water rushing past the side. She was certainly driving along. 'Now!' he yelled and Sonia put the helm down.

Charlie did not start the sheet until he was certain *Lyonesse* had passed through the eye of the wind. Then he worked frantically as the heavy canvas of the spitfire jig flogged wildly before the port sheet tamed it. A moment later they were heading north-east, stemming the tide and drawing slowly away from the Hound's Teeth.

Sonia cast a glance astern. High on the path she could just see two bright spots of colour that were Justine and Tegwyn.

'You'd better go below and try and get something more suitable on.'

'Aye, aye, skipper. Then I'll put the kettle on.'

'Good idea.'

Stanier was as much at sea in a metaphorical, as were Macready or Charlie Farthing in a literal sense. He consistently failed to get an answer from Caroline's

314

number, while David Smith's manservant grew tired of informing him that his master was at a late sitting of 'the House'. It was only when it dawned upon Stanier that Parliament was prorogued for the summer that he rang back and insisted upon speaking to Smith.

'I have already told you, sir, that Mr Smith is attending a late sitting of the House—'

'Don't fool with me, you damned scoundrel! I know the House of Commons is in recession for the summer—'

'If you'll excuse me, sir, but there is currently a play on in the West End, called *A Late Sitting of the House*, sir. A farce, I believe,' the man added dryly.

For a moment Stanier was speechless, then he gave his number and asked that Smith should telephone him the moment he got in. Ten minutes later the phone rang.

'Stanier, old boy, what can I do for you? My man says you're damned jumpy. Sorry about the confusion. Good play though; made me laugh.'

Stanier, worked up to a pitch of nervous tension, almost shouted, 'Where's my wife?'

'How should I know?'

'I've been trying to ring her number and there's no reply. You haven't seen her?'

Stanier mastered himself.

'No, not recently, anyway.'

'I tried Tegwyn Pomeroy, but I got Pom and he sounded drunk.'

'He probably was, old boy. She's left him.'

'What?'

'Tegwyn has left Pomeroy. It was inevitable in the end ... Perhaps Caro is with Tegwyn, or is it the other way round. Sorry I can't be more helpful.'

'There's something else,' Stanier said gloomily.

'What's that, old boy?'

'What's this about a flotation?'

'Oh that. Well, we had to act fast—'

'We? You mean you consulted Caroline?'

'Well no, actually she consulted me. That was the agreement, wasn't it, while you were enjoying your own little flotation on the briny.'

'So everything's fine?'

'Couldn't be better, old boy. Caro secured a contract for supplying coal to Costa Maya—'

'Yes, yes, I knew about that.'

'Well, we had to charter two extra ships, bareboat charters, and wanted some quick funds, otherwise we couldn't fulfil the schedule. Got two tramps on the Exchange and they'll be painting their funnels tomorrow, I should think.' Smith chuckled. He could hear Caroline saying, 'Tell Jimmy about their funnels being painted in Cambrian Steam's colours and he'll be happy as a sandboy.'

'As long as Caro's happy about it all,' Stanier said, slightly mollified, but still trying to wrestle with the sequence of events. There was something not quite right about it all, but he could not figure it out for himself.

'Look, Jimmy,' Smith was saying, 'Caroline is more than happy. She has everything well in hand. I saw her only yesterday and she told me, and I quote, "Everything is going just as we planned, David." Now that is what she said to me. I imagine that if you had been accessible, she would have said something along the same lines to you. She's a damned clever woman, Jimmy, you don't deserve her.'

And with that Stanier had to be content and take himself to bed.

Having cleared the Hound's Teeth, Charlie stood offshore for a mile or so before tacking again, heading roughly south-east until clear of Ynyscraven when he hove to, backing the jib and lashing the helm down. The motion of the ketch was much easier and although *Lyonesse* pitched heavily, she was no longer fighting the sea, but curtseying to it, acquiescing to its force, while matching it with her own, lesser but enduring strength.

'She's like a woman making love,' he shouted to Sonia when she re-emerged in hideous black oilskins holding mugs of hot, sweet tea.

'How many women have you made love to?'

'Enough.'

The cloud had covered the sky before sunset and the day that had begun in bright sunshine ended in gloom, fizzling out in a long twilight. Macready had turned *Caryatid* about and hove her to an hour or so earlier. He had also spoken by radio telephone to the keepers on the lighthouse. They too were concerned about the state of the oil reserves on the station, but thought they had sufficient for two more days.

'Mind you, sir,' said the Senior Keeper, 'we'll be scraping the barrel by then.'

Macready was much relieved. Two days was more than he could have hoped for, and although the matter might yet reach crisis point in the coming hours, while the easterly wind wound itself up to its climactic velocity, he could relax insofar as the Buccabu light was concerned.

Despite this remission of anxiety, however, he decided that he would remain

318

close by, ready to seize the first opportunity that offered to refuel the station. He signalled this intention to the keepers and as darkness fell, they could see the navigation lights of the lighthouse tender bucking up and down as, at slow speed, *Caryatid* shouldered aside the heavy seas that tore down upon her from the east-north-east.

Charlie decided he must get some navigation lights organised before the onset of darkness. It took him some time to locate the brass lanterns, only to find them empty of paraffin. Further time was lost locating their fuel and then he decided to fill all the lamps, including those for the compass and the cabin. It is a difficult enough matter to attend to in still water. By the time Charlie had replenished the reservoirs of all the lamps and wedged each filled lamp where it would not move, about a gallon of paraffin had been used, three quarters of which was busy finding its way into *Lyonesse*'s bilge, while it stunk the saloon to high heaven.

Nevertheless, Charlie persisted. He placed two small Argand lamps in their gimballed sconces in the saloon, then took the small light out and shoved it into the binnacle.

'Oooh, that's very cosy,' said Sonia, curled up in the corner of the cockpit.

'I'm glad you like it.'

'I do. I wouldn't be anywhere else on earth right now.' Charlie looked at her. He could just see her face peeping out from under the turned-back brim of the sou'wester.

'I almost believe you,' he said, laughing and ducking back into the saloon where he gingerly lifted the stern light up and, moving aft, hung it over the stern rail where its white light fell upon the oily swirl of the black sea a foot or so beneath him. Returning to the saloon, he next picked up the big port lantern and, bracing himself, carried it through the companionway and out into the cockpit.

'Are you going to open a house of ill repute?' Sonia asked as her face was suddenly bathed in the red glow.

'Yes, I'm going to hang it in the port rigging for all the passing sailors to see.'

Charlie struggled forward and set the lantern on the bracket screwed to the painted side-screen. He then locked the lantern in position by screwing the thumb screw as tight as possible. Afterwards he went back into the saloon for the green, starboard light.

'Oh, that's really weird,' Sonia said, as the ghoulish glare fell on her husband's face.

320

Forty miles to the north-east, *Galahad* steered to head through the 25-mile gap between Ynyscraven and Landfall Point. The tramp ship was deeply laden and wallowed in the following sea. As the waves overtook her, they washed along her side, sluicing in through the openings at the foot of her bulwarks, then poured out as trough followed crest, cleaning the accumulated dust of her lading off her well decks.

On the bridge at eight o'clock in the evening her young Third Officer took over from the Mate and settled down to the routine of watch-keeping.

'It's a filthy night,' the departing Mate remarked. 'And it'll probably get worse before it gets better. Good night.'

'Thank you for your cheery encouragement,' the Third Mate said.

'Don't worry, sir,' remarked the seaman at the wheel. 'It'll be four in the morning before he knows what's hit him.'

'Well, I'll be bloody glad when it's midnight.'

'So will I.'

As the first watch passed, between the hours of eight o'clock and midnight, the wind rose. The waves grew steeper under this assault, their crests toppling and breaking, the thunder of their dissolution adding to the shriek of the wind in the rigging of the three vessels. Then, at about half past eight o'clock off the Buccabu light, the tide turned. The strong force of a spring flood now made against the wind, heaping the seas into steeper and steeper gradients, so that they broke with heavy and destructive force.

One such wave swept *Lyonesse* from end to end, water pouring through the tightly shut skylight and waking Charlie who had sought an hour's shut-eye before taking over from Sonia. Sudden fear for her safety propelled him into the cockpit just as a second wave poured aboard. As he opened the companionway, his eyes unaccustomed to the darkness, there was no sign of Sonia. For a moment his heart stopped, then he saw her lying in the bottom of the cockpit, water sloshing round her. The next wave poured over the low roof of the dog-house and down his back, making him gasp.

'We'll have to turn round and run for it!' he yelled. 'I'll have to get the mizen off her!'

He was never quite sure how he got what he had hitherto considered a small triangular sail down and roughly secured to its boom. But sometime later he collapsed exhausted into the cockpit and recovered his breath. *Lyonesse* had already paid off the wind and it took only a moment of easing the jib sheet for her to start scudding before the storm.

'You'll have to steer,' he shouted into Sonia's ear. 'I'll get a mooring warp over the stern and stream it.'

'Be careful—' she urged, reaching out a hand and squeezing his arm.

With a warp astern, there would be less likelihood of the ketch broaching-to and capsizing in a breaking wave crest. Again, the task took him some time but immediately the line snaked out astern, Sonia reported the steering was a little easier.

'Thank the Lord for small mercies,' he said. 'I'm going below to change again.'

'Have you any more dry clothes?'

'No, I'm reduced to wearing Roger's cricket kit.'

'He's an earl now.'

'That's a bloody funny thing to think of right now.'

'I hope he marries Tegwyn.'

'That's impossible.'

'I'm not so sure,' Sonia said enigmatically, but Charlie had disappeared below in search of white flannels.

# Fateful Encounters

Charlie relieved Sonia and sent her below to rest, while he concentrated on steering *Lyonesse* downwind. The ketch's motion was still violent, for the hollow steepness of the seas flung her about, but it stressed both hull and crew less than trying to hold on, hove to and head to wind. Sonia, however, did not remain below, but soon reappeared in the cockpit. Even in the mean light diffused from the compass bowl, Charlie could see she was pale.

'Oh Charlie, the stink down there is unbearable.' She gasped in the fresh air, staring astern.

'The lamp oil?' She nodded without saying a word. 'Sorry. My fault.' She put out a hand and touched his shoulder. 'Don't look astern, darling. It can be pretty terrifying.' She slumped down in the cockpit, curled herself into a ball and tried to sleep. He could see her eyes close and, slipping in and out of the fitful, waking doze that hours at the helm of a sailing yacht can induce, steered like an automaton through the succeeding hours.

On the bridge of the *Galahad,* the watch changed at midnight. The young Third Mate handed over to the Second Mate. In the security and cosiness of the tramp's wheelhouse, the gale did not seem so very bad, not even when the wind rose to hurricane force, slicing the very tops off the tumbling seas, and sending the atomised water along the flattening surface of the sea with the velocity of buckshot.

The Second Mate supped his third mug of tea, enjoying a desultory chat with the helmsman. It was inconsequential nonsense, words intended merely to put the long voyage ahead into some sort of perspective and rationalise the demands of their odd, outlandish profession. It was only when they both heard the lookout on the bridge wing sing out:

'Right ahead! Something right ahead!'

The Second Mate lifted his glasses, saw nothing at all, then a small pinprick of light swung across his narrow field of vision, coming clear of the black column of the foremast. The angle at which he stared down at it, and its swirling reflection in water, made him realise instantly that it was no distance ahead of them.

'Hard a-port!' he snapped.

'Hard a-port!' came the grunted answer as the helmsman reacted. The Second Mate rushed out onto the bridge wing, alongside the lookout.

'What the hell?'

'It's a bloody yacht!' The incredulity in the lookout's voice was not surprising, but his report was accurate. The Second Mate saw it, a low white shape, a thin pale mast beyond which a triangle of sail flapped in the lee of the *Galahad*'s hull, a shorter mizzen. As the apparition drew swiftly astern, he thought he saw a face peering up at him. It was to haunt him for the rest of his life, for it had a spectral quality that, despite subsequent events, he was always to think of as supernatural.

Charlie had no inkling of the overtaking steamer until its approaching bulk blanketed the straining canvas of the spitfire jib. The sail collapsed, filled, and collapsed again, each time cracking like gunshot. His first thought was for Sonia, but she lay like a dead child in the foetal position, then he looked round.

The bow of the tramp steamer almost overhung him. The wallowing hull pushed a great wall of water before; this was as high, it seemed, as *Lyonesse*'s cross trees. Charlie stared up at the huge, black steel wall, speechless with horror. Then it swung ponderously away from him, exposing the flare upon which he read the stark white

326

letters of the ship's name: *Galahad.* Then the tramp was surging past, the sideways thrust of her bow wave striking *Lyonesse* and flinging her over to starboard. The yacht rolled back to port and was sucked closer as she fell into the trough which succeeded the bow wave. Charlie looked up but could see only the green glow of the ship's starboard navigation light, then she raced past, images of boats and boat davits passing quickly, followed by the low after well deck, a poop deck house and then another slam and roll and the kick of the protesting tiller as, lit by the *Galahad*'s rapidly diminishing stern light, *Lyonesse* wallowed for an instant, then drove after her tormentor, as the wind caught her again.

Charlie huddled shaking with reaction over the tiller. He had never been so terrified in his life and, seeing Sonia undisturbed by the appalling episode, resolved not to tell her.

Slowly he mastered himself. He recalled Macready telling him you could never run down a yacht, for the thing was inevitably shoved aside by the advancing pressure of the bow wave. In the light of his own experience, this seemed a hollow reassurance. They had survived an encounter with death, Charlie thought in that bleak and lonely hour. *Lyonesse* had saved them, he felt sure, and patted the tiller.

'Thank you, little ship,' he said to her, and Sonia stirred, waking in an agony of cramp with a whimper of pain. Charlie looked ahead into the screaming darkness, but there was no trace of the *Galahad*'s stern light. Then he saw the loom of a lighthouse. It was the Buccabu light, just over the horizon, a point to starboard. It was an immensely reassuring sight and he was about to point it out to Sonia, but she appeared to have drifted off to sleep again.

Despite the fact that he had had a disturbed night, Macready felt little inclination to retire to his bunk. That this might be his last night at sea in heavy weather was only one reason why he dozed fitfully in the chair provided for him on the bridge. He was also aware that, stout though *Caryatid* was, the conditions were extreme. Her low foredeck made her vulnerable to shipping green seas, and her large hatch, if stripped of its tarpaulin cover, would soon swallow sufficient water to sink her.

Besides, there was a rare majesty to the night, for the wind was scouring the sea so that it no longer presented the serried ranks of wave upon wave marching inexorably down upon them, but was one vast, undulating plain of grey-white and this, at about two o'clock in the morning, was suddenly dramatically lit by the full moon as the first rents in the overcast began to show.

In the next half hour, these first short moments of illumination grew longer. The stabbing light of the Buccabu, some five miles distant, grew less prominent, so that it was a moment before anyone, Macready, Wentworth, or the helmsman, noticed the light had vanished. Then they simultaneously reacted.

'The Buccabu light, sir! It's not there!'

'By damn, you're right!' Instinctively, Macready shook himself fully awake and checked the compass course. No, the ship's head remained roughly north-east, and the wind direction seemed steady. Surely they had not all been asleep and steamed past without noticing?

He went quickly to the wheelhouse door, flung it open and stepped out into the screaming night, almost blinded by the reflection of the moonlight on the sea and grazed by the salt-laden spray that flew horizontally through the air over the bridge dodgers. He stared astern, then swung round again and, leaning into the wind, lifted his glasses. He caught sight of the moonlight on the grey granite tower, a thin, pallid finger not three miles away.

He counted the seconds. By the time he reached twenty he knew for certain the light was extinguished.

Well, it had happened. He was shamed by it, but the fact stared him in the face: he had failed in his duty. As if aware of his shame, another curtain of cloud covered the moon and plunged the world into darkness again.

'Sir!'

'I've seen the lighthouse, Mister,' he told the Second Mate.

'It's not that, sir, there's a ship beyond the tower, sir!'

Macready lifted his binoculars again, and swept the horizon. He could see nothing. 'I don't see anything ...'

The Second Mate was silent, still peering through his glasses, then he lowered them. 'I'm sorry, sir, I could have sworn that I'd seen a ship.'

'Let's call up the lighthouse and see what's happened.'

'They must have run out of oil, sir.'

'Let's check, shall we,' Macready said patiently, 'before we jump to any conclusions.'

From the security of his wheelhouse, the Second Mate of the *Galahad* had seen the light of the Buccubu a few moments before Charlie. Unlike Charlie in the ketch, who, low in the water, had seen only the loom of the light as *Lyonesse* had been lifted up on a swell, the *Galahad's* Second Mate had seen the sweep of the full beam. He was still shaken by the shock of overtaking the yacht, and deferred taking a bearing, an unpleasant task in the prevailing conditions. The tramp ran on for almost half an hour then, as the chartroom clock edged up to three in the morning, the Second Mate stirred himself. He ought to put a position on the chart and went out onto the bridge wing and clambered up to the compass on the monkey island, the wind tearing at his body as he heaved himself up the ladder.

The moon had ducked in again, and the darkness seemed impenetrable. Then, as *Galahad* lifted on a great swell, he caught a distant glimpse of a ship's navigation light broad on the starboard bow. It was a long way off, he thought, bending over the azimuth mirror and twiddling it to take a bearing. Not as familiar with the Buccabu as the officers of the *Caryatid,* he waited for a full minute before he realised something was wrong. For five seemingly interminable minutes, the Second Mate waited for the Buccabu lighthouse to flash its warning of danger out over the heaving grey-white mass of the sea, but nothing happened.

331

The Second Mate of the *Galahad* calmed himself with an effort. They were all right. The bearing of the lighthouse had been to starboard. If they maintained a steady course, they must pass it clear. He went below.

'Bloody lighthouse has failed,' he said matter-of-factly to the helmsman. 'How much are you yawing?'

'Only about ten degrees either side of the course,' the man lied. In fact he was having difficulty holding the ship's head within twenty degrees, and once or twice she had nearly got away from him altogether.

'Steer as close as you can.'

'Aye, aye, sir.'

Aboard *Caryatid* the Second Mate had trouble contacting the lighthouse, but after about twenty minutes a voice came over the air acknowledging the call.

'*Caryatid*, this is Buccabu, over.'

'You'd think he'd know what we're calling about,' remarked Wentworth to Macready who was leaning in through the radio-room door.

'Well, ask him. He can hardly disguise the matter.'

'Buccabu, this is *Caryatid*. We see your light is extinguished. Please report the reason. Over.'

'It's pretty bad, sir. We've had the lantern stove in, sir.'

'That's the Junior Keeper,' Macready said suddenly, pushing his way into the radio room and taking the handset from the Second Officer. 'The poor bugger's in shock. Keep a lookout, I'll see to this ... Buccabu, this is Macready speaking, take your time and tell me what's happened. Over.'

'We took a big one, sir. Senior Keeper was on watch and it washed him to the foot of the day-room stairs, sir ...' That was a fall of at least twenty feet, down a steep staircase, Macready thought quickly. 'I think he's concussed, sir. It was some moments before the two of us realised what was the matter. Over.'

'And the lantern? What's the score with that? Over,' Macready prompted.

'The glazings are stove in, sir, and some of the astragal bars have come loose and damaged the lens. A lot of water got inside, sir. We've tried getting the emergency light going, but the wind up there is phenomenal, sir. Over.'

Macready thought for a moment. Then he put the handset to his mouth. 'Very well. Make the Senior Keeper, that's Mr Keeble, I take it, make him as comfortable as you can. Hold his head steady if you move him and assume that he's fractured

333

his skull and snapped his neck until we know to the contrary. Then you'll have to go on watch-and-watch. Keep out of the wind, but keep a lookout and call us to let us know if you see any ships approaching. You've a better height of eye than us, tossing about down here, so let us know what you see. It might give us time to intercept anyone hell-bent on dashing themselves to pieces on that reef of yours. D'you understand? Over.'

'Aye, aye, sir. Affirmative on Mr Keeble and we'll call you if we see any ships. Over.'

Relieved to hear the note of confidence back in the keeper's voice, Macready remembered the distant ship Wentworth had reported. 'Go up right away and have a good look round, then let me know—'

'Sir!' Macready turned. The voice was the Second Mate's, calling in from the wheelhouse.

'What is it?'

'There *is* a bloody ship out there, sir. And it's bloody close to the lighthouse.'

It was at that moment that Macready thought of the eddies which swirled about the Buccabu reef. Old Captain Jesmond had not believed in them until he had had first-hand experience. On the flood they could set a ship to the east of the reef bodily to the westwards if she hit

334

the inward curve of what was effectively a large whirlpool in the ocean itself.

At that moment several things happened at once. The moon came out from the obscurity of the clouds, the radio handset almost exploded into life and his own Second Mate blasphemed.

'Oh my God!'

'*Caryatid,* this is the Buccabu light. *There's a ship almost on top of us!*'

Macready dropped the handset and strode out onto the wing of the bridge.

On the bridge of the *Galahad,* the sudden moonlight fell upon the granite tower, reflecting pallidly from the smashed glazings themselves. Without orders, the helmsman, who had seen the lighthouse, put the helm hard over to port at the same time that the Second Officer screamed at him to do so. But it was too late. Although the *Galahad* had begun her swing and the eddy assisted the turning moment, her speed carried her down upon the reef and she struck her starboard bilge just abaft the engine-room bulkhead, tearing herself open the whole length of numbers four and five holds. The ship shook violently as her propeller hit an outcrop of rock, mangling the blades and severing two completely so that the engine raced and the tail shaft whipped.

'Oh, my God, my God,' the Second Officer whimpered as Galahad tore free, then lurched to starboard and began to settle by the stern.

'What in hell ...?' Her Master appeared on the bridge wing, staring incredulously aft where, looming over the starboard quarter, the granite tower of the Buccabu light rose above them.

'The light, sir,' the Second Mate tried to explain, 'the fucking light was out.'

'The ship's sinking, sir,' the helmsman called, and the Master leapt to the alarm bells and sent them jangling all through the ship.

# The Buccabu Light

Captain Macready saw quite clearly the moment of impact, saw the ship swing and strike, heel to port as her quarter rode up on the reef and then, as a gap opened between her and the moonlit finger of the light-tower, she began to fall over to starboard, her stern sinking.

'It's the *Galahad*, sir!' Wentworth called, his binoculars still clamped to his eyes and Macready recognised the ship the same instant. Within the next minute the moon slipped behind the clouds again and all they could see was the dark shape of the stricken ship and the green and white points of her navigation lights.

'Full ahead! Starboard easy!' Macready's seaman's instincts spurred him to action. 'Call all hands!'

'Ring the general alarm, sir?'

'Yes! Midships steady!'

*Caryatid* was thrust forward by her accelerating propeller. Butting through the seas, her bluff bow headed for the *Galahad* as the alarm bells rang throughout the accommodation. Studying the stricken casualty through his glasses,

Macready considered what he could do. It was clear that everything possible should be done to save the *Galahad*, but the weather ruled out lowering boats. *Caryatid* had towing gear and rocket apparatus and this seemed to offer the best option. *Galahad* was already lying beam on to the wind and sea, rolling abominably. While she had settled noticeably by the stern, she seemed not to be plunging to her doom. Perhaps they had had a chance aboard her to make an assessment of the damage, in which case it might be wise to try and call her up. Telling the Second Mate to reduce to half speed and continue to head towards the casualty, he strode into the radio room at the very moment the *Galahad* sent out her first SOS. Picking up the handset, Macready intercepted it.

'*Galahad*, this is Celtic Lighthouse Service Tender *Caryatid*, I am close to your position and have you under visual observation. I have towing capability and am willing to attempt salvage if there is no immediate prospect of you sinking. Please report your current state. Over.'

'*Caryatid*, this is *Galahad*. Master speaking. I am holed aft and immobile through damage to the screw. The after peak is intact and the after engine-room bulkhead is holding at the moment. Five and six

338

holds are breached. Your bloody light was out. Over.'

'*Caryatid* to *Galahad*, I am aware of the problem at the lighthouse, Captain. The lantern was stove in and a keeper is badly injured. I shall have to consider his life as a priority and will stand by you until daylight. If it comes to it, will you agree to towage under Lloyd's Open Agreement? Over.'

'Affirmative. Glad if you would keep us company. Over.'

'Very well, Captain. It's a bad night for all of us. Over and out.'

Macready emerged on the bridge to find Watson and the Bosun had reported there for orders.

'We've the hands mustered in the messdecks, sir.'

'Right,' said Macready. 'We'll get everything ready to tow, but the Senior Keeper on the Buccabu is suffering from concussion. If we steam away towing that ship, we risk the charge of putting pecuniary gain before safcty of life.'

'Yes ... But these violent easterlies usually blow themselves out quite quickly,' said Watson, adding, 'daylight should give us a better idea of how things stand.'

'Civil twilight's no more than an hour away now, sir,' offered Wentworth.

339

'Well, we'll need to get boats and towing gear ready. Get the cook turned-to for an early breakfast, I don't know when we'll have an opportunity to eat again once we commit ourselves to a salvage operation.' Macready looked round at them. 'Right then. Let's get on with it!'

It was already beginning to grow less dark and an hour later a grey daylight spread across the heaving waste. They were half a mile from the wallowing *Galahad*, a dark shape moving in the twilight.

'Breakfast, sir.' The steward arrived with a tray and the delicious smell of bacon and eggs filled the wheelhouse. He placed it in the fiddles on a small table in the corner and Macready fell upon the meal voraciously, unaware until that moment of his hunger. Food put new heart into a man. Behind him Watson relieved the Second Mate who slipped below to gobble up an even larger portion than his commander.

The Mate went out on the bridge wing and sniffed the wind, returning to the wheelhouse to report, 'You know, I really think that wind is easing.'

Macready sipped his tea and stared through the armoured-glass windows. Certainly less spray was driving aft and the air was no longer white with the suspended and atomised spume. He put his teacup down and began to con *Caryatid* up towards *Galahad*'s bow, seeing how close he could get to her in preparation for when the time came to fire a rocket and line across. *Caryatid,* pitching into wind and sea, edged up towards the tramp, at right angles to the heavily rolling casualty. The *Galahad*'s after well deck was awash, her after mast and Samson posts standing clear of the welter of white water surging across her. The poop looked like an island and a few men could be seen standing up on the docking bridge that ran athwart the poop deckhouse. At the other end of the ship, the bow stood high out of the water.

'I wonder how much of her cargo she dropped through the hole in her after holds,' Watson mused as he stared through his glasses.

'With all that deadweight forward stuck up in the air, the stresses on her hull will be immense. She could easily break up,' Macready said, raising his own glasses.

'The sea is dying a touch, sir, I'm damn sure of it.'

'Tide's turned,' Macready responded. 'Try not to let the prospect of salvage colour your judgement, Mr Watson.' He lowered his binoculars and looked at the younger officer. He wished he had Charlie with him.

'I'm trying hard, sir,' Watson said, a lopsided grin on his face. Then his face hardened as he swung his glasses to the right. 'What on earth? Is that a *yacht?*'

Macready lifted his own binoculars again and followed Watson's direction. He saw a small speck of white breast a wave and then the narrow curve of a sail above it. 'By damn, Mr Watson, I believe you're right!'

Charlie had seen nothing of the drama ahead of him. Huddling cold, wet and miserable in *Lyonesse*'s cockpit, the circle of his own visible horizon was limited to a few yards, bound by the restless and heaving seas. Nor had he noticed the Buccabu light had gone out. Navigation in a small yacht in such conditions is not a matter of precision. He had seen not just the loom, but several cycles of the double group flash of the light itself. Since this had shown sufficiently clearly on the starboard bow for him not to concern himself with the danger of hitting it on his present course, he continued to crouch over the compass, drifting half in and half out of a sort of cataleptic trance in which the tired body, like that of the deep-diving whales, simply shut down the extraneous bits of itself. In such a state, daylight came upon him quickly and he became fully conscious as Sonia finally woke from sleep, wracked with painful cramp.

'Ow!' she cried as she tried to straighten her stiffened muscles and finally drew herself up and peered round. 'The wind seems to have dropped a little ...' Charlie grunted agreement. 'Oh,' Sonia went on, 'there's a lighthouse.'

Charlie looked up and saw the familiar grey tower on the starboard beam some two miles away. At that distance there was no obvious sign of the damaged lantern.

'Charlie,' Sonia said suddenly, an edge to her voice, 'there's a ship ... and that's *Caryatid* ... Charlie!'

Suddenly desperately eager to relieve himself and have a cup of tea, yet alarmed by Sonia's tone he stood up, stretching and yawning. 'What is it?'

'I think I saw a funny ship.'

A wave ran up under the ketch's stern and lifted them forward in a great soaring arc of acceleration. Charlie felt the drag of the trailing warp keep them steady, then he too saw Sonia's 'funny ship' and beyond her the familiar, fond silhouette of *Caryatid*.

The wave passed and they fell into the succeeding trough, with a sluggish deceleration. Ahead of them the receding crest drove away from them, hiding the two ships. As *Lyonesse* lifted again, he saw clearly and understood.

'It's a tramp ship, by the look of it ...

343

Her after part must be flooded and she's broached-to.'

'You mean she's in trouble?' Sonia asked, still not quite grasping the fact that she was witnessing a maritime disaster.

Charlie nodded. 'Big trouble ... Look, darling, I need a leak and a cup of tea. Take the helm, will you? I'll get something to eat for us. We may be able to help.'

It was only when she found herself alone at the helm that Sonia wondered what on earth Charlie thought they could accomplish.

Macready's attention was diverted from the sudden appearance of the yacht. Yachtsmen were, in any case, a breed with which the good Captain had had only the most basic acquaintance. That this was usually when they were ashore at their most assertively unpleasant, was unfortunate, for it had inculcated a not unreasonable prejudice that they were over-privileged beings who had no business having anything to do with the stern preoccupations of sea-going. Aware that there were yachtsmen who achieved admirable voyages, Macready's attitude towards them generally was, therefore, ambivalent. He summed this up, dismissing the approaching ketch and her crew collectively as 'mad buggers!'

Hardly had this comprehensive assessment passed his lips than the radio telephone boomed into life again. Macready recognised the voice of the Master of the *Galahad* even as he saw what the man was appealing for help over. With a strange, brief but hideous squeal, clearly audible to the watching men aboard *Caryatid*, the highly stressed and neglected hull of the tramp ship twisted as she rolled and tore apart. Relieved of the weight of the submerged after part, the high-riding bow fell back into the sea, to find its own level. With more windage, this forward part drifted to leeward, leaving the after remnant to readjust itself. Consisting of the after two holds which were entirely open to the sea, and the after peak tank, steering engine and poop, this now turned through ninety degrees, the air in the extreme after body supporting the remainder. The most elevated part of the hull was thus the very curve of her stern plating and the rudder. As this small steel islet bobbed in the heavy seas, it alternately exposed and submerged glimpses of what had once been her propeller.

The few men remaining aft, a handful of firemen Macready supposed, could be seen scrambling over the after rail and clinging desperately to the wreckage.

'Looks like we've got three problems

now,' Watson observed dryly.

Macready went through to the radio room and spoke to *Galahad*'s Master, learning that they had evacuated two men from the poop through the shaft tunnel, but when the tunnel began to leak they had had to close the watertight door and seal the engine room. The engine room after bulkhead was now the effective after end of what was left of the ship and, although it was holding, the Master was clearly consumed by anxiety as to how long this state of affairs would last. When the Master had finished, Macready, well aware that his own part in this drama was as much to support this unfortunate man as to assist him in a more material manner, reassured him.

'We shall remain with you, Captain, and do whatever we can. First I'm going to try and take your men off the stern section, then I'll take you in tow. We'll take it step by step from there. Over.'

'Thank you, Captain. Over.' The voice was weary with anxiety.

Macready went out onto the bridge wing. 'Mr Watson,' he said, 'send in a signal saying Buccabu lighthouse extinguished through stress of weather, Senior Keeper Keeble believed concussed and steamship *Galahad* breaking up in close vicinity. Say we're standing by and will report situation as it develops. Signal via the coastguard as usual for Porth Ardur Lighthouse Base, to be repeated to headquarters ...' Macready looked at his watch. 'I suppose someone will be interested up there in about three hours.'

Watson grunted. 'Yes. Fun'll be over by then.'

'We'll see.'

Charlie was back in the cockpit with two wedges of bread and marmalade and two mugs of tea as they drew past the *Caryatid.*

'What are we going to do, Charlie? What can we do? That ship looks even funnier now—'

'Bloody hell, she's broken up!' He paused, seeing the bow section with its name. 'It's the *Galahad,* the bloody ship that nearly ran us down in the night!' Then he regretted the words, recalling that he had not intended mentioning the matter to Sonia. He looked at her, but she had not understood, instead she was pointing, her face screwed up in puzzlement.

'Are those men on there?' Sonia asked.

Charlie stared across the sea for a moment. 'Good God! Yes ... Look, Sonia, we've got to turn round and work our way back to Ynsycraven. You said yourself the wind had dropped and there's no doubt

347

that it'll go down during this morning; it's what always happens—'

'I know that.'

'Well then, let's put about now and tack up towards those poor devils—' He never finished, for she cut him short.

'All right then,' she said, 'let's get on with it.'

Charlie looked at her shining eyes. What a girl! 'I'll hoist the mizzen—'

'And get that warp in,' she ordered.

Charlie laughed. He was tired but suddenly Sonia's spirit invigorated him. What a girl!

'What's that fucking yacht doing?' Watson asked as he clambered up to the bridge from the boat deck. Macready had edged *Caryatid* as close to the *Galahad*'s drifting poop as he dared. Mooring ropes stowed there and now, fouled in the wreckage, trailed about the diminishing refuge of the six souls who stared desperately up at them, their dark faces revealing them as Lascars. Below the surface of the water the after Samson posts and derricks threatened a close approach like the outlying rocks of a reef. To hazard either *Caryatid*, stout though she was, or one of her boats, would be a risky, even a foolhardy business.

But their close approach had given the Lascar firemen hope and Macready felt the

348

moral obligation bind him to their fates. 'We'll have to *try* a boat, Mr Watson,' he said, lowering his glasses, 'that poop section is sinking. You can see air blowing out through an after port. We may not have very long.'

Watson nodded. It was not his job to make decisions and he did not envy Macready his responsibility, but the years of training brought his own professionalism unwaveringly to his commander's support. 'The men are all ready, sir. Port boat?'

Macready nodded. 'Yes.'

Watson turned away for the ladder. 'By the way, sir, have you seen this yacht?'

'Uh?' Macready turned. A white ketch lay under their port quarter, her sails just full as she edged in and out of the lee of *Caryatid*. A figure stood up in the bows, a hand at his mouth. Macready raised his glasses. 'Good God! It's Charlie! Nip aft and see what *he* wants. I'm damned if I can help him as well!'

Watson descended the bridge ladder and ran aft, past the men mustering round the port sea boat. Macready watched as Watson and Charlie exchanged remarks, recognising the ketch as that belonging to Lord Craven, then Charlie turned aft and clearly passed a message at whoever was on *Lyonesse*'s helm: Craven, Macready presumed, as the ketch bore away, disappearing under the stern, out of Macready's sight.

Waiting for Watson to come forward again, Macready recollected that Craven was now no longer the old earl's heir, but had succeeded to the title. He recalled the ketch had probably been off Ynyscraven when the storm blew up, then the irrelevant thought was swept aside as Watson came back up the bridge ladder.

'That was Charlie Farthing,' Watson said. 'They are going to have a go at picking the survivors off the stern section, sir.'

'Is that wise?' said Macready, irritated. 'Suppose they get into trouble. Then we've got him to worry about as well—'

'I put that to him. He said it was better to hazard the yacht and get the men off even if it meant damage. We could more easily take everyone off a drifting yacht in the lee of the ship if matters came to the push, and you would be relieved of the need to lower and recover our sea boat.'

Macready sighed. 'Well, I can see the logic of his argument ... I suppose it's up to Lord Craven ... I mean Dungarth. It's his boat, after all, and it might give us a chance to do something about getting Keeble off the Buccabu. Call up the lighthouse and see how he is.'

'Aye, aye, sir,' and as Watson disappeared into the radio room, Macready ordered *Caryatid*'s engines from slow to half ahead again, to keep *Lyonesse* under observation and try to resolve some of the more pressing of his problems. It never occurred to either Macready or Watson that the half-seen figure hunched over the *Lyonesse*'s tiller was anyone other than her owner, the latest Earl Dungarth.

Charlie scrambled aft and took up a position by the mizzen shrouds, conning Sonia as they steadied on a course which would take them as close downwind of the drifting stern section as he dared. He could imagine all the detritus trailing to windward, and while the windage of the poop would rob their sails of energy, he wanted to close the distance as quickly as possible and make an assessment.

As they beat up towards the *Galahad*'s stern they could see the frightened Lascars waving at them. More ominously, as they drew close, not only did the wreckage loom large and solid, it was also obvious from the jets of escaping air that hissed and poppled about its surging waterline, that it was sinking fast.

Charlie bent and let go the senhouse slips on *Lyonesse*'s upper and lower guard rails, making access to the deck somewhat easier, then he cupped his hands round his mouth. 'I come alongside next time—you jump—savvy?'

'Yes, sahib. Next time you come, we jump!'

'Right, darling,' he said, leaping down in the cockpit to handle the sheets, 'bear right away.'

Sonia pulled at the tiller and *Lyonesse* skidded to port, dipped her bow, flung spray high and then lay over as she came onto a broad reach and shot away from the wreckage. As soon as her speed built up, Charlie ordered: 'Gybe her!'

With only her small mizzen boom to worry about and the jib sheets to shift, the manoeuvre was less hazardous than might be supposed. Sonia turned the yacht's stern quickly through the wind, while Charlie worked frantically at the sheets. As the ketch came round, Sonia steadied *Lyonesse*'s leaping bow on the *Galahad*'s wrecked stern.

'Give me a compass course, Charlie, I can't look at this.'

'Steady as you go ... No, port five ... That's fine—'

'That's one-three-eight—'

'Good, keep on that then.' Charlie could feel adrenalin pumping into his system. He did not feel as though he had spent the night at the boat's helm, he just felt a great surge of focused elation as *Lyonesse* stood boldly towards the wreckage on the port tack. He would need all the acquired skill of his years at sea, an absolute faith in his own judgement and in Sonia's skilful obedience, if they were to succeed. For a second he felt the enormity of what he was intending to do and then he gave himself up to it.

'One-three-oh.'

She would just hold the wind on that course, Charlie judged, and Sonia said without looking up, 'Will she take it?'

Charlie looked up at the jib. The wind was below gale force now, but still blew strongly, while the seas still flung the ketch about as she swooped in towards the waiting firemen who were already clambering down the stern railings, using them as a ladder.

'Yes—'

It looked as though they were going to have to do this six times, Charlie thought, and then they were suddenly up with the rearing steel as it curved away round *Galahad*'s stern.

'Luff!'

Sonia thrust the helm down and *Lyonesse* came upright as she turned into the wind, rapidly losing speed as her rate of turn slowed.

'Jump!' Charlie roared, grabbing the arm

of a Lascar who fell on top of Sonia in the cockpit. She caught a glimpse of a rusty plate scabbed with chocolate paint and a row of rivets that seemed possessed of a kind of life of their own as they zipped up, down and then passed out of her sight as the man's weight knocked the breath out of her. Charlie lost his own balance and then felt another man on top of him and flung his own arm about the fellow's waist.

The confusion in the cockpit had thrown Sonia across the tiller, pushing it back to port, so that it arrested the port swing. Charlie frantically fought himself free of the man on top of him who, having reached sanctuary, was not intending to let it go, and required a huge heave. 'Get below out of the way! *Jildi! Jildi!*'

Then Charlie felt a thump on the deck followed by a second while the starboard mizzen shroud he was clinging to vibrated and a pair of plimsoled feet crushed his hand as a fifth man swarmed down it.

'Go! Go! Sahib! Go!'

'Hard over, Sonia!' he shouted. *Lyonesse* gave a jarring shudder as she came into heavy contact with *Galahad*'s stern. Charlie heard the splinter of wood and, forcing his way forward desperately, held the clew of the jib to windward.

There was another rending sound and

then *Lyonesse's* bow began to fall off to port, helped by the sudden surge of a wave as it poured round the wreckage to throw her clear. Charlie hastened aft again and flung the starboard jib sheet off the cleat. The sail flogged madly and the cockpit seemed full suddenly of excited, chattering, dark faces with Sonia, black clad and determined in their midst.

'Get below! Go bottomside! Fuck off into cabin! *Jildi! Jildi!*'

He shooed them down below, while trying to catch hold of and haul down the port jib sheet. As soon as he was done he looked at Sonia.

'We got five,' she said, her eyes shining with triumph.

'There were six. We've got to go back again,' he said.

'Oh no—'

'Not necessary, sahib.' A Lascar face in the companionway rocked happily and pointed upwards, over Charlie's shoulder. He looked round. Above his head, his feet on the mizzen cross trees and clinging to the mizzen rigging stood the sixth man.

'By damn, Charlie's done it!' Macready lowered his glasses. 'I'd not have believed it, had I not seen it myself.'

'Not a moment too soon,' Watson said. Astern of *Lyonesse* the stern section of the

*Galahad* was disappearing fast. As they watched, it took a sudden plunge and disappeared. 'I've got through to the Buccabu, sir,' said the Second Mate, coming out onto the wing of the bridge. 'I've just spoke to Keeble himself. He says he's all right. He's got a bump the size of an egg on his head, but he's more concerned with the light. He says he's tried to get the stand-by burner working, but the bronze astragals knocked it for six. It's smashed to smithereens.'

Macready nodded. The relief on his face was obvious. 'Well,' he said, his voice suddenly buoyant, 'let's see if we can get what's left of that rust-bucket under tow.'

# No Cure, No Pay

The news of the disaster at the Buccabu lighthouse reached the headquarters of the Commissioners for Celtic Lighthouses about mid-morning. Captain Sir Charles Mudge called an immediate meeting of the Board which was hurriedly scheduled for that afternoon. It was a day of extraordinary activity, unparalleled in living memory for, by a strange coincidence, in addition to the *Caryatid*'s attendance on the stricken *Galahad*, off the south-west coast, *Waterwitch* had just been released from standing by the grain ship whose cargo had shifted, but which was now under the tow of a salvage tug in moderating weather.

The Board was not so much concerned with the deployment of its ships, as the problem at the Buccabu lighthouse which clearly required the issuing of navigation warnings, notices to mariners and consideration of the means by which the effects of so catastrophic an event could be reversed. Reports of the disaster seemed to rule out a quick and easy answer for, in addition to the virtual destruction of the lantern structure and the lighting apparatus, some damage seemed to have been inflicted on the masonry of the tower. This was only discovered after the wind had dropped to a fresh breeze shortly before noon, arriving with the tidings that *Caryatid* had the *Galahad* in tow under the standard salvage arrangements of a Lloyd's Open Agreement.

This extraordinary legal instrument is unique in being the only one binding without signature. The difficulties of obtaining and exchanging formally signed contracts under the extreme circumstances prevailing in a rescue at sea in bad weather clearly preclude such a nicety. It was however, Macready afterwards thought, clear evidence that that strange brotherhood which existed between seamen of all nationalities, was one of the most civilised if unestablished institutions upon earth. Moreover, the formalities concluded an agreement which was exemplary in its essential fairness for, if the salvage attempt failed, no payment was due. This 'no-cure, no-pay' principle ensured that no salvage was undertaken lightly and for Captain Macready it was necessary that he sought the sanction of the Commissioners. This he did retrospectively, for he had had *Galahad* in tow for some hours before he transmitted his signal.

At about the same time as this in-telligence was passing along the wires to reach Sir Charles Mudge's desk at a quarter past twelve, and the Chairman's approval on behalf of the Board was returned as a matter of course, Captain Stanier was sitting hugging himself in a first-class compartment of an express train on the up line. The windy night had turned itself into a day of blustery weather with bright sunny periods sandwiched between patches of scudding cloud. His mood lightened; the forebodings of the night receded, dismissed as he sat and read the share prices in his newspaper. The wisdom of Caroline and Smith in chartering extra ships to fulfil the new contracts, impressed him. It was clearly a clever and necessary move, which would allow Cambrian Steam to maximise its opportunities. He had hoped that the financial pages of his broadsheet newspaper might have mentioned the economic impact of the revolt in Costa Maya, but was not unduly worried by the absence of any report on the event. It was an early edition and foreign news had a habit of taking time to percolate through the filtration of editing desks. There was, however, a fine photograph of the badly listing grain ship taken from an aeroplane. In the foreground of the shot he could see the Celtic Lighthouse Tender *Waterwitch* and it made him think of the more satisfactory events of the last few days. In the end the uncertainties as to the whereabouts of his wife receded as Stanier consigned his panic of the previous day to those recesses of his mind that processed his neuroses. As the journey wore on, Stanier found himself more bothered about where to go first when he arrived in the capital. The train would arrive at the terminus at four o'clock. He could go straight home, but Caro might not yet be there and he loathed going home to an empty flat. He ought to go to the city offices of Cambrian Steam and find out the details of recent events, but these were so clearly all under control and he would learn them from Caro herself later, that he thought it unnecessary. On the other hand, he had a bulging briefcase full of papers connected with the recent cruise of the Commissioners and would be happy to disencumber himself of their deadweight. Moreover, the most pressing matter he had on his own mind, was to report the disobedience of Captain Macready and this finally decided him upon dropping the briefcase off first at the headquarters of the Lighthouse Authority. It would be interesting too, he thought, to catch up on the latest news of *Waterwitch*'s involvement with the grain ship casualty, and to find out when she would head for Porth Ardur.

When Stanier arrived at headquarters, he was asked to go straight to the Board Room where the extraordinary meeting was still in progress. He was not surprised, though he meanly hoped that the Board had yet to hear of Macready's unilateral action. It was clear that Mudge and his colleagues were in sombre mood. Stanier guessed that the near mutiny at Porth Ardur was at the root of their deliberations. Mudge waved him to a seat.

'You've heard about *Caryatid*, Stanier,' Mudge said, thinking that Stanier's first preoccupation might be with his damaged ship.

'I know about him sailing from Porth Ardur without orders and in insubordinate disobedience—'

Mudge interrupted, matters were dragging inconclusively and he was anxious to get on. 'Well, it's just as well that he sailed, your *Galahad* would be in even deeper trouble than she is at the moment.'

'*Galahad?* What on earth d'you mean?' Stanier was frowning with incomprehension.

'You don't know? Damn it! Last night's severe weather stove in the whole upper part of the Buccabu lighthouse. A few minutes later Cambrian Steam's *Galahad* hit the reef and ripped her after bottom out. She drifted clear disabled, having

361

shed most, if not all her propeller blades. Fortunately *Caryatid* was in the offing.'

Stanier was white faced and it was a moment before he spoke. Then, in a quavering voice, he asked: 'You mean Macready has *Galahad* in tow?'

'Well the half of her that is still afloat.'

Stanier looked at Mudge, his face aghast. 'She's broken in half?'

'Yes,' Mudge nodded. 'Well, I'm sorry, but it is the Buccabu that we must consider. It looks as though it is going to be a major operation repairing the lighthouse and Blake is suggesting we may have to lay a lightvessel near the reef—'

'You said the light ... the Buccabu light was out?'

'Yes,' said Mudge impatiently, 'that is what we are discussing. How to make good the deficiency as quickly as possible—'

'No, no,' said Stanier leaning forward, 'I mean, you said the light was out before *Galahad* ran aground and this would have contributed to the grounding—'

'Look, that's as maybe, Stanier,' Blake said crossly, 'and I daresay you're concerned about your ship but we've a different concern which is our prime preoccupation—'

'While you're here, Stanier, you're wearing the hat of a Commissioner,' Mudge reminded him sternly.

362

Stanier looked from one to the other of them. 'You don't understand,' he whispered before sitting back and lapsing into silence, his face glazed.

Captain Macready looked astern with some satisfaction. His decision to sail was now thoroughly vindicated. His career was not to end on a note of whimpering, but a classic piece of good seamanship. He was in no doubt of this after the event just as before it, when competing priorities had been removed by Charlie's dashing act and the merciful thickness of Keeble's skull, he had had no doubt that he could do it. Nor did this confidence in himself arise from hubris; it derived from the sure and certain knowledge that, even with Watson as his mate, he commanded a ship and ship's company of unprecedented excellence.

It was in this knowledge that he had manoeuvred *Caryatid* so close in under the bow of *Galahad* that they had dispensed with the rocket line and found the distance could be bridged with a hand-thrown heaving line. This had been followed by a heavier rope and eventually *Caryatid*'s towing wire which, once shackled onto a length of *Galahad*'s port anchor cable, had finally connected rescuer and rescued.

The easterly wind died away as the day progressed, producing an evening of tranquil sunshine and a breeze backing quickly into the north and later the north-west. The sea dropped too, so that by sunset, when Ynyscraven was just abaft the beam on the northern horizon, only a low swell marked the passing of the storm.

Far astern of them on the starboard quarter, now no more than a sunlit speck of white, *Lyonesse* tacked up towards Ynyscraven. She had passed her happy Lascar 'passengers' across to *Caryatid* by way of one of the ship's boats after the tow had been connected, and then with a wave, Charlie had sheered away, setting the mainsail and a larger jib.

Having settled his human cargo safely in the messdeck, Watson came up to the bridge. 'D'you know who that was in the yacht with Charlie Farthing?' he said, to which Macready shook his head.

'She had red hair—'

'You mean Sonia ... his wife?' Macready asked incredulously, genuinely surprised.

Watson shrugged. 'There was no sign of anyone else.'

After the board meeting closed, agreement having been reached on the necessity of getting a lightvessel prepared immediately, Stanier had left the Lighthouse Authority's headquarters and taken a taxi to the offices of the Cambrian Steam Navigation

Company. As the cabbie fought his way through the traffic, Stanier reflected unhappily on how quickly all had been reversed. As he had cosily sought the downfall of Captain Septimus Macready, the bloody man was busy trying to save the wreckage of Stanier's ship. Stanier could hardly bear to contemplate the irony of it.

It was already late and, apart from a cleaner, only the charter manager was left in the shipping company's offices. He was a nondescript, middle-aged man who seemed incapable of existence without a cigarette. He looked up as Stanier approached.

'Ah, sir, thank goodness, do you know about the *Galahad?*'

'Yes. I found out this afternoon—'

'I tried to call you in Porth Ardur, but heard you had left your hotel this morning.'

'I was on the early train. What are the chances?'

'Oh, quite good, sir. There's been no loss of life and the men on the after bit were picked up. The after bit has sunk, sir, so there's the loss of that part of her cargo.'

'Yes, I know,' Stanier snapped sharply. That was another aspect he could hardly bear to think about. Then his other anxiety broke surface. 'What was her port of discharge in Costa Maya?'

The man frowned. 'Costa Maya, sir? No, she was bound for the Mediterranean.'

'Oh, I thought she had loaded under this new contract with the Costa Mayan government.'

'I er, I don't think I quite follow you, sir. We have no contract with the Costa Mayan Government—'

'We've a contract to supply the Costa Mayan Navy with navigation coal. We've chartered two additional ships to service it ...' Conviction ebbed from him with every word he uttered. To irony was now added terror.

The charter manager was shaking his head. 'If we had, Captain Stanier, I'd know about it.'

Stanier was feeling faint. 'Has my wife phoned? She was going to be in daily contact while I was away.'

'Ah, well.' The contract manager looked away. 'Well, she was, sir, for the first three weeks, then, well, we haven't heard from her recently.' He brightened and added, 'Everything was fine though, sir, until this morning.'

But Stanier was no longer listening, he was reaching for the charter manager's telephone and impatiently tapping the man's desk as the noise of unanswered ringing went on and on.

When he finally replaced the receiver, he turned and confronted the charter manager. 'I am ruined,' he said. *'Galahad,* like all my ships was uninsured ...'

From the empty flat Stanier reeled towards the Pomeroys' apartment, unsure why he had gone there, but with some vague idea that Tegwyn could help him, even give him a bed for the night. Pomeroy opened the door; he wore a yellow dressing gown and, with a lop-sided smile, ushered Stanier in.

'My dear James, you have come to tell me Caro has left you.' Pomeroy said, handing Stanier a glass half full of ncat Scotch whisky.

'How do you know?'

'The whole town knows, my dear, but don't worry, it is quite the fashion. You should count yourself lucky.'

'Lucky?' cried Stanier after a large, restorative gulp of whisky. 'Lucky?'

'You have only lost your wife ... I have lost my wife, my lover and half my fortune.'

'Your lover?' Stanier's capacity for surprises wearing thin.

'The beautiful, feckless, corrupt, devious and drunken David Smith. I am a queer, my dear. So was he, but he was queer-queer, if you see what I mean. Utterly corrupt, not just oddly orientated. He persuaded me to invest ... but it is pointless to go over and over the matter. Come with me. Oh, I shan't touch you, Jimmy, you are not my type at all. But just indulge me a little. Come.'

Stanier followed Pomeroy through into the room in which he kept his ethnographic treasures. Lighting a single lamp, Pomeroy set his glass down, picked up a Tasmanian wind mask and putting it to his face he suddenly blew through it. The thing emitted a howlingly piteous note.

Stanier stood dumbfounded, then stared as Pomeroy undid his dressing gown and stood naked. He lowered the mask from his face. 'Tell them about David, my dear Jimmy, there's a good fellow,' he said, advancing with mincing deliberation towards Stanier. 'Tell them it was due to David Smith, *Member* of Parliament and much else besides.' Pomeroy replaced the mask in front of his face and repeated the howling note.

Stanier dropped his glass and fled. He was seen by the apartment porter and would have been the prime suspect had Pomeroy not left a long note explaining everything. Nevertheless, the unfortunate Stanier spent a humiliating morning undergoing police interrogation until, convinced that the evidence against him was all circumstantial and Pomeroy's death was indeed suicide, he found himself on the street again.

Once on her homeward passage to Ynyscraven, Charlie inspected *Lyonesse* for damage. He had already ascertained that she was not taking water below, for she was pretty tight and he had pumped little water out of her bilge since he had first sailed on the ketch from Aberogg. But the beautiful line of her sheer was badly chewed in two places amidships, and below three ribs had suffered bad cracks. The most serious damage was down aft, on her starboard quarter, where her counter had been seriously damaged. It was, however, all above the waterline and all repairable.

Charlie was not quite certain how he was going to explain it to Lord Dungarth, for the damage seemed to put him in so untenable a position that he could no longer think of *Lyonesse*'s owner as Roger Craven. This was the only thing to mar the sense of joint achievement he felt. Sonia had proved her mettle, handled the ketch with absolute brilliance and earned herself, if such a thing were possible, an even greater measure of affection from her husband.

It was midnight before they got ashore and wearily tramped up the steep path. In their lit kitchen Justine was asleep at the table, her head on her folded arms. She woke as they came in and got up, her face smiling, her arms outstretched.

'I've a thick vegetable soup for you. I saw you tacking up at twilight.'

'Justine, you're an angel,' Charlie grinned, hugging her.

'And you two, I understand, are heroes.'

It was almost exactly forty-eight hours to the minute since he had left the bay, when Macready slipped his tow and *Galahad*'s starboard anchor rumbled out of the hawse pipe and brought her up, three cables south of the lighthouse pier of Porth Ardur. There was hardly a breath of wind.

## Winners And Losers

For a few days Porth Ardur enjoyed a curious period of frenetic activity. At high water later that day, edged inwards by *Caryatid* secured alongside, the forward section of *Galahad* was nudged into the dock entrance and thereafter warped back into her old berth. Here a mass of dusty men dug out the coal so easily poured into her capacious forward holds. It was a brief sunset flurry of laborious work before a prolonged period of idleness while the tortured hull awaited a decision as to its future.

Across the dock, *Caryatid* disgorged her own stores and sank into the inertia that was to precede her decommissioning. It was a state of affairs that lasted some weeks. In the meantime the Secretary to the Board of Commissioners for Celtic Lighthouses sought a buyer for her tired hull, finally agreeing to her being broken up.

There *had* been a revolt in Costa Maya, and the state navy *had* brought out of reserve two ancient monitors. These had steamed down the coast and bombarded

371

half a dozen villages with their huge 12-inch guns, after which Costa Maya sank back into obscurity. That was all; no contracts for navigation coal had been sought on the spot market, no tramps had been taken up on bareboat charter.

In the succeeding months, a society magazine called the *Tittle-Tattler* contained several reports from the Côte d'Azur of the flamboyantly extravagant excesses of Caro Blackadder, a woman, it was averred, whose marital distress had led her to adopt the highly creditable initiative of absconding with a substantial amount of her cruel husband's assets, after acquiescing to his putting them in her name to avoid tax himself. Feminist opinion praised her highly, admired her resumption of her maiden name and in particular, her adoption of what they called 'inalienable rights to pursue happiness through freedom of expression'. Caro Blackadder was thereafter frequently seen assisting the consumptive former Member of Parliament, David Smith, to enjoy the last years of his tragically short life.

By a trick of fate, the cruel husband avoided the scandal of bankruptcy. Tegwyn Pomeroy took pity upon her former lover and, wanting nothing associated with Pomeroy, whose physical betrayal she

372

found herself unable to forgive despite the fact that he had left the residue of his fortune to her, made it all over to Stanier. It was a considerable sum, enabling him to pay off the modest salvage claim submitted by the Celtic Lighthouse Authority on behalf of Captain Septimus Macready and the ship's company of the *Caryatid*. Stanier was compelled to scrap the remains of *Galahad,* covering the cost of her towage to the breakers, and compensate the consignees of her lost cargo. The consignees invoked the reversion clause and cancelled their contracts. The salvaged remains of *Galahad*'s cargo, discharged upon the quay at Porth Ardur, was loaded into four coasters and shipped out, to be resold at a net loss, to another buyer.

Faced by the loss of his job, the Cambrian Steam Navigation Company's contracts manager secured three cargoes for the remaining ships in the fleet. These, two of iron ore and one, oddly a logwood cargo from, of all places, Costa Maya, began the slow process of rebuilding the shipping company. This skilful saving of his Cambrian Steam in the face of extreme difficulties, not only earned Stanier a measure of admiration from his fellow shipowners, but secured his seat on the Board of the Commissioners of Celtic Lighthouses. It was not the business of the Commissioners to kick a man when he was down and, as Sir Charles Mudge remarked, 'Any damn fool can get into a mess; it takes a real man to get out of one.'

This fortuitous consequence decided Stanier to promote his contracts manager to a place on his own Board of Directors and the Cambrian Steam Navigation Company entered a phase of its existence characterised by substantial reinvestment.

In Porth Ardur, Mrs Gwendolyn Macready, like Mr Sinclair of the Pendragon Bank, grew wiser, acknowledging the sin of greed. Sinclair, a widower, found himself retired early and, sharing his humiliation with the only other living soul who knew of it in Porth Ardur, formed a scandalous attachment with Mrs Macready. It would be indelicate to pry too deeply into this odd and quite unexpected liaison, particularly as the Macready house was put into the hands of an estate agent and divorce proceedings followed. Both Mrs Macready and Mr Sinclair left Porth Ardur at the same time. Some said together, and occasional rumours surfaced. Families on holiday reported seeing them in seedy seaside resorts and one incredible account suggested they had been positively identified running a troupe of pierrots at an end-of-the-pier show. The truth does not greatly matter; they fade from this history, finding perhaps a small contentment amid the shame in the twilight of their lives.

A month after *Caryatid* had arrived at the breakers' yard and Macready had turned his back on the old ship for the last time, Parliament reassembled. The Upper House was held spellbound for half an hour, while Roger Craven, eleventh Earl Dungarth, lambasted the Government in his maiden speech for its coercive policies towards the public services, policies that reduced them to levels of such penury that they were unable to carry out their functions.

'... They might just as well not exist!' he declaimed. 'Indeed, would it not be better for the Government to approve the complete abolition of these institutions? They could, with the money thus saved, refund every freeholding taxpayer in the land, a measure, my lords, that recommends itself to a self-serving coterie, anxious to secure re-election!

'Consider, my noble lords, the consequences of which you have read in your newspapers of the extinguishing of the Buccabu lighthouse. It is not something your lordships normally worry about! Why? Because for one hundred and nine years a light has shone out from the Buccabu lighthouse every single night in that period. But, my lords, a cut-back on putty ... yes, putty, caused the glazings to fail, whereupon this structure, my lords, as noble as ourselves, was filled with the ocean which it had withstood for over a century ...'

Creeping crabwise towards his objective, Lord Dungarth precipitated a protracted debate the result of which, some two years later, led to the commissioning of a new, modern diesel tender, named *Caryatid* after her predecessor. She would be based at Porth Ardur, whose facilities would be modernised.

But we anticipate. Long before this outcome, reading of the decision to build this new ship in the newspapers which had Dungarth brought to Ynyscraven, Macready looked up across the dining table about which were crowded the Farthings, Justine and Tegwyn, and smiled at his lordship.

'That's wonderful,' he said, his eyes bright with emotion.

'Someone else will command her of course, Septimus, but you should not let that worry you.'

'No, of course not, my lord,' Macready said, seeing no obliquity in his lordship's remark, but putting out his hand and squeezing that of Justine, who smiled happily back at him.

'Now, Septimus,' Dungarth went on, 'I have a favour to ask you. Will you give Tegwyn away? The silly girl agreed to marry me this afternoon.'

'I shall be honoured, my lord—'

'Septimus, you will not call me that on this island. Indulge me thus far ... please, there's a good fellow.'

Macready smiled. 'On one condition, my lord.'

'What is that?'

'You give Justine away!'

'Septimus!' breathed Justine, while Tegwyn reached out and squeezed his lordship's noble hand.

'Honoured, Captain Macready! Charlie, where's that case of bubbly I brought ashore?'

The cork-popping rituals over, the glasses charged, Dungarth gave a series of toasts to which everyone drank enthusiastically.

'Now,' Dungarth said as the jollity subsided. 'I must not leave you two out of this. Here we are.'

He drew a rather crumpled brown paper envelope from his blazer pocket and tossed it towards Charlie, who caught it. Drawing a linen document from it he unfolded it, then looked at Dungarth, his face puzzled.

'Since you treated the old lady as if you owned her, and since you make such a brilliant crew, you two might as well have her.'

Charlie's mouth gaped in incredulity while Sonia lent forward and kissed Dungarth on the cheek. 'You absolute sweetie,' she said, turning to Charlie. 'He's given us *Lyonesse,* you numb-skull.'

'But what will *you* sail, Roger? You love that boat.'

Dungarth pulled a face and looked at Tegwyn. 'I'm not certain Teggy wants to go sailing and, if she does, I've enough spondulicks to build something new. I'd rather set my mind on a schooner.' Dungarth turned his attention to Charlie. 'Anyway, Charlie, there are a few repairs to see to and, frankly, I can't be bothered.'

'Well, thanks, Roger—'

'I think you need to lay a proper mooring for her, but then that's right up your street, isn't it?'

'I'd like to extend the breakwater—'

'Well then, get on with it. Don't keep asking me.'

'Right. Thanks.'

'There's something else as well. You've both won Lloyd's Medals for your rescue of those firemen. Congratulations ... No, no, don't thank me. It was Septimus who put in the recommendation.'

Charlie looked at his old commander and mumbled his thanks.

'He's a lovely man,' said Justine, tears flowing down her face.

Embarrassed, Macready cleared his throat. 'There's one thing I must ask you, er, Roger ...'

'What's that?'

'About the putty in the Buccabu light ... You know the whole thing was wrecked by a huge wave and the bronze astragals were simply torn out. I doubt if it was just putty. Besides, no-one had stopped any requisition order for putty, certainly not to my knowledge, and I doubt if old Dale would have done it.'

'Well, Septimus, politics is the art of the possible. I was pretty certain that no-one in either House would have the slightest acquaintance with the Buccabu lighthouse and I backed my hunch.'

'You ought to get a medal for that, Roger darling,' Tegwyn said to general laughter.

'I've always,' Dungarth said charging everybody's glass, 'deeply deplored the effrontery of the peerage. Cheers, everyone!'

That is not quite the end of the story. Its last twist took place not long after this happy evening in the Farthings' cottage on

Ynyscraven, in the distant Board Room of the Commissioners for Celtic Lighthouses.

It was, it will be remembered, a tradition of the Celtic Lighthouse Service that every Commissioner had the right to nominate the man he considered best fit to succeed him. It was urged upon Commissioners to make such a nomination soon after their appointment and while their selection was in no way binding upon the assembled Board, it was unusual for a nomination to be black-balled, the nominee usually being duly elected into the vacancy.

In due course that autumn the Board's attention was directed to the matter of filling the post left by the untimely death of Captain Jesmond. The old shipmaster's sealed letter, deposited many years earlier, was reverently opened by the Secretary and solemnly unfolded.

The waiting Commissioners ran through their minds the likely nominees, commanders, no doubt, of ocean liners, large oil tankers or smart cargo-passenger ships, men whose candidacy they would easily approve.

'Captain Jesmond's nominee is ...' the Secretary intoned, as Mudge struck the bruised table top with his ceremonial gavel, calling the attention of all to this important moment, '... Captain Septimus Macready.'

There was a stunned silence. The

election of a service officer was unheard of! Such a thing was without precedent. The man did not have a formal certificate of competence as master, having been promoted in the days when the Commissioners themselves examined their own officers, unhappy with the government department who seemed insufficiently rigorous in its standards.

'Any objections?' asked Mudge, looking at Stanier, whose mouth seemed about to open.

'He's a damn fine seaman who just about saved your bacon, Stanier,' said Captain Blake.

'It's certainly breaking the mould of tradition,' offered Gostling, 'and we want to be seen moving into the modern world of business practice, don't you agree, gentlemen?'

'Well,' asked Mudge, 'what d'you say, Captain Stanier? It's traditional to ask the junior man first.'

'Like a council of war,' added Blake sententiously.

'Well? Any objections?'

Stanier swallowed, then slowly shook his head. The matter was passed unanimously.

The publishers hope that this book has given you enjoyable reading. Large Print Books are especially designed to be as easy to see and hold as possible. If you wish a complete list of our books, please ask at your local library or write directly to: Magna Large Print Books, Long Preston, North Yorkshire, BD23 4ND, England.

This Large Print Book for the Partially sighted, who cannot read normal print, is published under the auspices of

## THE ULVERSCROFT FOUNDATION

---

## THE ULVERSCROFT FOUNDATION

. . . we hope that you have enjoyed this Large Print Book. Please think for a moment about those people who have worse eyesight problems than you . . . and are unable to even read or enjoy Large Print, without great difficulty.

You can help them by sending a donation, large or small to:

**The Ulverscroft Foundation,
1, The Green, Bradgate Road,
Anstey, Leicestershire, LE7 7FU,
England.**
or request a copy of our brochure for more details.

The Foundation will use all your help to assist those people who are handicapped by various sight problems and need special attention.

Thank you very much for your help.

995C